Deception on All Accounts

Deception on All Accounts

Sara Sue Hoklotubbe

The University of Arizona Press

Tucson

The University of Arizona Press
© 2003 Sara Sue Hoklotubbe
All rights reserved

www.uapress.arizona.edu

Library of Congress Cataloging-in-Publication Data
Hoklotubbe, Sara Sue, 1952–
Deception on all accounts / Sara Sue Hoklotubbe.
p. cm.
ISBN 978-0-8165-2311-5 (Paper : alk. paper)
1. Women bank employees—Fiction. 2. Cherokee women—
Fiction. 3. Bank robberies—Fiction. I. Title.
PS3608.04828 D43   2003
813'.6—dc21   2003005023

Manufactured in the United States of America on acid-free,
archival quality paper and processed chlorine free.

14   13   12   11   7   6   5   4   3

To Eddie,

who has never stopped believing in me and my dreams.

Acknowledgments

Grateful appreciation goes to Faith E. Horton, my good friend and co-worker, who had to face the gun barrel of a robber instead of me; David "Big Mac" McWhorter, for his inspiration and expertise in law enforcement and weapons; Dr. Michael Chang, for his extensive understanding of mental trauma and its effect on victims; Harold Winton, who survived more than one rattlesnake bite and lived to tell his stories; Chad Smith, Principal Chief of the Cherokee Nation, and Dr. Richard Allen, for their words of support; Wynema Smith and Dennis Sixkiller, for their expertise with the Cherokee language and knowledge of Cherokee culture; Linda Boyden, Mary Ellen Cooper, Audrey Eggers, Rachelle "Rey" Hanan, and Pamela Rentz, who cheerfully and tirelessly read my manuscript and made helpful suggestions; Wordcraft Circle of Native American Writers and Storytellers, for their moral support; Paul Wood, who helped me visualize my name on the front of a book and launch my writing career; Geary Hobson, who gently nudged me in the right direction by suggesting I contact the University of Arizona Press; Patti Hartmann, acquiring editor, and Judith Allen, managing editor, who are both a joy to work with; Debra Makay, my manuscript editor, who somehow knew exactly what I wanted to say; Rosa, my Cherokee grandmother, who taught me I could do anything and to always persevere; and to my Choctaw husband, whose enduring love and generous support made it possible for me to write this book, you are a gift from God.

Deception on All Accounts

With the skill of a nocturnal animal, he slipped to the end of the alley. He crouched to absorb his surroundings. The stench of forgotten trash permeated the darkness and a sudden gust of wind carried a whiff of freshly cut grass up his nose. He gasped and choked back a sneeze.

From his hiding place behind a stockade fence, Johnny could see through the windows of the small bank. A spotlight above the teller counter reflected off the vault door, a golden glow that rivaled the light of the full moon. A sticky sweatshirt clung to his back as an irritating trickle of sweat slid below the waistband of his underwear. The only sound came from an occasional vehicle in the distance as it rushed down an empty street.

Johnny chose this bank because it sat on the quiet corner of Martin Luther King Boulevard and Harvest Street. He had watched the corner street lamp that shed a ray of light on the small building. As the cars traveled down the steep hill toward MLK Boulevard, their headlights would invariably hit the photocell, causing the lamp to temporarily go dead. The automatic sensor, recognizing the sunny illusion, would then turn the light on again. Over the last several weeks, Johnny had timed the duration of these mini blackouts. They lasted three and one-half minutes.

At 4:15 A.M., as expected, a police officer drove down the hill at Harvest Street. As the headlight beams of the vehicle bobbed down the hill, the street lamp flickered and went dead right on cue. As Johnny had watched him routinely do, the officer eased through the stop sign by the bank, downshifted, and drove off into the blackness.

Johnny slipped across the parking lot and slid behind the shrubbery next to the building. With a swift and fluid movement, he drew an odd-shaped circle with a glass cutter in a window near the ground. Then, with his glove-protected hand, he punched out the glass. After what seemed like an endless minute of silence, he lay on the ground and slithered into the bank like a snake.

Once inside the building, Johnny crouched on the floor and listened, allowing the pounding in his chest to subside and his eyes to adjust to the surroundings. Losing no time, Johnny verified what he already knew—the room contained no glass-break sensors and no motion detectors. Like the other small bank branches he had encountered during his illustrious criminal career, the only alarm was installed on the vault to protect the money, with little thought given to the rest of the building or the safety of the employees.

The street lamp relit as he moved out of the office and into the lobby. The best place to wait, he decided, was behind the teller counter.

Chapter 1

Sadie Walela's old Chevy sputtered and died just as she reached her designated parking space. She looked at her watch, then scanned the lot. The policy and procedure manual strictly prohibited anyone from entering the bank alone. Since none of the other employees had arrived yet, she would have to wait.

She understood the purpose of the rule. First of all, no one should be left alone with access to the bank's money. With two people present, cash was less likely to come up missing. The second issue dealt with personal safety. The other employee's role was to wait in the vehicle until the first employee gave the predetermined "all clear" sign indicating the bank was safe to enter. If the correct sign was not given, the employee could drive off and summon help.

Sadie's dilemma at this point was the fact that the vault had a twenty-minute time lock on it. Once she dialed the combination, she would have to wait for the time lock to expire before she could try to open the vault door. If she was unsuccessful on her first attempt and it didn't open, she would have to redial and wait another twenty minutes.

Soon she would have to make a decision. Which was more important? Not following procedure and going in alone, as she had witnessed the manager do countless times before, or not having enough time to open the vault and get the cash drawers in place before it was time to open the bank? The last time a branch manager missed the combination and had to wait for the time lock to recycle, the bank's doors didn't open on time and he was fired. Sadie didn't want to suffer the same fate.

While she waited, she lowered the car window and gazed at a honeysuckle bush growing up over the wooden fence bordering the east side of the parking lot. It reminded her of how as a young girl she had harvested honeysuckle vines for Rosa, her grandmother, who would then weave double-walled baskets using the same technique passed down from her ancestors.

Sadie knew that, before long, if left unchecked, the flowering bush with its heady fragrance would sprout into an indestructible woody beast, pushing its tender vines through every knothole and crevice it could find, slowly overtaking and destroying the fence. Things were never as they appeared, she thought.

Tiny blooms fell from the Oklahoma sky, released by a nearby pear tree making way for tender spring leaves. A morning breeze carried the white flowers through Sadie's car window, attaching the delicate works of nature to her hair. She flicked at the flowers with her fingers and then applied a quick stroke of lipstick, using the rearview mirror to check her appearance. The honey-colored tint of her flawless complexion, her jet-black hair, and her high cheekbones reflected her daddy's Cherokee lineage. But the icy-blue color of her eyes, an unwanted gift from her white mother, revealed the secret of her mixed blood. She put away her lipstick and continued to wait.

The branch manager, Tom Duncan, had scheduled the day off, leaving his assistant, Sadie, in temporary control. It was his way of dodging the mischievous April Fools' Day pranks the young tellers liked to play on a preoccupied manager. He had returned one too many calls to Mr. Lyon or Ms. Wolf, only to find himself sputtering in the phone when the voice on the other end of the line answered for the Delaware County Zoo. His method of defense was simply to take the day off.

Sadie checked the time again and wished someone would arrive. If she didn't get the combination right the first time, she would have to redial and the entire morning schedule would fall twenty minutes behind. If the bank didn't open on time, she would have to answer for it.

Finally, she gathered her purse under her arm, pushed the car door open, and headed for the bank. After a brisk stride across the parking lot, she unlocked the front door and entered. Once inside, she turned the key and felt the heavy dead bolt fall between the glass doors. Before entering the second set of doors into the lobby, she checked the parking lot one more time. Still empty.

The lush burgundy carpet muffled her footsteps as Sadie moved across the lobby. She placed her sweater on the back of her chair and looked at the messy stack of papers in her should-have-been-done-yesterday tray. She had spent over twelve years at this bank, harboring an unquenchable desire to be a successful banker. It was a respectable career and a good way to make money, she had decided, when she started at the bottom of the ladder all those long workdays ago. She had been a naive young woman who believed she could be the first to break the glass ceiling at this good-old-boy bank. Now, she was ready to move up or move on.

A shriveled violet beckoned to Sadie, begging a reprieve from its sunny location on the corner of her desk. While she deliberated the fate of the fuzzy-leafed plant, Sadie pulled a brush from her purse and ran it through her hair. Long, shiny strands fell behind her shoulders, the tips clinging to the small of her back, static electricity wrapping flighty strands around the top of her arm. The violet would have to wait.

She straightened her collar, picked up her keys, and walked back across the lobby. Under her right arm she hugged the notepad bearing the instructions to open the vault and methodically unlocked the door to the small equipment room. Holding the door open with her foot, she flipped on the light switch with her elbow, punched in the code, and rotated the shunt key to disarm the vault alarm. She turned out the light and moved her foot. The door closed automatically, stopped short by a sticky hinge just before it slammed.

"Hold it right there," a loud voice commanded.

The notepad fell to the floor in slow motion as Sadie gasped for air. Every muscle in her body froze and the room began to swirl. A huge man covered in black from head to toe stood up behind the teller counter, a gun in each hand.

"No need to get excited," he added. "We're going to transact a little business before the bank opens. That's all."

For a split second, Sadie thought the crew had gotten carried away with their April Fools' jokes. Then, reality set in as she stared down the barrels of what appeared to be two huge cannons. One, shiny as a new nickel, and the other black. Her mind switched gears, and in a fleeting moment she filed away the information her stunned senses were gathering. The pounding of her heart deafened her ears, but she could hear her grandmother's voice telling her to remain steadfast. *This animal must not smell your fear.*

The man wore mirrored sunglasses under a ski mask to conceal his eyes. Black electrical tape, positioned around the eye holes of the mask, held the glasses in place. His hooded jogging suit, gloves, and shoes covered the rest of his body. Sadie could see no skin anywhere. The only distinguishing mark was a small rip on the top of his hood. It appeared to have been caught on a sharp object, leaving a tear that looked like a run in a pair of pantyhose.

"Open it," he demanded.

No answer. Instead, Sadie glanced through the huge windows wondering who was going to be next to walk into this man's trap. A feeling of helplessness rushed over her like hot air.

"Hurry up!"

Sadie picked up her notepad and reluctantly moved toward the vault. With trembling hands she dialed the combination. Her limited experience opening the vault left her with a track record of about fifty-fifty on the first try, and this attempt was going to be shaky, at best.

"There . . . there's a time lock," she said, suddenly afraid this man would go berserk and shoot her because the door remained locked.

"Shut up," he said. "I can wait. Stand right there and when your friends show up keep your mouth shut or I'll kill them."

It was obvious the man already knew about the time lock on the vault. Sadie stood as still as she could and waited, trying to analyze his voice. He sounded educated, but his voice was unnaturally cold and unemotional. She didn't think he sounded Indian, but she couldn't determine if he was white, black, or anything else for that matter. Frozen in time, she glanced at her watch. Only two minutes had passed.

The sun flashed on a moving windshield announcing the arrival of another bank employee. With the manager gone, there would be only four people in the small branch today. The robber leveled his guns at Sadie and crouched once more behind the teller counter.

"Keep your mouth shut until they get in here, or I'll shoot. Do you hear me?"

Tessie, a young teller with wild, curly blond hair and a personality to match, arrived first. Sadie cringed when she realized Tessie would assume it was okay to come inside when she saw Sadie's car. With the decision to come in by herself, she had placed the others' lives in danger. Sure enough, the young girl let herself in through the front door and started talking across the lobby.

"Hey, Sadie, you know that cute guy with the funny glasses in Dunkin' Donuts? He almost spilled coffee on this—"

"Come on in and join your friend." The robber's voice boomed from behind the teller counter.

Tessie let out a shriek, dropped her purse, and almost fell to her knees. Her face drained of color and her mouth hung open until the robber gestured with one of his guns for her to move out of the middle of the lobby to where her co-worker stood motionless. Leaving her purse where it fell, Tessie walked over to Sadie. A wet spot began to appear on the front of her slacks between her legs. She started to speak, but Sadie cut her short with a quick shake of her head.

"That's right," he said calmly. "Just do as you're told and nobody will get hurt. We have a few minutes to wait, that's all."

Tessie bit her lip and stared at the ceiling as the scene replayed twice more—for Gordy and then for Heather. With each arrival, the gunman crouched and waited for them to enter and relock the door before making his presence known. Sadie studied the robber and tried to memorize everything about him. She looked at the height marker on the exit door, and guessed him to be less than six feet tall. He didn't have big hands, she thought, but it was hard to tell since he wore black leather gloves. He seemed to be extremely calm. Too calm.

Sadie mentally berated herself for entering the bank alone and wondered if she would lose her job. She could hear it all now. If she had done everything by the book, she would have waited for someone else to arrive. Then she would have entered and checked the entire building before giving the "all clear" sign to the other employee. Without the signal, they could have driven away and called for help.

However, Sadie had studied that procedure before and decided it was not exactly foolproof. Summoning help was a good idea, but in Sadie's mind it opened up the possibility of being held hostage if someone was already inside. Opening up a bank without a security guard made for a bad situation any way you looked at it.

As the minutes slowly ticked by, Sadie remembered the off-duty police officer who had held security seminars for the bank. He warned them about this very scenario. But now she had been careless and landed the entire group in the middle of a nightmare. It was all her fault. Twenty minutes dragged by. Tessie whimpered and shrunk against the wall.

"It's time," said the robber. "Get at it."

Sadie prayed as she turned the big silver handle. CLUNK. A feeling of relief came over her as she pulled the vault door open exposing several drawers, four of which were locked. A white canvas bag with the words "Federal Reserve" stamped on the side sat in full view next to a cup containing an assortment of keys. Sadie knew the bag held thousands of new twenties for their regular Monday-morning routine of refilling the automatic teller machine.

"Okay, you." Johnny pointed the black gun at Gordy. "How many cash drawers are there?"

Gordy was twenty-three years old and working at the bank while he finished his degree at Northeastern State University. As he was the only male employee present, Sadie feared his macho sense of duty would kick in, and she was right.

"Two," said Gordy.

It was apparent that the small branch was set up to house only two tellers. But Sadie knew Gordy was lying. Yes, there were two cash drawers, but what about the other cash drawer in the vault used to replenish the tellers when they got low on cash? She made no indication he was lying. She thought he was stupid to risk their lives to save a lousy stack of paper money. His misplaced loyalty to the bank gave her a sinking feeling. After all, it was insured and she didn't care whether the robber took it or not.

The robber removed a black canvas bag from his pocket and threw it on the floor at Sadie's feet. "Fill it up with both cash drawers. No coins. You can start with that bag there." The robber pointed with his right gun at the bag of money.

Her knees felt weak but she never faltered as she dumped the ATM money into the robber's bag and then added all of the bills from the top two drawers. The money in the second drawer included a dye pack concealed in a bundle of twenties. With no hesitation, she dropped it in with the rest.

She knew the dye pack would not explode unless it got close enough to or crossed the two transmitter beams at the front door. It didn't appear to her that he had come in that way. But if he did choose the door as his escape route, and the dye pack exploded, it would spew tear gas and fluorescent-pink dye everywhere, unmercifully marking the money and anything or anyone else around. Sadie hoped that wouldn't happen until long after he was gone.

She also pulled the bait money out of the drawer and added it to the bag. The serial numbers on the bait money had been recorded. If the bills were ever recovered the bank could prove the money belonged to them.

"Open the other two drawers," said the robber, once again motioning with a gun at Gordy's head.

Gordy bent over, fished for a key, and opened the bottom drawer revealing deposit stamps, a box of money orders, and a stack of cashier's checks.

"I don't want that shit. Open the other drawer."

Gordy froze.

"I said," the robber raised his voice, "open the other drawer."

Gordy stared, eyes wide as if he were an animal caught in the headlights of an oncoming vehicle, unable to move.

"You." The robber directed one of his guns toward Sadie.

Realizing there was nothing else she could do, Sadie plucked another key from the cup and unlocked the fourth drawer, exposing twice as much cash as in the top two drawers together.

"You son of a bitch," he said as he turned toward Gordy. "You lied to me."

Gordy started walking backward, holding his hands out straight in front of him. "I . . . I didn't mean to . . ." Then, in a panic, he turned and ran toward the door.

Very coolly, the robber raised his gun, aimed, and fired once. Gordy catapulted forward and fell facedown right next to Tessie's purse, his arms and legs sprawled like a rag doll's. The blood from his collapsed body began to seep into the dark red carpet and disappear.

When Sadie saw the robber aim, she pulled the other two women to their knees, her arms around them as if creating an invisible shield. When the gun rang out, Tessie screamed, Heather sobbed, and Sadie clasped them tighter.

"Shhhhhh . . . be quiet." Sadie tried to comfort them. Somehow, she thought, if they showed no threat to the robber, maybe he would spare their lives.

"Get off your ass and get the rest of the money. We're wasting time."

The coldness of the robber's voice cut through Sadie's heart. She jumped to her feet, took the rest of the money, and crammed it into the black sack. While she took care of the money, she watched him from the corner of her eye as he bound and gagged the other two women. He had instructed each one to collect a spiral phone cord from the phones on the teller counter. Then he used the pliable connectors to tie their hands to their feet behind their backs. Sadie handed him the sack, silently praying he would not hog-tie her, too.

"Get on the floor."

Sadie obeyed and the robber wrapped tape around her mouth and head. He hurriedly tied her hands with another phone cord and her prayer was answered when he missed her feet. When he crammed her face into the carpet, she noticed the bullet's brass casing that had landed on the floor nearby. He scooped it up and added it to the money along with the tape.

"Now listen to me and listen real good," he growled. "I'm going into this room and wait for my ride. If anyone makes a sound or tries to get up, I'll come back in here and kill you." Then he disappeared into the empty office.

Sadie lay on her stomach listening for sounds of the robber's movements. She could hear nothing except the faint ticking of the time clock. If she rolled onto her side and pulled her head up, she could see numerals II through VI as the red, toothpick-shaped hand jerked around, second by second. She rolled onto her back and turned her head to the side. From her new vantage point, she could see an assortment of paper clips, pens, calculator tape, and dirt that had accumulated under the bottom edge of the teller counter. She wondered why no one ever cleaned under there and then realized how absurd her thoughts were given her current circumstances.

The phone rang and Sadie hoped someone would figure out something was wrong when no one answered. She assumed Gordy was dead and it was too late to help him. Tessie sobbed through her gag and Heather lay paralyzed with shock.

After what seemed like an eternity Sadie sat up, pulled her feet under her, and rolled up onto her knees. She used her strong legs to push her body into a standing position. Rubbing her wrists against the edge of the counter, she loosened the phone cord just enough to wiggle her hands free. She estimated it had been about ten minutes since the robber had left. When she pulled the tape off her mouth, she could taste blood from her torn lip. The rest of the tape hung from the back of her hair. She silently cautioned her co-workers to be quiet and gathered all of her courage to peek around the corner into the office through which the robber had fled. There in the corner of the glass wall, the lower pane was missing and all she could see was a bushy, outside shrub. To her relief, the robber was long gone.

She ran to Gordy, fearing the worst. She felt for a pulse. Nothing. She tried to turn him over and realized he wasn't breathing. Suddenly, she felt sick to her stomach. At least he had died quickly, she thought to herself. Tears streamed down her face as she pulled her sweater from her nearby chair and placed it over Gordy's head and shoulders. Then the sound of Tessie crying forced her back to the present. She ran to the phone, frantically reattached the phone cord, and dialed 911.

Sergeant Charlie McCord stopped at the Sycamore Springs Waffle House by six o'clock every morning before heading to the station to start his paperwork. He lived on black coffee, and the biscuits and sausage gravy reminded him of those his mother had made when she was still alive. Besides the greasy food, though, Charlie liked to make small talk with Gladys.

Gladys Goins worked the early-morning shift at the Waffle House six days a week. She had spent the better part of her forty-nine years serving food to friends and strangers alike in first one small diner and then another. Her dreams of leaving northeastern Oklahoma for the bright lights of a city were no secret to Charlie, and he was quite sure she would take the first offer that came along to do so.

Most mornings she would sit cross-legged on a high stool, swinging her foot in the air, resting her chin on one hand, and holding a long, thin cigarette in the other while she chewed gum and listened to him tell stories of cops and robbers. She hung on to every word, interrupted only when other customers began to arrive. He teasingly called her "Red" when no one else was around, and her cheeks would turn just a few shades lighter than her fiery, bottle-red hair. Although Charlie held no romantic attraction to Gladys, he liked the wide-eyed attention she gave him. Somehow it seemed to help ease the image of his wife, Lilly, still home in bed with pink curlers stuck all over her head.

Charlie was a burly man with a dense head of brown hair, heavy eyebrows, and friendly green eyes. Gladys affectionately called him "Big Mac," and although he wasn't particularly fond of the name, he never objected. The fair skin on his face and arms had been tanned to the texture of soft leather, the result of long days spent in a squad car in the Oklahoma sun. His middle-aged waistline reflected his love of southern cooking, and he threatened on a regular basis to start working out at the gym in the evenings. You have to stay in shape, he would tell Gladys, to keep up with the bad guys.

Charlie routinely finished his paperwork and had his troops on the street by a few minutes after seven every day and then made another stop at the Waffle House for more coffee. Just as he spooned an ice cube from his water glass into his coffee cup, his radio began to sputter. He dropped his spoon and lumbered toward the front door.

"See you later, Gladys, we got a stop-and-rob at the bank this morning."

While they waited for help to arrive, Sadie freed Tessie and Heather from their restraints and set the girls down on the floor where they could not see Gordy's body. The first police car arrived and Sadie walked across the lobby and unlocked the front door for a brawny policeman. He looked familiar, maybe a customer.

The next few hours were a blur as each employee recounted over and over the events of the morning, first to the police and then to the FBI. Stan Blackton, senior vice president, arrived and took over as spokesman. Television crews descended like flies to a picnic and Sadie couldn't find anywhere to hide as onlookers gawked through every crevice they could find. By the time Gordy's body had been removed from the lobby, Sadie was exhausted. When Blackton appeared to be finished posing for the television cameras, he turned his attention to Sadie.

"I guess we'll talk about the violation of policy later. In the meantime, you can go to another branch to finish out the day, or if you want to go home you can take a sick day. We'll have this mess cleaned up and be open for business tomorrow."

"You mean . . . Monday?" Sadie's words sounded more like a corrective statement than a question. "Today's Friday," she added, as if he needed clarification.

She threw her hair behind her shoulder and felt something rub against her. A chill involuntarily ran through her body when she realized a piece of the killer's tape was still attached to her hair. Quickly, she dispensed with the tape and flung it to the floor. A nearby police officer motioned for her to leave it where it had fallen.

"Uh, yeah. Monday, I guess it is." Blackton rubbed his forehead with his fingertips and then crammed his glasses tight up against his eyebrows and looked at Sadie. "Monday."

"Well, color me sick. I'm going home."

She turned and hesitated for a moment, then picked up the dead-tired violet and dropped it in the trash before she walked toward the door.

"Ma'am?" The police officer who had been first to arrive now stood at attention by the front door. He had been eavesdropping on the conversation. "Here's my card if you think of anything else."

Sadie stopped and acknowledged his kind eyes with a nod.

"This is kind of personal for me," he added. "This is where I bank."

Sadie took his card and smiled weakly. Without saying a word, she held the card in her hand until she reached the security of her old brown car. Dropping the card on the seat next to her, she said a silent prayer, pumped the accelerator twice, and turned the key. When the cantankerous engine came to life, she noticed the name on the card— Sergeant Charles McCord.

Chapter 2

When Johnny slipped into the empty office where he had made his entry several hours earlier, he removed his gloves, mask, and sunglasses, stuffed them in the bag with his loot, and made his escape through the opening in the glass. He checked the parking lot and street for any movement. It was clear. He emerged from behind the bushes and took off trotting into the quiet neighborhood. Adrenaline pumped through his veins like lightning striking in a thunderstorm. He had tried drugs a couple of times but hated the feeling, the loss of control. Adrenaline was better. As he briskly moved along, the black jogging suit concealed the black bag under his arm and its deep pockets bulged under the weight of his guns.

The corner of Jefferson Street and High seemed deserted except for the melody of the birds in the tall elm trees that lined the sidewalk. The small businesses on each corner appeared latched up tight, not open for business until mid-morning. Johnny unlocked the back door of his white Dodge panel van and jumped inside.

With the door secure, he opened the black bag and carefully removed his mask, gloves, and sunglasses. He fished in the bag until he found a stiff packet of money. He cautiously pulled up two top bills and uncovered a dye pack discreetly hidden in the carved-out innards of the altered bundle of twenties. What a waste of good cash, he thought, as he popped the battery out of the colorful maze of wires. He knew how the dye pack worked—without the battery connected, it was harmless. He disrobed and wrapped the jogging suit around the dye pack. From a blue gym bag wedged under the front seat, he retrieved a clean set of clothes and a plastic garbage bag. Quickly he dressed and stuffed his disguise, including the dye pack, into the trash sack. He then stowed his bag of loot, along with his guns, in an empty tool chest sitting against the inside wall of the van.

He crawled into the front seat, picked up a comb from the floor, and smoothed his hair. He checked his appearance in the rearview mirror, then scanned the area for anyone who might be watching. On the other side of the street, a young woman race-walked past the parking lot where the van was sitting. Her earplugs firmly planted in place, she sang out loud to herself and never looked toward the van. He watched her ass jiggle as she proceeded out of sight.

Johnny liked women. No, he was a connoisseur of women. As far as he was concerned, the variety of females in this world made living worthwhile. But they were for pleasure, and he never mixed business with pleasure.

The escape route took him down Jefferson Street to the expressway. He shifted and started up the ramp just as a patrol car sped past him in the opposite direction, lights and siren blasting. At the second exit, he left the highway and drove north to the big Wal-Mart Super Store. The sign screamed "OPEN 24 HOURS EVERY DAY." Behind the store, he stopped at the second Dumpster. And as he tossed the trash bag over the top, he could hear his dad's laughter in his head. Johnny laughed, too.

He had done his homework and knew that every morning between nine and ten o'clock a massive blue trash truck would arrive and collect the store's refuse. His disguise would soon be crushed along with tons of trash and on its way to the city dump. He drove the van around the opposite end of the building and waited for a few minutes. Confident that he had not been seen, he pulled back around the building and joined a group of cars waiting to merge into the rush-hour traffic on Tenth Street. Just as he gave it some gas, a grimy derelict carrying a trash sack walked right in front of the van.

"Watch it, scum," shouted Johnny. "Get out of my way before I run over you." Then as he edged his van toward the street he added, "Why don't you go climb under a rock somewhere?"

The man never stopped walking, just waved his hand in the air and laughed. Johnny gunned the van and pulled into traffic. "Somebody ought to do something about people like that," he muttered under his breath.

The short drive home presented no problems since most of the commuters were traveling in the opposite direction. Johnny turned down a quiet lane and hit the garage door opener as he nosed the van into the driveway. The garage door gave a groan and opened wide.

He parked inside, then carefully closed the garage door before un-locking the connecting door and carrying his goods into the house. He placed the tool chest on the kitchen floor, removed his guns, and put them on the seat of the chair next to him. He pushed back the place mats and dumped the contents of the black bag onto the center of the table. Carefully, he studied the money, looking for any bills that might be marked or for any more dye packs. It looked okay, but he couldn't be sure about some of the loose bills. The woman had added a dye pack, so she could have added bait money, too. There was no way to be sure.

Johnny removed the paper clips and money straps and placed them together in a pile. Dividing up the bills, he grouped each de-nomination into its own stack. He clipped together the fives and fifties in bundles of twenty each; the ones, tens, twenties, and hundreds went into bundles of twenty-five bills each. Then he began to count. The tally came to a little less than $75,000. He wasn't sure what the extra bag of money had been for, but appreciated the added bonus. Not bad for a morning's work. He placed the money inside a large satchel, snapped it shut, and rolled the combination lock.

A pack of cigarettes lay on the other side of the table. Johnny pulled one out, lit it, and took a long drag, propelling smoke across the room. Then, holding the cigarette between his front teeth, he raked the remaining paper clips into his hands and threw them into the trash. He wadded the paper money straps and placed them in the middle of a square, green ashtray and sat down once again at the table. He took the cigarette and held it to the wad of paper and stared as it began to turn black, smolder, then grow into a flame.

As Johnny watched the fire in the middle of his kitchen table burn, he began to replay the morning's events. Everything had gone exactly as he had planned except for the stupid kid trying to run away. Killing someone had not been in the plan, but that was just a hazard of the business.

The bank had been easy to hit. No motion detectors, no glass-break alarms, and a diligent woman who was sure to come in early to open the vault with the manager gone.

He thought about how he had stood in the lobby weeks ago and listened to the manager arguing with one of the vice presidents about their lack of security. The manager had been trying to make a case for a security guard, but the bank officer wasn't listening. Instead, he was busy watching a young teller, bent over a file cabinet in a skirt that barely covered the cheeks of her ass. When the manager stopped talking, the vice president looked at the manager and said, "You've got a time lock on the safe, what else do you want?" Then he strolled over to where the young girl was working and struck up a conversation.

Johnny had cased the branch for several months. Periodically, he would overhear the tellers talking among themselves. The best information came from the blond teenager, who seemed never to stop talking. That's how he had learned about the manager and his predictable three-day weekends. Careful not to say too much while in the branch, he made small deposits into the savings account he had opened by mail in his mother's name.

With each visit he tried to learn something new about the bank. He had determined there were no perimeter alarms or motion detectors. It was easy to see there were no video cameras and that the still camera located at the front door would photograph a robber only as he left the bank. That camera was most likely triggered when the alarm was set off. This would be done by panic buttons or when the bait money was pulled from its trap in the teller drawer. That was easy enough. Make sure no one could reach a panic button, don't leave by the front door, and get the money before the money drawer was transferred from the vault to the teller window and plugged into the alarm system.

The shrieking of the smoke detector in the hallway jolted Johnny back to the present. He was standing with both guns pointing at an imaginary being before realizing his little fire had made too much smoke. He put the guns down, walked to the hallway, pulled the front off the smoke detector, and yanked out the battery.

"Enough, already," he yelled. The battery reminded him of the dye pack he had disposed of earlier. "Gutsy broad," he muttered under his breath as he walked back to the kitchen and thought about the danger of the game he was playing. Then, he smiled smugly to himself while his thoughts returned to how cleverly he had outsmarted the bank and its lackluster attempt at security.

The only thing left on the table was the brass casing from the bullet that had killed Gordy. Johnny picked up the casing and walked out into the garage where he pulled the plastic lid off a red coffee can and let the casing fall in a pile of brass casings, all identical. He made a practice of picking up all of his brass when target shooting so he could trade them later at the gun show. That casing was no different from all of the others.

He returned to the kitchen and picked up his government-issued Colt .45 semiautomatic. He couldn't afford to take the chance that Gordy's deadly bullet could be matched back to his favorite piece. His daddy had given him this gun and he didn't want to lose it. He held the gun in his left hand, pushed in the recoil spring plug, and turned the barrel bushing. The procedure was second nature to Johnny. His dad, a Korean War veteran, had taught him to take apart this gun when he was only twelve years old. When the gun's internal notch disengaged, the spring plug fell on the table and the barrel came off with ease.

He walked down the hall to the bedroom and picked up a piece of hand luggage that resembled a bowling bag. He unzipped it, pulled out a red cloth, and unwrapped a shiny new gun barrel. He held the barrel up to his face and felt it, smooth and cold against his cheek.

He carried the barrel back to the kitchen where he began reassembling his gun with the new barrel. Now his Colt could never be matched to the bullet that had killed Gordy, and they would have no casing to match to his firing pin.

Johnny then walked out to the garage and placed the sacrificed barrel on the workbench. He reached to a high shelf, felt for an empty beaker, then placed it on a small hot plate. He cracked the back door of the garage and flipped the switch on the box fan. He carefully removed a blue glass bottle of nitric acid from a nearby cabinet and set it next to the burner. Gingerly, he removed the stopper and poured the caustic liquid into the beaker. As the hot plate began to heat the acid, Johnny picked up the gun barrel with bamboo tongs and placed it in the beaker, careful not to allow a splash. He unplugged the hot plate before the acid got too hot, before it started to boil. Then he left the warm acid to do its work and went back into the house.

First, he turned on the television. Nothing yet. Then he tried the radio. Finally, the hourly newscaster reported the horrible crime that had taken place that morning at a small branch of Mercury Savings Bank. The information was sketchy, she reported, and there were no leads on the gunman.

Johnny turned off the radio and slipped into the shower to clean up. When dressed in khaki pants, pullover shirt, and loafers, he stood in front of the mirror and stared at his face. "Willie would be proud of you, Johnny Boy," he said to the reflection in the mirror.

Willie was Johnny's dad and resided in Huntsville now. He had been convicted of murdering two women as they sat in their car outside a beer joint in Jasper. The women looked to Willie like they were rich, but when he tried to rob them they didn't have a cent of cash on them. So he had just capped them right there anyway, gotten into his car and driven away. There hadn't been any eyewitnesses, but Willie had gotten careless and, a few months later, after having one too many drinks, his secret slipped out. The sheriff went to Willie's house and talked him into letting him in and there lay his gun, in plain sight on the coffee table. After matching the bullets that killed the women to Willie's gun and his fingerprints to those on the door handle of the car, Willie was sentenced to death row. Johnny always thought his dad got a raw deal. The sheriff had no search warrant and therefore should not have been able to get at Willie's gun. But they did, and that was that—indisputable proof. Willie was a killer.

Johnny picked up his car keys and satchel and went back to the garage. The gun barrel had already disintegrated into the acid. Johnny turned off the fan, closed the back door, and poured the acid back into its original container. The garage door groaned once again as he backed his ten-year-old Mustang out of the driveway and drove toward Blue Lake.

The lake road was fairly empty as he drove past Glory Park, around the lake toward the dam. He could see three sailboats, their puffy white sails blowing in the strong breeze. Several fishermen dotted the side of the lake, perched on rocks, holding on to fishing poles and staring into the water. Johnny hadn't grown up in the country and had never been fishing. But it was something he thought he'd like to do.

He parked in front of Blue Lake Bank and entered the lobby carrying his satchel. He walked straight to a buxom woman with blond, streaked hair sitting at a desk in front of the vault.

"Hi, hon, I need in my safe deposit box. Can you do it for me?"

"Oh, sure. Just follow me, sir."

Johnny followed the woman into the safe deposit vault where he signed for entry to the box and handed her his key.

"Did you want to use one of the privacy booths, sir?"

"Yes, ma'am." Johnny winked at the woman. "And I'd love for you to join me. How private are they?"

"Oh," she giggled. "Not today, sir."

Johnny locked the door of the privacy booth and quickly transferred the contents of his bag into the metal box—except for $500 he decided to hold out for spending money. He closed the box, carried it back to the vault, and relocked the outer door.

"Thanks, honey," he said as he walked past the clerk's desk.

The clock in the lobby chimed and Johnny looked up. It was twelve noon. He hadn't realized it, but he was hungry. He threw the empty bag into the trunk of his convertible, climbed in, and drove toward Tulsa.

The Tulsa Oil Center office building housed a very plush restaurant and Johnny loved the atmosphere. He could sit for hours and eavesdrop on the big-bellied oil men in ten-gallon hats and lizard-skinned boots making million-dollar deals. He loved to watch the old geezers make contracts over liquid lunches and stinking cigars, sealing them with only a nod and a handshake.

If he was lucky, he thought, he could get one of the secretaries there to buy him lunch.

Chapter 3

It was almost 3 P.M. when Sadie turned off the highway two miles southwest of Eucha, crossed the cattle guard, and drove up the lane toward the small, white farmhouse. Joe, her beautiful paint-horse stallion, saw the car coming up the hill and ran the entire fence line to greet her. Sadie didn't usually make it home until after six o'clock, but today was different. They could count it as a sick day, a vacation day, or whatever they wanted, but she had had enough. Gordy was dead and she felt responsible. She wished she could somehow start the day over, erasing the horrible events of that dreadful morning.

She eased her car to a stop beside the faded blue pickup that had once belonged to her dad. She rolled down her window, turned off the ignition, and stared at the old truck. She missed her dad, Jim Walela. His friends had called him "Bird," shortened from the English version of his name—Hummingbird. He always knew how to handle tough situations, and Sadie wished he was here so she could revert into a little girl, crawl up on his lap, and cry on his shoulder. But he had been dead for almost ten years now and the only thing she had left of him was the farm, that old truck, and her paint horse, a stallion named Joe.

Sadie's mom, Cathryn Walela, had tried to sell the 80-acre farm right after Sadie's dad died, but the Bureau of Indian Affairs stopped her. Bird was a full-blood Cherokee and the farm was Indian land, part of the original allotments handed out to Indians just before Indian Territory became the state of Oklahoma. By federal law, half of the land belonged to Sadie, the only heir with Indian blood. Sadie was half Indian and her mother loved to call her a half-breed. But Sadie didn't care anymore what her mother called her—the farm belonged to her now. Cathryn Walela had remarried, moved away, and finally given up interest in the farm.

Sonny, a huge wolf-dog, ran up to the car, placed his front paws on the driver's door, and gave Sadie a lick on the face. Sadie smiled as tears welled up in her eyes and trickled down her cheeks. She reached out and rubbed his soft, furry head.

"You always know when I need a kiss, don't you?"

Sonny barked and eagerly followed her inside the house where she exchanged her skirt and blouse for a pair of jeans and a shirt. As she picked up the white blouse she had worn to work, she noticed, for the first time, a smudge of blood on the sleeve near the elbow. For a moment, she felt sick as the vision of Gordy came rushing back to her. She folded the blouse and placed it in a used grocery sack, grabbed a book of matches, and carried the bag outside. There, she placed it in the trash barrel as if giving the piece of clothing its own ceremony and final resting place. Then she dropped a match on it and watched it slowly burn.

When she came back inside, she realized not only did she not want to be at work, she didn't want to be at home, either. The breakfast dishes stared at her from the sink and suddenly the walls of her tiny farmhouse began closing in on her. She plucked one of three cowboy hats that hung in a row by the back door and pushed it down firmly on her head. Sonny, who had been watching her with curious eyes, knew hat meant horse. The wolf-dog jumped to his feet, ran to the back door, and barked.

"You're right, Sonny. Let's get out of here."

Sonny had come to the farm when he was only a few weeks old by way of her uncle Eli Walela, who had found the mother wolf hit by a car. It took the old man almost an hour to find the den, hidden less than fifty yards away. There, he found the two youngsters patiently waiting for their mother, who would never return. Eli took the pups home and decided to keep the scrawny one, naming him Little Wolf. He carried the other pup through the pasture to Sadie's house, knowing she would never refuse an old man and the smell of puppy breath.

Sadie named her pup Sonny and fed him warm baby cereal and milk every four hours, night and day, until he was big enough to eat puppy food. Exactly how much wolf blood flowed through Sonny's veins, Sadie wasn't sure. But the fear of owning a wolf-dog had dwindled away after six years of companionship unequaled by any dog Sadie had ever known. Sonny's beautiful silver coat and stunning blue eyes reflected his heritage, as well as his natural instinct to distrust strangers. His love for Sadie was apparent, and today he seemed to feel Sadie's pain.

When she entered the barn, tiny particles of hay dust floated in the air around her, reflected by the sunshine that filtered through the cracks in the side of the building. Sadie slung Joe's halter over her shoulder and gave a whistle at the back door of the barn. The stallion trotted toward her in all his splendor, tossing his head. Sadie clicked her tongue against the roof of her mouth and Joe stuck his big nose against her shoulder. She stroked his forehead with one hand, grasped his mane with the other, and whispered gently to the huge animal. Then she took the bridle off her shoulder and slipped it over his big wide nose, past his baby-blue eyes, up and over his mousy ears. The horse accepted the bit between his teeth and ducked his head so she could fasten the buckle of the bridle. The reins fell to the ground and the grand horse waited patiently as Sadie returned to the darkness of the barn.

She came back with the saddle and horse blanket almost dragging the ground. With Joe standing perfectly still, she placed first the blanket on his broad back, then heaved the saddle up and over him. As she tightened the cinch, he snorted in anticipation. Sadie took the reins in her hand, tucked her boot in the left stirrup, and threw her right leg over Joe's back.

This strong, big-headed stallion had been a surprise present from her dad the day she graduated from college. The spindly-legged colt was snow white with a brown spot on his forehead, centered right between his ears. A long, fluid brown marking covered his throat, spreading down and across his chest. Another covered his underbelly and flank, cresting just short of his backbone. Last, a brown tip punctuated his long white tail. These were the markings of a champion, and now as a full-grown horse he had the attitude to match. Sadie loved Joe and felt alive on his back as he responded to the slightest movement of the reins and the touch of her knees.

Sadie and Joe, with Sonny close by, turned down the trail toward the creek, which carved its way indiscriminately through her land. The afternoon sun felt good on her back. She patted the horse on the neck and talked to him as they rode slowly into the pasture. At last she was light-years away from the bank and the political machine that ran it, away from the madness, the robber, the death that lay on the floor just a few hours earlier.

This farm, this horse, and this dog gave Sadie a refuge and a lifeline back to her ancestors. Her father had ridden these hills before Sadie was born and had promised they would always be hers. She had to fight to keep them, but they were hers.

Sadie relaxed and let Joe proceed at his own pace. Sonny, busy sniffing out rabbit holes, made a playful, mad dash for one and then another. Sadie contemplated the balance of nature. She knew Sonny would kill other animals—it was a survival instinct. She wanted to believe that humans were on a higher plane. But were they? For a moment, her thoughts strayed back to Gordy as he fell forward, dying in a pool of blood. He had died so needlessly. She wrestled away from the gloom by concentrating on her surroundings.

Springtime in northeastern Oklahoma brought the color and fragrance of blooming wildflowers, and Sadie savored the aroma of moist black soil as they rode closer to the creek. She dismounted and walked over to the bank of the stream. With her boot, she pushed back the grass while Sonny bounced over to help her investigate. Suddenly, she could smell the slight odor of onions.

"Look, Sonny. Look at that. It's our wild onion patch."

Sadie looked around for something to dig with while Joe grazed on tender green Bermuda grass. When she picked up a short stick and began to dig in the soft soil, tears began to well up in her eyes and stream down her face. She stopped digging, sat down on the bank of the creek, and sobbed.

She cried for the loss of her friend and comrade, Gordy. She cried for the loss of her father and grandmother. She cried for the loss of her childish innocence and for the sudden overwhelming loneliness she felt. She cried for an angry corporate world hostile to her very being, and she cried for the dark soul of a killer. She cried for the violation and the vulnerability she felt in her heart at that very moment.

Sadie sat on the bank of the creek, pulled her ankles up against her buttocks, and stared into space, transforming her senses into a blank slate. After the tears had cleansed her head, memories of her grandmother began to emerge. She smiled and wiped the tears from her face with the back of her hand. It had been Rosa who had taught her to survive no matter what came along in life, including the verbal abuse she would eventually endure from her white mother. And now today, Sadie needed that strength more than ever.

She shoved the sharp end of her stick in the ground, fighting with uncomfortable thoughts of her mother. Living in a house with her mother and grandmother had taught Sadie, at a tender age, what it took to swim in the river that flowed between Indian and white— and not drown.

After she made holes close to the young plants, she relaxed, then turned the stick around and used the wishbone shape at the other end to gently push up the soil while she pulled the onions upward with her other hand. The white, pearl-shaped onion heads easily broke free.

Sadie gathered her onions, carried them over to Joe, and placed them carefully in her saddlebags. The sun had begun its descent in the western sky, casting a tangerine-pink glow over the meadow.

With Sadie on Joe's back again, the horse walked easily, and his movement rocked Sadie into a peaceful state. As they reached the pasture next to the barn, Sonny barked a warning and ran ahead to meet a man leaning against the corral gate.

From a distance, Sadie recognized her uncle's bowed legs, created by decades spent gripping the girth of a horse. His clean, faded jeans hung low on his slender hips, held up by a tooled leather belt and silver buckle.

"*Osiyo*, Sadie." Eli held his white straw hat over his head and waved.

"'*Siyo, 'siyo*." Sadie echoed the Cherokee words of greeting as Sonny returned to her side, wagging his tail.

Eli dropped what was left of his Camel cigarette on the ground and pushed it into the dirt with his old cowboy boot. Sadie slid off Joe's back and gave her uncle a hug.

Her uncle Eli lived on adjoining property with his wife, Mary. He had returned to live on his portion of the family's Indian land after he and Sadie's dad had spent their high school years at Chilocco Indian School in north-central Oklahoma. There the teachers had tried to rid both of the young Indians of their native language and assimilate them into the white man's culture. The school was only half successful. They did indeed learn to live shoulder to shoulder with their neighbors without the animosity their father had held toward the white intruders. But, working together, they never forgot their language.

While at Chilocco, Eli made friends with two Ponca boys. He followed them to a few local powwows, where he learned to dance. A Ponca man had just created a new flamboyant dance called the Fancy War Dance and it caught his attention. It turned out to be quite an experience for Eli when he discovered he could turn the heads of the young Indian girls when he danced—especially the fancy dance. So, he spent his summers traveling the powwow circuit with his Ponca friends and honing his skills, finally winning prizes and earning the nickname of Dancer. After he graduated and served a tour in the army, he returned home to Delaware County to raise horses and live a simple life off the land, next door to his brother.

Now at the age of sixty-three and no longer interested in impressing the ladies, Eli occasionally attended social powwows with his wife. When they did, he proved he could still dance a few songs with the best of them. He spent the rest of his time with his horses, fishing, or playing bingo.

"Uncle," said Sadie. "What brings you out on a Friday night? Isn't it about time for you to be heading toward the bingo hall?"

Eli grinned, revealing his sparse, yellow teeth. His eyes, though slightly clouded, still sparkled when he saw his niece.

"Do you need a ride to bingo?" she asked. "I'll be glad to take you."

"No, no ride."

Eli placed his sweat-stained hat back on his head as they entered the barn. He removed Joe's saddle while Sadie filled a two-pound, red coffee can with oats and dumped them into Joe's feed tub.

"Heard about the stickup." Eli's statement sounded matter-of-fact.

Sadie picked up a currycomb and ran it down Joe's wide chest and over his strong shoulders.

"Want some wild onions to take to Aunt Mary? I have more than enough." Sadie pointed to her saddlebags.

"No, no onions."

Sonny lay in the shadows and patiently watched Sadie brush Joe. Eli kneeled and silently stroked the wolf-dog's head.

"Saw you come home early and ride out on Joe," said Eli. "Saw you were okay."

"You know I can see it as clearly as if it were yesterday," said Sadie. "You know, the way Grandma would bend at her waist, knees locked in place, pulling dead grass and leaves away with her hands ..."

Sadie stopped brushing Joe long enough to demonstrate how her grandmother dug wild onions. Sonny's ears came to attention. He wrinkled his forehead and cocked his head to one side at Sadie's theatrics.

"'Don't be greedy,' she'd say," continued Sadie. "Then she'd say, 'Be sure and leave enough to reseed the patch.'"

"Came to tell you about the *yonega*," said Eli, as he pursed his lips and then added, "*asgaya*." Eli unconsciously sprinkled his speech with Cherokee words out of habit.

"White man?" she asked. "What white man?" Sadie stopped brushing Joe and turned toward her uncle, a puzzled look on her face.

"Before you came home today, I was checking on one of my mares, walking the fence line up by the pond . . . the upper pasture. I can see your place real good from up there, you know."

"Yes, yes I know." Sadie frowned. "Who was it?"

"The boy you married. The one with all the trouble."

Sadie's shoulders slumped. *Michael? Oh, God, please don't let him be talking about Michael.* She placed Joe's grooming brush on a nearby shelf and dumped the onions out of the saddlebags. "Do you remember how she used to wash them on the rocks in the creek?" she asked.

Eli leaned against the wall of the barn, crossed his arms, and slowly shook his head.

"Then we'd come home," she continued, "and she'd take a milk bucket and turn it over so I could reach the sink and then she'd let me finish cleaning them. Then she'd fry those onions up with some bacon and eggs. Why, I thought that was the best eating ever was. And then Mother would get so pissed off because the whole house smelled like wild onions." Sadie smiled. "And then Grandma would lean back in her chair and just laugh."

"Bird was a good brother," said Eli. "And when he died, I promised him I'd watch out for you."

Can't be . . . surely to God it can't be . . . he's in jail . . .

"That boy's bad medicine," said Eli, shaking his head.

Sadie picked up some of the onions with her hand. "Sure you don't want to come inside?"

"No, no. Got to go." Eli winked at Sadie.

Sadie followed her uncle to his old pickup.

"You'll be all right?" he asked. "Mary said you could come stay with us if you wanted."

"I'll be fine. I'll take her some onions."

Eli climbed into his truck and slammed the door. "I'll keep my eye out for you, Sadie. But, you know you got the best protection ever was in that dog there."

"Don't worry, Eli. If we need help, we'll send for Little Wolf."

Eli rested his arm in the open window of his truck. "Took Little Wolf down to Tahlequah to Mary's sister, Essie."

"No. What if you need him?"

"Essie needs him worse. She's got him guarding the chicken house. A bunch of teenagers down there been stealing her chickens."

"Must be hungry kids."

"Hell, no. They're using them in a crazy ritual to get into some college fraternity. Boys need more than a scare from a dog, if you ask me." He looked at the ground, shook his head, and looked back at Sadie. "But, Little Wolf will take care of Essie just like Sonny will take care of you." Then he stomped the accelerator, turned the key, and his truck rumbled to life.

"I know, Eli. Don't worry."

Sadie watched until her uncle pulled onto the highway, then made sure the house was locked tight before inviting Sonny to ride in the back of the pickup. She drove behind the house and followed a well-worn path through the pasture to her aunt and uncle's home.

A black-and-white, paint-horse mare stood in the nearby corral, a gangly colt with identical markings at her side. Sadie slowed to a stop so she could admire the awesome works of the Creator before rolling around the barn to the house.

Mary Walela stood at the kitchen door, drying her hands on a dish towel, when the blue truck pulled through the gate. Sonny bounced off the tailgate as Sadie parked and waited for the dust to settle. She could see Mary open the screen door and wave. It was nice to know she was always welcome at this house no matter what time of day or night. She would never be ridiculed or talked down to, or asked to explain her actions. But she would always be expected to eat. Sadie let herself in through the kitchen door. The strong aroma in Mary's kitchen assured Sadie that her aunt had been expecting her.

"*Siyo*," said Sadie. "I saw Eli a while ago and he didn't say anything about the paint mare having a new baby. When did she have it?"

Mary turned toward Sadie holding a spatula in midair. "Eli got worried about her a couple of days ago and put her in the barn. Spent most of the night up with her night before last. Little thing showed his face early in the morning, about the same time the sun came up. He's a pretty one, isn't he?"

"He's beautiful," said Sadie. "Looks just like his momma. How'd Eli manage that?"

"Oh, just luck, I reckon." Mary continued tending her iron skillet. "Used that white stallion, I think."

Mary picked up a saucepan from a back burner, using her dish towel as a potholder, and poured a weak-colored liquid into a mug and set it on the table. The distinct smell of sassafras filled the air.

Sadie laid the onions in the sink, then pulled out one of the wooden chairs from the table and sat down. "Mmm. Where'd you get the sassafras root?" she asked.

"Eli dug it up and brought it in a while ago. Said you'd need some."

"Oh yeah? And why is that?" Sadie took another sip.

"It's good for what ails you."

"Eli think I'm ailing?"

"Don't argue, just drink it. You're bound to need something to soothe your soul after all that killing going on."

Sadie held the warm cup close to her face. "Brought you some onions," she said.

Mary turned around, studied the pile of greens in her sink, and returned her attention to the skillet. One by one, she pulled out sizzling crawdads and piled them in a mound on a plate. Then she handed Sadie a clean dish towel to use as a napkin and slid the plate in front of her.

"Aunt Mary, why don't you peel these darned things before you cook them? You know the only good part is the tail and I'd much rather you peel them first."

"What kind of Cherokee are you?" asked Eli as the screen door slammed behind him. He deposited his straw hat on a nail next to the door and walked to the sink to wash his hands. "Wanting your crawdads peeled," he teased. "I never heard of the like. You've been working in that bank too long." Eli pulled out a chair and sat across the table from Sadie.

Sadie picked at a crawdad, then finally grabbed it by the head and bit off the tail. "Yeah, Eli, you're right. They're trying to civilize me."

"Or kill you, one or the other," Eli added.

"Here, now," interrupted Mary. "We'll have no talk about that at the table." She sat a bowl of brown beans in the middle of the table and then poured a cup of coffee for Eli.

He spooned himself a helping of beans, picked up several crawdads, and piled them onto his plate next to a hunk of cornbread. Then he spilled some coffee into his saucer to cool.

"They will never succeed," said Sadie, "civilize nor kill." She got up and walked to the window to check on Sonny. She could see him patiently waiting near the back steps. "I better go. This has been a long day. Just wanted to bring these onions to you."

"No need to run off." Eli raised the saucer to his lips and sipped coffee. Then he set the saucer down and sloshed more coffee into it. "Say," he said, "have you been in that Wal-Mart store lately? They got the biggest danged crawdads I ever saw. And they're alive. Got them in a big tank of water."

Sadie laughed at her uncle's tease and played along. "Uncle Eli, those are called lobsters, not crawdads."

Eli grinned. "Look like big crawdads to me."

Mary stood at the kitchen sink cleaning the tender onions. "If you'll wait just a minute, I'll fix these up for you."

"No, really. I'm bushed and I've got plenty more where those came from."

Mary opened the refrigerator and took out a bowl of brown eggs. "Here, honey, you need some eggs?"

Sadie never turned down gifts of food from her aunt. "I always need eggs," she said. "Especially brown eggs. They taste better than the white ones, you know."

"Well, I don't know about that." Mary opened a drawer and pulled out a couple of blue, plastic Wal-Mart sacks, placed a loaf of home-baked bread in the bottom of one, and carefully laid the eggs in the other. "Here, be careful with these eggs until you get home. It'll give you something to eat with your onions."

Sadie took the food, thanked her aunt, and then kissed her on the cheek. "Let me know next time you're going to be midwife to a horse and I'll help."

Eli laughed and Mary waved as Sadie headed toward the truck for the short drive home.

It was dark when she parked the truck next to the Chevy. Sonny jumped out, marked the corner of the porch, and waited for Sadie to let him in. She placed the fresh bread and eggs on the table, then locked the kitchen door behind them.

"This day had better end soon," Sadie spoke aloud as if Sonny could understand. "I don't think I can take much more."

Sadie placed several slices of bacon in her own iron skillet and started cleaning the onions in the sink. As soon as the bacon finished frying, she poured off the grease, saving just the right amount of drippings to cook the onions and the eggs together. Then she savored an indulgence she seldom allowed. Although wild onions were a traditional Cherokee dish, she usually ate them only at church gatherings or special wild onion dinners offered in the community. Tonight was different. The smell of onions flourished throughout the house and Sonny's nose twitched in anticipation. She always saved the last bite for him.

Sadie searched the refrigerator and on a bottom shelf found a forgotten bottle of Budweiser. The cold beer tasted good and she chuckled to herself at the thought of her mother and how aggravated she would be if she were there. She lifted the beer bottle in the air and stuck out her chin. "Here's to a smelly kitchen, Mother. Kiss my ass."

After she ate all she could, she placed her plate on the floor. Sonny quickly licked the plate clean of every last tidbit before checking the floor to see if any got away.

Leaving the dishes for later, she crawled into bed and held a pillow tight to her chest, her body exhausted, her mind racing. The day began to recycle. Maybe she could have done something different, she thought. Feelings of guilt for entering the bank alone flooded her soul. Then the sounds of the day, the robber's voice and the blast of his gun, echoed in her ears. She forced her thoughts to shift. Maybe Eli was wrong about seeing Michael.

Sadie had not seen him in over fifteen years. During that time, she had managed to erase a six-month period of her life from existence. Suddenly, a cold shiver ran up her spine and she sat straight up in bed. Desperately, she searched her memory for the sound of Michael's voice, tried to visualize his stature, wondering what he might look like after years of incarceration.

After a few minutes, she lay back down. No, she thought, I'm becoming hysterical. I've got to relax. And with that thought, she began to think about Michael.

She had been only sixteen, working at the soda fountain, when she first met Michael. He drove into town in his fancy blue-and-white Ford truck with Texas plates and parked next to the Hilltop Drug Store. By the time he walked up the sidewalk, opened the worn screen door, and stepped inside in his tight Wrangler's and black T-shirt, every young girl in town had her eye on him. He placed his shiny boot on the soda fountain foot rail, pushed his cowboy hat back on his head, and ordered a cherry limeade from a young, starry-eyed Sadie. He ordered cherry limeades until she ran out of limes, then switched to Pepsi.

When Sadie's mother saw her get out of Michael's truck and walk up the lane toward the house, the arguing and yelling never stopped until two years later when Sadie ran off in that same truck, only to return home a week later, wearing a thin golden wedding band.

The small ceremony took place at the Benton County courthouse, just over the Arkansas border. Sadie, barely eighteen, held a handful of fresh daffodils Michael had picked for her from the courthouse flower bed. *Do you, Sadie Sehoya Walela, take Michael Jonathan Mills to be your . . . . Do you, Michael . . .*

And then her mother's words, seared into her very being, came out of nowhere. *Well, I guess you proved one thing, didn't you?* Sadie tried to push her mother's words away. *You proved you really are a blanket ass . . .*

Sadie had walked away from her mother and into a nightmare, which ended six months later with a dead man and Michael on his way to the state prison in McAlester. And now, she thought, the nightmare had returned.

The wind banged a tree limb against the window. Sadie got up from her bed and walked into the dark kitchen, still filled with the aroma of wild onions. Curious, Sonny followed as she methodically moved from room to room checking the locks on every door and window.

"Sonny, come."

Sonny followed Sadie back into the bedroom and curled up on the floor next to her bed. She fell asleep, her hand resting lightly on his back.

Chapter 4

Donnie Tenkiller watched through the front plate-glass window as Sadie pulled up to the curbless sidewalk in front of the Eucha General Store. Then he poured a fresh cup of black coffee into a large white Styrofoam cup and placed it on the counter next to a jar of coffee creamer. The cowbell tied to the front door jangled as Sadie swept into the empty store.

"Oh, you've got coffee for me," said Sadie. "You're a sweetheart, Donnie."

Donnie grinned as Sadie stirred lots of sugar and powdered cream into the coffee before raising the cup to her lips and blowing across the top of the steaming liquid. A strand of shiny black hair fell across her cheek, unleashed from the colorful, beaded barrette. She smoothed the straggler against her head with the palm of her hand.

"Donnie? When's some sweet, young thing going to snap you up so you can have coffee ready for her every morning?"

Donnie laughed and Sadie returned the cup to the counter, freeing her hands so she could collect her Monday-morning goodies.

"I heard about the robbery, Sadie."

Donnie's statement was laced with both compassion and morbid curiosity. The young Indian wanted to hear what had happened, but was too polite to ask for a personal account. Now with her back to the counter, Sadie pretended not to hear his comment.

For the last few months Donnie had been working the early shift at the store when Sadie made her daily stop there. His physical appearance belied his true age, barely out of his teen years, and Sadie got the feeling he was secretly offering his heart to her on a regular basis. He seemed to enjoy their early-morning conversations while she stood at the counter injecting her body with caffeine before making the twenty-five-minute drive to Sycamore Springs.

While she drank coffee and talked, she darted through the tiny store picking up first one thing and then another, none of which looked like items befitting a woman like Sadie. This morning it was three ready-to-open cans of beanie-weenies, a small jar of crunchy peanut butter, a loaf of bread, and a large bag of potato chips.

Sadie placed the items on the counter and returned to her cup of energy. She blew across the top of the cup, took another drink, and put it back down on the counter.

"Say, Donnie, you haven't seen any strangers around here lately, have you?"

Donnie tilted his head while he thought, his face showing surprise at Sadie's interest in the local gossip. "Old man Johnson has a new girlfriend. She stayed in the truck while he came in to buy a six-pack a couple of weeks ago."

"No, I mean anyone . . . you know, not from around here."

Donnie thought for another moment before he answered. "No, can't say that I've noticed anyone. Why?"

"No reason, really. Just curious."

Sadie resumed her early-morning treasure hunt, adding two apples, a container of orange juice, and a large bottle of water. Donnie pecked at the cash register and bagged the items one at a time.

"That'll be nine thirty-six, Sadie."

Sadie pulled out a ten-dollar bill and handed it to Donnie. She picked up the brown paper sack and headed for the door.

"You'd better keep all of that, Donnie. You forgot to add my coffee."

The young clerk blushed and looked down.

"And thank you for not asking about the robbery. I've spent all weekend dodging phone calls and trying to forget it, and, well, I'm afraid when I get to work this morning all that trying won't amount to much."

Sadie smiled and waited for him to look at her before she winked at him. The cowbell clanged again and then the store fell silent as Donnie watched Sadie drive off.

The Monday-morning traffic in Sycamore Springs reminded Sadie of how much she disliked the thirteen and a half miles of twisting highway she drove to work every day. Then, it seemed like she always managed to catch every red light on MLK. As she sat at the

Harvest Street intersection, she could see the bank parking lot. Stan Blackton stood flailing his arms, deep in conversation with Tom Duncan, the branch manager. She wondered if Tom had stayed out of reach the entire weekend. If so, he would be suffering the repercussions of Stan's wrath for it now.

A quick check of the time showed she had twenty minutes before she was officially due to clock in. Careful to evade Tom and Stan's parking lot meeting, Sadie drove past the bank and up the Harvest Street hill. When she got to Jefferson, her luck changed and she sailed through two green lights in a row. Moving away from the major flow of traffic, she turned left on Tenth Street, then took a quick right down an unmarked alley that ended under the expressway. There, beneath the shelter of a concrete embankment, she could see the large cardboard box. Sadie gathered up her small bag of groceries and walked a short distance through an empty lot of overgrown weeds and broken glass. She stopped at the corner of a broken fence, her self-imposed boundary.

"Happy?" Sadie's voice was soft against the hum of traffic rushing overhead.

Her arrival generated no movement in the box. No sign of anyone. She placed the brown bag in the regular place and picked up a sack of trash that included empty cans from her last delivery.

"Happy, I brought orange juice."

Still no one stirred. Sadie waited for a moment, looked at her watch, and went back to her car. She would check on him again in a few days. She realized she couldn't support all the homeless people in Sycamore Springs, but Happy was different.

The first time she met him, her front tire had gone flat just as she was leaving the Wal-Mart Super Store. She had pulled back into the huge parking lot and while attempting to retrieve the spare tire from her trunk, he appeared from nowhere. His presence, first announced by the pungent smell of body odor, caught Sadie off-guard. The man's kinky, black hair and beard harbored tiny flecks of dried grass and he clenched a green garbage sack in his filthy right hand.

Sadie picked up the tire tool from the trunk and stepped back. "Don't come any closer," she warned.

Ignoring her stance, the man placed his trash bag on the ground, walked over, and took the spare tire and jack out of the car. He got down on his hands and knees and carefully pushed the jack stand under the edge of the bumper. With a puzzled face, he looked at the tire tool in Sadie's hand as if he knew he needed it but was unsure how to get it. Sadie hesitantly surrendered the tool and watched while he changed her tire.

Dumbstruck by the man's kindness and embarrassed for her initial reaction, Sadie offered to pay for his help. He just shook his head, unable or unwilling, Sadie was unsure which, to say a word. He left her standing and sauntered over to the nearby Dairy Queen to pick through the trash for something to eat.

Sadie slammed the trunk of her car, drove to the fast-food eatery, and ordered cheeseburgers, French fries, and chocolate shakes until he could eat no more. The unlikely pair, a young woman in her business suit and a smelly, disheveled man, sat at an outdoor picnic table while he ate and she talked.

"What do they call you?" she asked.

The man chomped on his food, filling his mouth until his cheeks stretched like a chipmunk storing nuts for the winter.

"Do you live around here? Where's your family?"

The man laughed, then took a gulp of chocolate shake before cramming more greasy French fries into his mouth with his dirty fingers.

"Can I take you somewhere?"

Try as she might, she could not budge a word from his lips. Finally, they sat in silence. The painfully thin man stopped eating and rubbed his belly. Sadie ordered him two more burgers, which he promptly put in his front pockets. Unwanted tears pooled in the corner of her eyes when she saw the happiness she had managed to generate in this silent, gentle man.

She offered once more to take him home, but instead he stood, belched, and laughed again. Then, to her animated protests, he walked away.

Intrigued, Sadie decided to follow at a distance. The man walked south on Tenth Street. He stopped here and there, dawdled and picked through trash. Finally, after almost thirty minutes, he reached home— a big brown, empty appliance box under the expressway. When he saw she had followed, he laughed and disappeared into the box. That's when she decided to call him Happy.

For an entire week after Sadie's encounter with the homeless Samaritan, she called every social service agency in the phonebook trying to find someone to help Happy.

"I'm sorry, ma'am." The voice on the other end of the telephone line sounded uninterested. "If he is not a threat to anyone and not a danger to himself he's free to live in a box all he wants."

Later that day the blue-haired woman at the Shelter of Grace gave Sadie a boxed dinner. "Here, take this to him and tell him he can come to the shelter. But, you know, honey," she said, "some people would rather live on the street."

Sadie thanked the woman and delivered the warm meal to Happy, leaving it near his brown box. She returned the next day to find the empty food container folded neatly where she had left it. That was when she had started her routine of delivering food and removing trash twice a week, usually on Mondays and Thursdays.

On this Monday morning, after leaving Happy's homeless world, Sadie sailed through green lights all the way back to MLK and Harvest. She had three minutes to spare. She parked in her usual space and walked toward the bank. Tom stood at the front door meeting each employee as they arrived. Stan was already gone.

"I see you decided not to come in early by yourself this morning, Sadie."

Sadie had to remind herself it was not worth the hassle to verbally duel with Tom. She stopped just inside the glass doors and stood in the vestibule while he turned the key in the dead bolt behind her. She could see in her peripheral vision that the burgundy carpet was gone, replaced with a navy blue berber.

"It's nice to see you, too, Tom."

"Hey, don't look at me like that," said Tom. "Blackton is the one considering hanging you from the highest tree at sunrise. Only thing stopping him is the fact you're a woman."

Sadie frowned. "You mean I'm an Indian woman, don't you? Give me a break, Tom." Irritation echoed in her voice. "And, can we dispense with the cowboy-and-Indian humor this morning, please?"

"Okay, Sadie. Sorry." Tom opened the second glass entryway door for Sadie. She stopped for a moment and stared at the place where Gordy had fallen. Two new overstuffed chairs and a small table were arranged directly over the dreadful spot, flanked by two potted scheffleras. New-account brochures lay scattered across the top of the table.

Attuned to Sadie's question before she asked, Tom said, "It was Thelma's idea. You know, that way we walk around that area for a while."

Thelma worked in the personnel department at the main office. Her main job was to act as troubleshooter and pacify the employees in whatever manner deemed necessary. Her signature went on all the employment records even though the decisions were always made by one of the men.

"Oh." Sadie hated the feeling beginning to overtake her. She thought for an instant she heard Gordy's voice coming from the teller area and jerked her head in that direction.

"We've got some new tellers this morning, Sadie."

Sadie realized she didn't recognize any of the employees in the branch.

"I think Stan half expected to get a resignation call from you, too. But I told him I was sure you could weather this storm."

Sadie continued to stare inside the lobby from the safety of the doorway.

"You *are* all right, aren't you, Sadie?" Tom's bantering had softened and compassion began to creep around the edge of his voice.

"Why, yes. I'm fine." She stepped onto the new blue carpet and walked over to her desk. Tom followed. Her desk looked just as she had left it, as if somehow it had been suspended in air while the old carpet had been ripped away and the new carpet rolled across the floor. Her small picture of Joe sat right next to her phone where she always kept it, a reminder of strength and beauty.

"I guess you know," Tom continued to talk, "the memorial service for Gordy is today at five o'clock."

"Oh? No, not really." Sadie smoothed the front of the black jumper she had unconsciously chosen to wear that morning. "No, I wasn't sure when it would be. Five o'clock?"

"Yes. Stan asked the family to have it after we closed so the employees could go."

A curious look crossed Sadie's face. "You're kidding, aren't you? You're saying Stan told the family when to have their son's memorial service? I can't believe it. On the other hand . . ."

"Sadie, do you mind if we go to the service together?"

"That man is disgusting. Why couldn't we just close down for the afternoon . . . oh, never mind." Then, as an afterthought, she answered his question, "Yeah, sure."

"Sadie, I'm going to need you to go through Gordy's desk. They've already taken his personal things, but I have no idea what he was working on."

The mention of Gordy's name brought a sad smile to Sadie's face just as the phone on her desk rang in short, double bursts, piercing the air.

"Good morning, this is Sadie. How may I help you?" Sadie's voice took on the sound of a prerecorded message.

"Sadie. Stan here. You need to get in your car and go down to police headquarters. They've arrested that robber and they need you to identify him."

Sadie reached for her chair in slow motion and sat in it as if she thought it would break.

"Sadie? Are you there?"

"Uh . . . yes, sir. I'm here."

"They are expecting you. Be sure and clock out."

Sadie hung up the phone and looked at Tom. "I don't think I'm going to be much help today, Tom. They need me to identify the robber."

"Damn. It's about time they finally caught that guy." Tom seemed flustered at the news. "Okay . . . okay, go ahead and go . . ."

"I can't identify him." Sadie had dismissed Tom and was staring out the huge glass window next to her desk. "It's not like I really saw him . . ."

An elderly woman with starched, silver hair drove into the handicapped parking stall directly in front of the bank entrance. Her wooden cane appeared from underneath the open car door and began to probe at the concrete as if testing to see if it would hold the delicate old lady up. When she had cleared the sidewalk ramp, she leaned on her cane and shielded her eyes from the morning sun to see if the bank was open.

"The world just keeps right on turning, doesn't it?" said Sadie.

"I don't know, Sadie," said Tom. "I've got to make sure these tellers are ready." Tom walked away from Sadie and then added over his shoulder, "Just come back here when you get through so we can go to the service together."

Sadie unlocked the front door and held it open while the shriveled woman entered the bank, filling the air around her with the fragrance of gardenias. Once the lady was safely inside and teetering toward the teller line, Sadie stepped into the morning sunshine. She looked at the sky and thanked God to be leaving the discomfort of overstuffed chairs and navy blue carpet.

Chapter 5

The morning traffic began to thin as Sadie drove the three short miles downtown. She decided to go south on Martin Luther King Boulevard instead of looping onto the expressway, even though that route would take longer. Her mind wandered and then resurfaced, detached and replaying the events of last Friday. And once she arrived at the Sycamore Springs Police Department, she could not remember the familiar scenery she had passed along the way.

Black-and-white police cars crawled in every direction and Sadie felt like an intruder among members of a secret society. She wavered between the thought of complete safety and a sudden fear of increased scrutiny. Then she noticed a good-looking Indian cop standing next to a parked car, scribbling on a small metal clipboard. "Working on your monthly quota of traffic tickets, handsome?" She spoke aloud to herself and smiled.

She grabbed a parking space near the front entrance of the police station and disposed of her last three quarters in the parking meter. Pushing her way through the heavy front door of the old building, Sadie found herself engulfed by a large bustling lobby with a shiny, faux marble floor and a high, ornate ceiling. A myriad of sounds echoed in the heavy air as she made her way toward a large, box-shaped directory stationed in the middle of the floor.

As Sadie searched the board for guidance, two uniformed officers, deep in serious conversation, walked out of a crowded elevator and stopped. One large officer stood with his back to Sadie, while the other young man talked expressively with his hands. The two officers both broke out in laughter as the ticket writer she had seen a few moments earlier joined them. She watched the trio from the corner of her eye while she searched the directory for the Robbery Division.

The Indian officer continued to capture her interest. He appeared to be about her age, in his mid-thirties. Yet he wore his uniform well with what she imagined to be washboard abs, broad shoulders, and a rock-hard chest. She couldn't help but notice his raven-black hair, shorn in a crewcut, and how it complemented the strong lines of his face.

When she reached a decision on which path she should take, she turned on her heels, almost colliding with the large officer who was still engrossed in conversation with the ticket-writing Indian while they walked across the lobby.

"Ma'am?" The sergeant instinctively nodded his head. "Can I help you find someone?"

"Oh, hello," said Sadie, relieved to see his friendly face. "Sergeant McCord, isn't it?"

"Indeed it is, young lady. But you can call me Charlie. You're, uh, from the bank."

"You remember me?"

"Of course I remember you." Charlie struggled for the pronunciation of her name. "It's Miss Wa—"

"Walela," she offered. "But, please, call me Sadie."

"Yes, ma'am." Then he turned and motioned toward the other officer. "This is Officer Lance Smith."

"*Siyo,*" said Lance.

"Hello." Sadie shook the officer's hand and smiled. His light grip reminded her of her father's handshake, unlike the aggressive, firm clasp demanded of all employees by the superiors at the bank. Then she wondered if this handsome Indian might be a descendant of Redbird Smith, the legendary Cherokee who had devoted his life to preserving the old ways.

"What brings you all the way downtown?" asked Charlie.

Sadie returned her attention to the big man. "Well, one of the vice presidents at the bank called and said they wanted me to come down and identify the robber."

"Oh, they did?" A crease grew between his thick eyebrows and then he laughed. "I wondered why all those federal boys were crawling around here this morning."

Sadie relaxed temporarily, enjoying the sergeant's good mood.

"Listen, Miss, uh, Sadie, just have a seat and I'll see what I can find out for you. Monday mornings can be kind of hectic around here." Charlie guided Sadie to the corner of the lobby to a small waiting area. Then both officers disappeared in separate directions.

A slim woman with a complexion the color of weak coffee sat on a bench with a preschool-aged child propped against her shoulder. She wore her frizzy, black hair slicked flat against her head. The woman leaned forward, placed her elbows on her knees, and took a drag from a thin smoldering cigarette. Dark circles encased the woman's eyes, sinking them deep into her face. A short skirt barely covered the tops of her long legs, and her tight blouse gaped between her breasts where the fabric was held together with a safety pin.

Disturbed from her resting place, the child silently climbed toward her mother. The young girl, neatly dressed in worn clothes, bore the sad woman's unflattering facial features. Several small, pink clasps fought to contain her hair.

"Hope you ain't in no hurry," said the woman. Before making a place for her daughter on her lap, the woman dropped her half-smoked cigarette on the floor and twisted her worn, high-heeled shoe on it twice before kicking it into the corner where several other discarded cigarette butts lay. "Name's Christine," she continued. "I been waiting here near all night. They suppose to already let me see my man, Leroy."

Sadie could not tell if the woman's slurred speech resulted from lack of sleep or perhaps some other form of incapacitation. "Hello." Sadie smiled weakly and chose a chair across from the woman. "No, I'm in no hurry," she added.

The restless child descended from her mother's lap, walked straight over to Sadie, and stared at her with curious eyes, then held up three fingers.

"I'm this many," she said.

"Candy, don't bother the nice lady." The woman patted the seat beside her.

"She's okay." Sadie opened her purse, pulled out a small box of raisins, and held them up for the mother's approval. "Is it all right if she has these?"

Before the mother could answer, the child jammed her thumbs in the end of the box, opening the container and scattering tiny brown pellets across the floor. Suddenly, Charlie appeared out of nowhere and almost tripped trying to avoid the runaway raisins.

"What the . . . ?"

Behind him, a man in a navy blue suit, white shirt, and tie stopped at the outer edge of the waiting area.

"Ma'am," said Charlie. "This is Federal Agent Victor Robinson. He's heading up the investigation on the robbery."

Sadie stood and the photo badge around the tall agent's neck swung forward as he took one step and leaned over to shake her hand. She did not recognize him as one of the agents who had come to the branch the morning of the robbery.

"Thank you for coming down," said the agent. "This will only take a few minutes."

The young child sat on the floor, stuffing raisins in her pockets. Sadie hesitated for a moment. "Yes, thank you. But, did you know this lady has been waiting here all night?" she asked.

Yeah, I'm still waiting," piped the mother of the child. "What's the deal?"

The agent ignored the woman and walked toward the elevator. With a nod, Charlie silently urged Sadie to comply. Reluctantly, she followed him into the elevator.

The doors slid open on the third floor revealing a long hallway of dull institutional gray sliced by an endless, shiny-red horizontal stripe running the length of the corridor. A large sign facing the elevator shouted: "RESTRICTED AREA—ALL VISITORS MUST SIGN IN HERE." An arrow pointed to a small opening that resembled the outside window at the Dairy Queen. Two black metal chairs sat in the hallway to the right of the window. Agent Robinson leaned into the window and waved to three uniformed officers who shared the small office behind the makeshift welcome desk.

"Ready when you are, Max."

A silver-haired Sergeant Maddox walked up to the window, tilted his head at Sadie, and made a limp, one-fingered salute at the agent.

Sadie followed Robinson to the end of the hall and into a room the size of a large broom closet. A row of four brown plastic chairs faced a large dark window. After the door closed behind them, Charlie stood in back of Sadie as if trying to find an inconspicuous place in the small room. A very young FBI agent, wearing the same navy suit uniform and swinging identification badge, stood staring into the void.

"This is Agent Daniel Booker," said Robinson. "He will be assisting in the investigation."

Booker glanced at Sadie, nodded, and then returned his attention to the window.

"Have a seat, ma'am," continued Robinson. "We have a few people we would like you to take a look at. Hopefully, one of them will look familiar."

Sadie continued to stand. "Mr. Robinson . . . I don't think you understand. I never really saw the robber." Sadie turned and looked at Charlie, hoping he could help explain to these two men how everything had happened. "He was completely covered . . ."

Charlie stood silently with his feet apart, his big arms resting across his broad chest.

"Yes, ma'am, I know," said Robinson. "We're just hoping you'll see something about one of them that's recognizable or familiar. Perhaps the way he stands or maybe his physique, you know, his build."

"I heard him speak," said Sadie. "That's all. Maybe if I could hear his voice. He had a really cold voice . . . hard to describe." Sadie rubbed the palm of her right hand on her left forearm. "It makes me shiver just to think about it."

The second agent turned away from the window. A silent message passed between the two as they glanced at each other. Then as if on cue, the lights came on in the room behind the large glass window and five men walked into view. They were all wearing black, hooded sweatsuits and Sadie's mind temporarily flashed backward. For an instant, she thought everyone she saw was the robber.

Unaware that she was trembling, Sadie involuntarily dropped her purse. Charlie stepped forward, retrieved her purse, and gently guided her into one of the plastic chairs.

"Relax, Sadie," he said. "They can't see you."

Sadie's reaction seemed to ignite something in the FBI agents. Excitement began to show in their eyes. Booker smiled at Robinson with an arrogant air of success as if he was sure they had their man.

Regaining her composure, Sadie began to study each suspect. Although their faces were partly obscured by their hoods, she could not help but stare, searching for some unknown clue.

"The first one is too tall and skinny," she said.

"Are you sure? Now, take your time," urged Booker.

"I'm sure." Sadie's voice began to show confidence.

Only a few seconds passed.

"Number two is too stocky."

The room was quiet.

"It isn't number three either. He's just not built right."

"What about number four?"

"No, he's too short."

"And five?" The question from Booker was almost a plea for recognition.

"Oh, I don't think so . . . he's really too skinny."

Booker flipped a toggle switch next to the window and spoke into a small speaker. "Max, have them step forward and turn to their right."

Sadie withdrew from the window.

"If they can't see me, why are they looking at me?" she whispered.

"It's okay." Charlie sat beside Sadie and leaned forward, his hand on the chair behind her as if offering protection. "They can't see you."

Sadie looked back at the five men. The hair on her arms stood on end.

"Oh, God," she gasped, raising her hand to her mouth. "That one's hood. It looks like the robber's . . . the torn place on his hood."

"Which one, Sadie?"

"That one," she said, pointing at number five.

"Okay, Max, have them turn forward again."

"Oh, no." Her voice full of relief, she almost laughed. "It's not him. I know him."

"You know the robber?"

"No, he's not a robber. He's Happy." Sadie could see the scared man's face, his mouth drawn into a frown.

"Happy?" Both agents turned and looked at Sadie.

"Who's happy?" asked Booker. "We're trying to pick out a robber here."

"He's a homeless man and he lives under the bridge."

"And his name is Happy?"

"No, I just call him that because I don't know his real name. He laughs a lot."

"And you know him?" asked Robinson.

"Yes, well, sorta. He helped me fix my tire one day—"

"He what?" Robinson's voice suddenly sounded angry. Then in a calmer tone he added, "And his voice is not the robber's voice?"

"He doesn't talk."

"How do you know?"

"I've tried to talk to him before."

"When did you try to talk to him?"

"All the time. I take him food twice a week."

"You what?"

"Food?" Booker came alive. "Well, here, let me get a bandage for your bleeding heart. Is he the robber or not?"

Charlie's eyes flashed a warning straight at the young agent. "Cool it, Junior. You're out of line."

"Hey, Sarge." Booker stuck his chin in the air. "Don't you have some traffic to direct somewhere?"

"Knock it off, you two," snapped Robinson. "Save it for later." Robinson then turned his attention back to Sadie. "I'm sorry, ma'am. Now, what about the hood?"

"I don't know. I thought for a minute it looked like the one the robber had on . . . it was torn in the same place as his."

"You think it's the same hood?"

"I don't think that's gonna stand up for you boys in court." Charlie's voice reeked with sarcasm. "You cannot . . . identify a perp . . . by the hole in his hat." Charlie separated each phrase for emphasis and then laughed a schoolboy laugh.

Both agents ignored Charlie.

"What did the robber say to you, ma'am?" asked Booker.

Sadie told him, and Booker walked back over to the toggle switch. "Okay, Max. Have number five repeat 'We're going to transact a little business.'"

Sadie could hear the officer in the lighted room barking at Happy. Happy looked scared and made no sound.

"Stop yelling at him," begged Sadie. "It's not him. I told you he's not the robber."

"That's okay, Max." Booker tried to hide the disappointment in his voice. "Take number five back to the holding cell." His voice then accelerated to a command. "The rest of you clowns can go back to work, now. Show's over."

Sadie felt a wave of relief rush over her body. Thank God, she thought, she would not have to face the killer today.

Charlie stood up. "Do you need the lady for anything else?"

"Well, I'm not sure." Robinson looked first at Charlie and then at

Sadie. "Exactly how well do you know this man?" His voice had become sweet, almost sickening, and Sadie reacted by backing away from the agent.

"I told you. He's homeless. He helped me change a tire one time and I found out where he lived and started taking him food."

"Do you ever carry on a conversation with this homeless helper?"

"No, I told you. He can't talk."

"And you're sure about that?" Booker chimed in from behind Robinson.

"Yes . . . well, I guess . . . I don't know." Sadie's head began to spin. What was happening? Why were they turning on her?

"That's enough, boys." Charlie took Sadie by the elbow and guided her to the door. "I don't know where you're going with this, but there's a difference between robber and robbee. Try to keep it straight."

"We'll keep in touch, ma'am. Don't be taking any long trips any-where."

Right after Sergeant Charlie McCord escorted a shaken Sadie through the lobby, Christine took Candy by the hand and slipped onto the elevator. She wasn't sure where she was going, but she was tired of waiting.

"What do ya think, Candy?"

The child held up three fingers again. "This many," she said.

"Three it is."

Christine punched button number three. In a moment, the doors magically opened to a new world for Candy and her eyes grew big with astonishment. Suddenly, an urge struck the young girl.

"Momma, gotta pee."

"Shut up," snapped Christine. "You'll have to wait."

"Gotta pee." Candy began to whimper.

A door opened at the end of the hall and Sergeant Maddox emerged with his prisoner. Happy was handcuffed, his black sweatsuit confiscated and replaced with an orange jumpsuit with "Inmate" sten-ciled in black letters across the front and back. Instantly, Maddox spotted the woman and child at the elevator.

"Hold it right there, ma'am," he said. "You want to wait there by the window? Someone'll help you there in a minute."

Candy crossed her legs and began to cry. "Pee, Momma, pee."

The child grabbed at her crotch with one hand and pulled at the bottom of her mother's short skirt with the other.

"Good grief, Candy. You can pick the worst time . . ."

Maddox tightened his grip on Happy. "Hold on, buddy, you don't need no trouble right now," he said.

Simultaneously, two officers arrived, flanked Christine, and began to escort her and Candy back to the elevator. The child broke loose and ran straight at Happy and then stopped abruptly. She could hold it no longer and a puddle began to form between her feet. Her face turned bright red and she began to scream.

Maddox shoved Happy against the wall as Christine, both officers in tow, quickly moved to retrieve Candy. Happy slid down the wall, sat on the floor, and looked at the little girl. Tears began to flow down his face and, to the sergeant's surprise, he tried to speak. Maddox looked at his prisoner and then back at the woman and child.

"Ma'am," yelled Maddox. "Do you know this man?"

"Hell, no. I don't know him," she yelled. "I'm lookin' for Leroy, and that sure ain't Leroy."

Christine jerked Candy's arm as the elevator door closed behind them.

Chapter 6

The evening sunlight filtered through the stained-glass windows creating a temporary mosaic of color on the walls of the Sycamore Springs Baptist Church. The casket sat in front of the pulpit, covered with a huge spray of white carnations, with a high school graduation picture of Gordy nestled in the center. Bouquets of flowers covered the entire area where the choir usually sat and blooming plants created a blanket of color on the floor.

Sadie and Tom Duncan found seats near the back of the crowded sanctuary, near an outside wall. She discreetly shifted, searching for a comfortable spot on the unpadded, wooden pew. Organ music floated in the air but she could see no organ anywhere. Eventually, the melodies of the hymns began to repeat and she realized it must be a tape. The family had gathered in an adjacent room, and as the time for the service neared, they filed into the three front pews.

A young man sang "Beyond the Sunset," after which the pastor recited the Twenty-third Psalm. Then friends and family members came to tell stories about Gordy and what a bright future he would have had.

A girl about Gordy's age joined the first singer and together they sang "Amazing Grace" in harmony. On the last stanza they asked the congregation to sing along. Unconsciously, Sadie sang quietly in Cherokee. *"Unelanvhi uwetsi igaguyvhei hnaqwu tsosv wiulose igaguyvhona."*

The song brought a sense of comfort to her. It reminded her of her grandmother's wake after she succumbed to pneumonia, an aftereffect of influenza. She remembered how the choir from the Oklahoma Indian Missionary Conference Church had sung Cherokee hymns for hours as friends and neighbors got up one by one, speaking good words about her. Then, only ten months later, she would have to sit through the same ordeal again after her father suddenly died. He had fallen into a diabetic coma, never to reawaken. With his aversion to doctors, she hadn't even known he'd had diabetes, the disease that millions of Indians suffer from every year.

The singing stopped and the preacher began to read from his Bible. "Let not your heart be troubled . . . . In my Father's house are many mansions, if it were not so . . . . I go now to prepare a place for you . . ."

Sadie's mind wandered again as she thought about the fragility of life. She wondered if Gordy had any idea this photograph would someday be displayed in front of a group of people as they recounted the good things about his life. It so easily could have been her who was dead in place of him. Agonizing memories steeped in guilt began to wash over her again.

A young man about Gordy's age, visibly shaken, stood up near the front and began to tell a story about his friendship with Gordy. Then a group of young people sang two more songs. After an hour and a half, the service finally came to an end and Sadie felt a sense of relief. She preferred to grieve privately.

As Sadie left the sanctuary of the church, she found the vestibule crowded, full of bank employees. Stan Blackton stood in the middle of a group of executives talking and laughing. While Sadie was not surprised, she thought his behavior offensive. She recalled Tom's comment about Blackton's request to hold the service after hours, so the bank would not have to lose a minute of work time, and her grief became mixed with disgust. Embarrassed to be associated with such people, she purposely turned her back to Blackton.

Adam Cruthers, the bank's chief financial officer, stood near the door speaking in quiet tones to a man she did not know. The man was striking, well dressed in a dark suit and tie. He stood with feet apart, hands clasped in front of him, head bent, listening intently to Adam. As Sadie wove her way through the crowd toward the front door, Adam reached out and touched her on the arm.

"You okay, Sadie?"

"Yes, Adam. Thanks."

Sadie and Adam's friendship had begun over twelve years earlier when they went to work for the bank on the same day. He managed to successfully climb the corporate ladder, securing a coveted slot at the top, while Sadie continued to laughingly classify herself as lower-middle management. Her position ranked too low in the hierarchy of the bank to receive credit when something good happened, but high enough to be blamed when something bad happened. However, even with the disparity in the levels of their positions, Adam and Sadie remained distant friends.

"Sadie, this is Jaycee Jones," said Adam. "He handles some of the investments for the bank."

Sadie greeted the man and offered her hand.

"Please accept my condolences," he said softly and held her hand between both of his for a few extended moments. His hands were warm against her cold fingers and she felt an instant attraction to him.

About that time, Tom attached himself to her elbow and interrupted. "Sadie, I thought I'd lost you in this crowd," he said. "Can you give me a ride to pick up my car?"

"Yeah, sure," said Sadie, pulling her hand free.

"Nice to meet you," said Jaycee.

Sadie smiled and nodded before walking out into the evening dusk with Tom. The air, cool and damp, smelled of rain and held the eerie stillness of an approaching storm. Silent flickers of lightning illuminated the outer edges of a bank of clouds in the western sky.

"Why does it always seem to rain when you go to funerals?" asked Tom.

"It's the Creator talking to you, Tom," she said. "You should try listening once in a while."

Tom did not know what to say. He could tell from the tone of Sadie's voice she was not in the mood for conversation.

"Do you think we should hang around?" asked Tom.

Sadie stopped walking and turned toward her colleague. "For what?"

"I don't know," he said. "Maybe we should see what Stan has to say when he comes out."

"This is a memorial service, Tom . . . and it's over. And I sure don't need Stan Blackton's permission to leave."

"Go ahead, then," said Tom. "I think I'll wait. I can catch a ride with someone else."

"Suit yourself." Sadie turned and continued walking toward the parking lot.

Tom waited on the sidewalk while Blackton and the rest of the crowd began to emerge from the church.

Sadie sat in her car and watched as Tom and others swarmed around Blackton as if trying to make sure he knew they were there, perhaps win points for attending. As she started her car, she caught a whiff of Jaycee's cologne on her hand. She held the tips of her fingers to her nostrils and inhaled. The musky smell stirred something deep inside. What an intoxicating fragrance, she thought.

The crowd dispersed among the vehicles and Tom waved at her, indicating he was riding with someone else. She acknowledged him and waited her turn to pull out of the parking lot. Three cars down, she watched as Jaycee got in the car with Adam. She couldn't help but wonder about the handsome stranger.

Finally, it was her turn to go. The sky moaned in the distance and she drove away into the evening.

Chapter 7

To the steady stream of customers, frantic over the impending tax deadline of April 15, the new blue carpet in the bank seemed to be invisible. One of the regulars stumbled into the newly placed chairs and complained about the unfamiliar display in the middle of the lobby. Sadie buried herself in her work, trying to ignore the trauma of the robbery, hoping it would quietly seep to the back of her mind.

She watched as customers parked their cars and hurried into the bank. From time to time, she would find herself distracted from her work, gazing through the huge plate-glass windows and critiquing the physique of each man, comparing it to her memory of the robber.

She saw Charlie McCord get out of his squad car and lumber toward the bank. The sight of the officer set off a flash of panic. The big man entered the branch and walked directly to the teller line and pulled out a check. Sadie relaxed and reminded herself that he, too, was a customer and needed to carry on business like everyone else. Then he turned and walked straight toward Sadie's desk.

"Is there somewhere we can talk in private?" he asked.

"Sure, is there something wrong, Sergeant?"

"No, no." Charlie shook his head. "Actually, I'd just like to visit." He smiled and Sadie stood.

"In that case, you can join me for lunch," she said. "I was just getting ready to walk over to the Blue Dumpling Café."

"I've never been known," said Charlie, "to turn down an invitation to a meal."

The two left the bank and walked across the street to a row of small shops. The morning chill had disappeared, replaced with the radiant warmth of full spring sunshine. A strip of Bermuda grass next to the sidewalk sported a hearty crop of bright yellow dandelion blooms with an occasional fuzzy head waving in the breeze. Purple blossoms covered the ground below a large redbud tree that had begun to surrender its dainty blooms near a freshly painted white park bench.

As they walked toward the café, Sadie realized she was beginning to like the sergeant. He gave her a sense of security, a feeling she had missed since her dad died. And although she thought many people might find Charlie's size intimidating, she liked to think of him as a giant teddy bear in a police uniform.

"It's nice to get out of the bank for lunch," she said. "I like to get some fresh air during the day, if I can. I mean, we have a lunchroom and all, but if I stay there, well, I never get to finish without someone interrupting me. And then I end up scarfing it down, or just leaving it and returning to work before I'm finished."

"You shouldn't let them bother you like that."

"Yeah, well, they know if I'm within earshot of a ringing phone, they've got me," Sadie laughed. "This way, they can't get to me and I can enjoy my lunch. I guess what I'm trying to say is—thanks for coming by at lunchtime."

"Glad I could help out," said Charlie, rubbing his round belly. "Especially since I love to eat."

Charlie and Sadie picked a corner booth for privacy and studied the menu. Charlie placed his portable radio on the edge of the table, adjusting the volume as low as possible without completely shutting out the drone of the dispatcher. They both decided on the special of the day—chicken-fried steak, mashed potatoes, and gravy. Each plate lunch included a small serving of the house specialty—blue dumplings.

"Just one thing," began Charlie. "What exactly are these blue dumplings? Lance Smith is always carrying on about them."

"*Unitelvladi digalvnv,*" Sadie said.

"Do what?"

Sadie laughed. "Cherokee words for grape dumplings. Blue dumplings are the same thing as grape dumplings, a traditional Cherokee dish made out of grapes—possum grapes. You boil the juice and then drop in the dumplings. I love them. You never see them in restaurants, just Indian gatherings. That's why I like to come here. The owners of the café are Cherokee."

"Possum grapes, you say?" Charlie raised his eyebrows. "I'm going to have to ask Smith about that."

"Speaking of Lance Smith, how is that good-looking Indian cop?" Sadie embarrassed herself before she could stop the words from leaving her mouth.

"Lance? He's a good man. Eats here all the time. Should have known he'd be eating something like possum grapes. I'll have to tell him I know his secret for staying so slim."

"Don't worry." Sadie could hardly hide her amusement. "You can rest assured these are probably made from canned grape juice and I doubt they contribute to anyone being slim. But, I don't think you came here to get the recipe for blue dumplings."

"No, not really. I just thought you might want to know they arraigned John Doe this morning."

"John Doe? I don't understand."

"The homeless man. The one you call Happy."

"Oh, Happy? They arraigned Happy? Does that mean they really think he's the robber? How could they do that? I told them it wasn't him."

"Sadie, do you remember the hole in the hood of his sweatsuit?"

"Yes."

"The lab matched slivers of glass from it to the broken windowpane at the bank where the robber made his point of entry."

Sadie looked perplexed. "Well, I'm sorry, Sergeant McCord. If he was the person who held a gun on me . . . on us . . . and killed Gordy . . . well then, I'm just crazy."

"Sadie, you're not crazy. And I'd feel better if you would call me Charlie."

"Okay, Charlie. But, I still don't believe it could have been him."

The two ate in silence for a while. Then Charlie continued, "That's not all." He hesitated for a minute while the waitress refilled his coffee. "They also found the unexploded dye pack. It was with the rest of the disguise in the box where he lives."

"The dye pack?"

"The battery had been pulled out of it. Somebody from your corporate office identified it. They matched the serial number to some list they had. Said it was the one you put in the money bag."

Sadie put her fork down, placed both hands in her lap, and looked blankly at Charlie. She felt uneasy—alone in a sea of madness. Why hadn't somebody from the main office told her they found the dye pack?

"No one told me," she said softly.

"And guess whose fingerprints were all over it?" Charlie continued. Then before Sadie had a chance to say anything, he answered himself. "The wordless wonder boy, that's who. And those federal boys ran those fingerprints everywhere but loose, and this old boy is not in the system anywhere."

Sadie continued to eat in silence for a few minutes, questions swirling in her head.

"Mine," she said as she sipped from her glass of water.

"Pardon me?" Charlie continued to eat.

"My fingerprints. I guess my fingerprints were on the dye pack, too."

"I'm sure they were," said Charlie, "if you're the one that handled it. I'm surprised those federal boys haven't been out to get your fingerprints so they could identify them."

"I haven't heard from anyone. But you know I think the bank has my fingerprints on file from a long time ago . . . for the insurance company or something." Sadie resumed eating. "And speaking of fingerprints . . . can't somebody run some kind of DNA test or something on those clothes they found to prove they belonged to somebody else?"

"Wouldn't do any good. Looked like your friend had been sleeping in them. A test would just match back to him."

"What if they found DNA that didn't match him?"

"But, we don't have any other suspects to match, Sadie. It's not like the DNA is going to have somebody's name on it so we can just show up on their doorstep and charge them with robbery—or murder, I guess it is."

"I see," she said. "What about the money? Did they find the money?"

"Nope. No sign of the money so far. And your guy still doesn't want to talk."

"I don't think he can, Charlie."

Charlie pushed his half-empty plate to the side, moved his heavy coffee mug to the center of his attention, and took a long sip.

"You want to tell me just how much you know about this guy?"
"What do you mean?" Sadie became defensive. "I told you the other day . . . he's homeless . . . he helped me one time and . . . "
"You see him on a regular basis just because he helped you change a flat tire?"
"I felt sorry for him." Sadie avoided Charlie's eyes.
"And you're sure he can't talk?"
"Well, I've never heard him say anything . . . except laugh."
"Okay, okay," soothed Charlie. He waited a moment and then changed the subject. "You ever heard of a woman named Christine Wiley?"
"Christine Wiley? No, doesn't ring a bell. Why?"
"Well, I talked to Maddox, the sergeant who was helping out that day with the lineup. He said he and John Doe had a run-in with this Wiley woman and her little girl. I'm not exactly sure what happened, but the little girl was crying about something. Maddox says John Doe got really upset and tried to talk to her."
Sadie paused, dumpling in midair. "Happy tried to talk to this Christine Wiley woman?"
"No, the little girl."
"Wait a minute. Christine? The woman in the lobby with the little girl?"
"Yeah, that's the one."
"I thought she was waiting for someone named Leroy." Sadie took a bite of dumpling. "What did he say? Did the woman know him?"
"He never really said anything, I guess. More like a whimper. The woman swears she never saw him before in her life."
Sadie put her fork down and dabbed at her mouth with her paper napkin. "Charlie, the man who robbed me isn't capable of whimpering. This is absurd. They've got the wrong man. And I'd bet my life on it." Sadie rifled through her purse, placed some money under her water glass, and slid to the corner of her seat. Then she looked straight into Charlie's eyes. "I'll admit I was scared, Sergeant, but I'm not stupid." She flipped her hair behind her shoulder and headed toward the door.
"Whoa, lady. Slow down. I'm on your side." Charlie threw some money on the table and rushed to follow her out of the café.

Sadie waited outside on the sidewalk for Charlie to catch up.

"You need to know, Sadie, the FBI's going to show up. They have to follow every lead and they don't have much more to go on. And an inside job theory . . ."

Sadie stared at Charlie in disbelief. "You can't think I had something to do with all this. How could you?" She fought the lump rising in her throat.

"No, I don't think so. But, it doesn't matter what I think right now. This is a federal case. And if you didn't do anything, well then, you don't have anything to worry about, do you?"

"What's going to happen to Happy?"

"The judge sent him to Eastern State Hospital in Vinita for evaluation. They'll clean him up and decide if he can talk or not. If he can't talk and isn't capable of defending himself, the court-appointed attorney will probably ask for a dismissal. Or they'll just leave him there. That is, unless they can get him to talk and you can identify his voice."

"Thanks for having lunch with me . . . and for the information." Sadie grimaced. "At least I know I'm a suspect now."

"Don't look at it like that right now, Sadie. You're the only one who can identify the robber's voice. The other two girls are not reliable enough."

Sadie frowned, feeling the uncomfortable weight of this new responsibility.

"And we'll be able to clear Happy," said Charlie, "when the real robber is caught."

"Thanks, Charlie." Sadie looked at her watch. "I gotta go. Duty calls."

The static hum of the sergeant's radio escalated into a high-pitched voice of alarm. Charlie turned up the volume and listened for a moment.

"Yeah," he said. "Duty calls."

Warm breezes and billowy blue sky suddenly turned into a blinding, white light and Happy wondered if he had somehow passed from this life into another. Maybe this was heaven, he thought. But when he tried to reach out and touch the stark surroundings he realized his hands were still restrained by steel handcuffs.

A loud buzzing noise startled him as a set of double doors automatically swung open revealing the bustling world of Eastern Oklahoma State Hospital. The doors closed with a heavy thud and the days that followed turned into a blur for the unhappy homeless man Sadie called Happy.

Chapter 8

Memorial Day weekend was only three days away, and, as usual, the Oklahoma weather promised to add its own fireworks to the holiday, signaling the unofficial start of summer. A thunderstorm, poised directly over Sycamore Springs for most of the day, continued to soak the city, sending most people scurrying for cover.

Sadie placed her trench coat on a crowded coatrack just inside the front door of the salon and then sat on a hard vinyl chair close by. She thought if she changed her mind at the last minute she could make a run for it without making too big a scene. The chrome, mirrors, and black enamel fixtures reflected the chill of her sweaty palms and numb fingertips. A stoic pink flamingo stood watch over the buzzing tube in the window that formed the letters for "Roberto's, A Hair Extravaganza."

Sadie mused to herself. How could this establishment have ever evolved from a small-town beauty shop? She touched the back of her hand to the tip of her nose in an attempt to filter her breathing. The unpleasing stench of permanent-wave solution and acrylic nail glue permeated the air.

She pulled her long black hair in front of her shoulder and fingered the ends nervously. Then she pushed it back and snatched a magazine from the glass coffee table. The glossy, oversized pages boasted pale, thin models sporting outrageous hairdos, darkened eyelids, and unnatural pouty lips. A knot began to form in the pit of Sadie's stomach. Just as she contemplated a plan of escape, a young girl with orange-sherbet hair rounded the corner and fingered the appointment book.

"Sadie Wa . . . how do you say your last name?" she asked.

"Wa-le-la, just the way it's spelled," answered Sadie.

"What kind of name's that?"

"It's Cherokee. Means hummingbird."

Sadie had spent most of her life spelling and explaining her name, amazed at how rude some people could be about a non-Anglo name.

"Cool," said the young girl. "I'm Crystal. Come on back and I'll get you shampooed for Bo."

"For who?" Sadie wrinkled her forehead.

"I mean, for Roberto," Crystal laughed. "His friends all call him Bo."

"Oh?"

This was getting scarier by the minute, thought Sadie. The name Bo created the image of a clown holding a giant pair of scissors. She followed the young girl into the bowels of the salon, silently surrendering to the unfamiliar world. After an herbal shampoo and mint conditioner, Sadie sat with a towel wrapped around her head waiting for Roberto, hair designer extraordinaire. Or should she call him Bo, she wondered.

The decision to cut her hair had not been made lightly. Sadie had been appalled after listening to Thelma's comments one day in the personnel department.

"We would like to look at you for a middle-management position, Sadie," Thelma had said. "But you have to look the part. The hair has got to go. Get a nice haircut and get some new suits," she added. "Your performance rating is good on everything else. We can move you into an assistant vice-president position and get you into the corporate office where you belong. But you've got to cooperate a little. You need to look like a banker, not an Indian."

Sadie's first reaction to Thelma was defiance. Who did this white woman think she was to make such absurd remarks? She vowed right then and there to never cut her hair, not for Thelma or for anyone else. That is, until Soda Pop came along.

Soda Pop Andover had introduced herself to Sadie one day in the lobby of the branch. Sadie remembered thinking that the little girl possessed the biggest brown eyes she had ever seen for a six-year-old child. And she always wore her straight, black hair pulled back in a ponytail, barrettes tightly applied to each side of her head and her bangs slicked neatly onto her forehead. Nicknamed for her love of the sugary drink, Soda Pop had explained to Sadie that it was far better than her real name, Agatha Gertrude, or any variation thereof for that matter. Although small for her age, Soda Pop's personality made up for every inch of stature she lacked.

Soda Pop and her mother came into the bank again a few weeks after the robbery. Unusually quiet, Soda Pop climbed into the chair her mother designated, next to the tall schefflera plant. She sat on her hands with a serious look on her face, gazing around the busy office as if absorbing every detail while her mother visited with one of the customer service employees. Soda Pop's feet and legs, too short to touch the floor, bobbed a pair of white patent shoes in unison. A colorful scarf neatly covered her head. Not a fleck of hair could be seen.

Sadie walked over to the young girl, bent over, and whispered something in her ear. She looked first at Sadie, then at her mother just a few feet away. Sensing the child's apprehension, Sadie caught the mother's watchful eye and said, "Is it okay if Soda Pop waits for you at my desk?" The mother smiled weakly, then gave her permission with a nod of her head.

Sadie held out her hand; Soda Pop took it and followed. Sadie retrieved a glass jar from her credenza, opened it, and held it out for the little girl. Soda Pop stood on her tiptoes and peered suspiciously into the jar with one eye closed. When she saw the red, white, and yellow balloons tucked inside, she backed away, her face danced, and she let out a laugh.

"Go ahead," said Sadie. "Pick out one and we'll blow it up for you."

Soda Pop placed her tiny hand in the middle of the balloons and came out with two—one red and one white.

"Okay, two it is." Sadie blew up the balloons, tying a knot in each one so the air could not escape, and handed them to Soda Pop.

Soda Pop thought for a moment and then handed one back to Sadie. "You can have one, too," she said. "You have pretty hair." And with a big gesture, she handed the red one back to Sadie. They bounced the balloons back and forth to each other while the rest of the customers in the lobby looked on—some with smiles, some with disgust.

Soda Pop jumped for a balloon high in the air. Her arm caught the edge of her scarf and it slid backward off her head, revealing a bald scalp with just a few tufts of hair on one side.

"Uh-oh." Soda Pop's small voice sounded panicked. She grabbed and repositioned her scarf, simultaneously checking to see if her mother had seen what had happened. Relieved to see the back of her mother's head, Soda Pop quickly climbed into Sadie's lap, carefully running her fingers around the edge of her scarf and tightening the knot.

"Is it okay?" she asked. "Did I mess it up?"

"You look fine," said Sadie, trying to hide her disbelief. "You look fine."

Sadie shifted the frail child on her knee and began a conversation that would eventually land her in a beauty salon, waiting for someone to cut her hair. Soda Pop's hair had been sacrificed to the chemicals used to treat a monster named leukemia. It broke Sadie's heart to see the child with no hair, so she decided to give her some of her own. The hair would be fashioned into a wig that would fit her small head precisely. Sadie wished she could do more.

Soda Pop's mother had come to the bank that day to ask for help in securing a second mortgage. The insurance company had stopped paying for the expensive medical treatments after the bills had reached the maximum amount allowed on the policy.

After Soda Pop and her mother left, Sadie spent weeks working with the loan department on the application. Overextended. Not enough collateral. The reasons from the loan clerk had been endless. Under the circumstances, the bank would never make the loan. So here sat Sadie, doing the only thing she knew how. She would share her hair with the little girl who wanted to share her balloons.

Roberto handed Sadie a glass of wine and droned on in an irritating, nasal voice. "We could sell your hair, girl," he said. "There are women out there who would kill for a piece of this gorgeous stuff."

"I don't think so," she said. "Just save it in this paper bag like I asked, please."

Sadie placed her untouched wine glass next to a collection of scissors and combs on a shelf covered with tiny flecks of hair. She didn't mind a glass of wine now and then, but this didn't seem like the time, or the place.

"We'll leave it one length. You know, just below your chin with a side bang," he said, holding her hair up and to the side to help visualize the finished product. "Your hair is so thick and straight. You'll look very chic."

The ordeal began and Sadie tried to concentrate on breathing. She glanced in a side mirror at the other people in the salon, wondering if their visit was as traumatic as hers, then returned her gaze to the reflection of her own face in the mirror. She studied the shape of her face, her eyes, nose, and chin, and tried to imagine which part came from her father and which from her mother. All from her Cherokee father, she decided, except for her sky-blue eyes. They undeniably belonged to her mother and she wished her mother had kept them.

The double-tone bell at the front door announced the arrival of a customer and Sadie sensed the presence of a man. Her view was distorted, obstructed by heavy strands of hair covering her face. The man removed his navy blue sport coat, rolled up his white shirtsleeves, and loosened his tie as he walked over to Crystal, who was now perched on a stool at the receptionist desk. The man looked almost out of place in the salon, yet very sure of himself, very comfortable. Sadie watched from a distance as the man settled in at the workstation of the salon's manicurist.

Good grief, he's here to get a manicure.

Sadie smiled inwardly. She couldn't think of a man she knew who would be caught dead in a salon getting his cuticles snipped.

The scissors sliced closer to her ear and she could feel the clumps of hair falling from her head. She closed her eyes.

What on earth was I thinking?

Clip, clip, clip.

Soda Pop—think of Soda Pop.

Sadie tried to relax. Her shoulders ached from the tension that had invaded her neck and worked its way down her back and spread throughout her body. Roberto, or Bo, or whoever he was, chattered about something, but she couldn't hear him. Suddenly she felt hot— very hot and unduly claustrophobic.

It'll grow back. She doesn't have any.

Thoughts buzzed around in her head like dizzy bees while Roberto pulled the round hairbrush through her shortened locks to the hum of the hair dryer. The deafening sound stopped abruptly and Sadie opened her eyes.

"You can give up that death grip you've got on my chair now," said Roberto.

"Oh, I'm sorry. I didn't realize . . ."

"I don't know what you're worried about, girl. You are gorgeous."

A reflection of the new Sadie stared back at her from the huge mirror. Her hair was parted just left of center, and gave way to feathered bangs. Her shiny black hair bounced with a fluid movement as she moved her head. The length of her new coif fell just below her strong jawbone.

Maybe this is what a banker's supposed to look like, anyway.

"Want to see the back?"

Sadie took the handheld mirror as Roberto spun the chair so she could see the reflection of the back of her head. Sheepishly, she placed her limp hand on her bare neck as if it were a new discovery and maybe, just maybe, if she touched it her hair would instantly reappear.

"We call this a bob, and it's perfect for your hair." Roberto tugged at the towel, loosening the plastic cape covering Sadie's shoulders.

She very graciously thanked Roberto when he presented her with the brown paper sack, then walked back to the reception area. Crystal sat on her stool behind the counter moving her head from side to side, mouthing invisible words. Two thin wires ran from a small contraption attached to her waist and disappeared into her vibrant hair. When she saw Sadie approach, she pulled out the earphones and hopped down, and began to write on a pink ticket.

Sadie stood at the glass counter, rummaged in her purse for her billfold, and pulled out two twenty-dollar bills. As she waited for the young girl to finish writing, she rubbed Andrew Jackson's face with her thumb and wondered if she would ever be able to look at a twenty-dollar bill and not think of how Jackson had lied and turned his back on the entire Indian population of the New World. Her grandmother had repeated the story to her so many times, she knew it by heart.

After the Cherokees had fought alongside Jackson to defeat the British, he repaid them for their loyalty by stealing their land. He cost the Cherokees thousands of lives as he sent his army to remove them by force from their homelands in North Carolina, Tennessee, and Georgia to be resettled thousands of miles away in Indian Territory, which would later become the state of Oklahoma. The money Jackson promised as compensation to the Cherokees for their land was never paid. Now, the memory of the Trail of Tears for most people had been reduced to an annual stage production at the Cherokee Heritage Center in Tahlequah and Jackson had been immortalized, his face patriotically displayed on the most widely used piece of currency in the country—the twenty-dollar bill. "Just don't seem right," her grandmother had always said.

"That'll be twenty-five dollars," Crystal said, handing Sadie a copy of her ticket.

As Sadie handed her the two bills and waited for her change, she shifted her thoughts back to her new haircut as she looked at her reflection in one of the salon's many mirrors, turning her head from side to side and poking at her bangs with her long, slender fingers. *Not too bad . . . I still look like me.*

Crystal handed her a ten and a five. Sadie dropped the five back on the counter. "Can you give this to Roberto for me?" she asked. Crystal nodded that she would as she replanted the speaker wires into her ears.

Sadie stood tall, pulled her trench coat tight around her shapely body, turned the collar up around her ears, and walked toward the door. She stopped, folded the paper bag holding her hair, and slid it into her coat pocket. From the corner of her eye, she couldn't help but sneak a closer look at the manicure man. A flash of a glance and their eyes met. Sadie blushed. It was Adam's friend, Jaycee Jones.

"Well, look at you," he said.

The manicurist, a young woman with bleached blond hair, stopped buffing his fingers, looked up and smiled.

"Oh, uh, hi," said Sadie. She didn't know what to say. Her excitement in seeing Jaycee again was tempered with embarrassment for what she was sure was an uncomfortable position for a man.

"I almost didn't recognize you," he said. "Whatever possessed you to cut your hair?"

"It's kind of a long story." Sadie looked around as if worried someone might see them or overhear their conversation.

"Say, I'm almost finished here. Can I buy you a cup of coffee?"

Sadie looked at her watch and silently searched her mind for an excuse. Her thoughts became a tangled mess within a millisecond. *I don't know him . . . yes, I do, he has a business relationship with the bank . . . it should be all right, Adam introduced us at Gordy's funeral . . . damn, he's good-looking . . . he could be Jack the Ripper in disguise . . .*

"I promise I won't bite," he added, as if he could read her mind. "There's a diner down the street that has great apple pie."

"Well, I love apple pie, and I guess just one cup of coffee would be all right. But after that I've got to get home."

Sadie waited by the front door of the salon while Jaycee paid Crystal for his manicure. The thundershower had passed, leaving the air clean and fresh. They walked slowly toward the Coffee Cup Corner. Jaycee absentmindedly removed a Hershey's kiss from his pocket, handed it to Sadie, then peeled another and popped it in his mouth.

"Well, I don't know why you cut your hair, but all I can say is you are a beautiful woman."

"Thank you." Sadie smiled with her eyes and stashed the chocolate candy in her coat pocket for later.

They entered the diner, chose a booth near the front, and placed their orders for apple pie and coffee. Jaycee began to talk.

"I'm an investment banker," he said. "That's how I met Adam. I handle several accounts for the bank. My company provides risk management and investment services to corporate clients like your bank."

Mechanically, he reached into his wallet and pulled out a card and handed it to her. She took his card, held it tightly in her hand, and read it. His name was printed in red ink as Jaycee Jones. Below this was the name of an investment company in Dallas—Powerhouse Investments.

"I travel a lot," he continued. "My company is out of Dallas but I maintain two homes, a small place not far from here between Sycamore Springs and Tulsa, and my main home in Plano just north of Dallas." Then he turned his attention to her. "What about you?"

"Well, you already know where I work. I've been at the bank a little over twelve years."

"Twelve years? I'd think you'd be running the place by now," Jaycee laughed.

"Let's just say Adam has been a little better at playing their game than I have. Kind of a good-old-boy network, wouldn't you say?" They waited while the waitress served their desserts and filled their cups with steaming coffee. "You work directly with the higher-ups," she continued, "you should know." Sadie poured a double helping of cream and sugar into her coffee, then held her cup with both hands and sipped, her elbows perched on the edge of the table.

"Unfortunately," he said, "I guess I'll have to agree."

Sadie put her coffee cup down and picked up her fork. "Maybe this new haircut will help."

"Help? Help what?"

"I've been told not to look like an Indian if I want a crack at a promotion."

"You're kidding. They can't tell you to cut your hair. That's blatant racism."

"Well, I didn't exactly cut it for them. I cut it for a little girl. Her name is Soda Pop. But they don't have to know that. They can think it was for them if they want. I don't care. It's just a game." The air between them fell silent. Jaycee finished his pie while Sadie picked at hers. "I made a promise to myself," she finally continued, "that I would make something of myself. And I think I can do that as a banker. I promised myself that I would not be pulled down like so many of my friends have . . . alcohol . . . drugs . . . everything else. So, I guess I'll play the white man's game and do what it takes, as long as it doesn't compromise my values. I have to be smarter than the man." Sadie laughed. "And as for my hair? It will grow back."

"You're quite a lady, my dear. Not only are you beautiful, you're smart. And on top of that you know what you want and how to get it. That can be a pretty dangerous combination, don't you think?"

They laughed and infatuation began to trickle through Sadie's veins. She fought the sensation. What was it with this guy? Was it his wavy black hair and liquid brown eyes? His well-groomed fingernails? His witty stories, lavish compliments, or his remarkable laugh? He had a kind, soft voice and she began to feel like she had known him her whole life. He was mysterious, and unpretentiously handsome. She loved and, at the same time, unexplainably, hated how she felt. And true to her word, after finishing her apple pie and one cup of coffee, she excused herself.

"You have my card," he said. "Give me a call sometime."

"Thanks for the pie and coffee. It was nice. But I've got to get home."

They said their goodbyes and she walked out into the damp air, seeking relief from an overwhelming feeling of intoxication. She needed to leave this man's presence to regain her wits.

She headed up the street toward Tango's, a quaint little dress shop tucked between a fancy Italian restaurant and Toby's Shoes.

She walked with a spring in her step. She felt fresh. New. Her emotions had run the gamut, and she had finally transcended her fear of short hair. She couldn't help but think her life had taken a turn toward the future, and she secretly hoped Jaycee would be a part of it.

For a split second before she disappeared into the dress shop, a man jogging away from her in the distance caught her attention with a certain familiarity. She stopped and looked again, but the jogger was gone.

Chapter 9

Sadie teetered somewhere between excitement and trepidation. When she had first seen Cindy handing out invitations to an evening pool party, she hadn't thought much about it. She was used to being excluded from the unofficial get-togethers of the social crowd at the bank. But this time an envelope for the "Memorial Day Bank Bash" for a Friday-night party magically appeared on Sadie's desk with her name on it. Boldly, she accepted.

Now that the day of the event had arrived, she began to question her decision to go. But she had already committed and couldn't turn back now.

She stopped at the Colonial Grocery Store on her way home from work to pick up a tray of vegetables she had ordered earlier by phone. She had requested whatever vegetables they had with a good mix of colors. Serving contrasting colors of vegetables was important. It was the only lesson she could remember from her junior high home economics class and for some reason the "vegetable rule" had stuck in her head all these years. She almost felt obliged to explain this to the deli clerk. But she didn't.

She brushed her bangs to one side, pushed her new short locks behind her ears, and impatiently waited for the clerk to insert the container of dip in the center of the tray. She could see the broccoli, cauliflower, and carrots arranged around a smattering of cheese. Adding the other garnishes of sweet pickles, black olives, and flower-cut radishes made the wait worthwhile. She wanted everything to be perfect.

When Sadie got home, she pulled out her grandmother's favorite serving dish. Pink roses adorned the center and edge of the antique plate. She carefully transferred the vegetables, dip, and other goodies to the dish and covered the entire creation with clear plastic wrap.

Smiling, she knew her grandmother would approve of the use of her dish. Now she was ready to get dressed.

The occasion had definitely called for something new to wear. She held the plastic hanger with her new purchase high in the air with one hand and tugged at Tango's trademark gold-and-navy plastic covering with the other. Trying not to obsess over what to wear, she had asked the saleslady for something casual, but nice—classy, but not too revealing.

The invitation had noted that swimwear was optional, so she opted for a compromise. She didn't want to be the only one there unprepared for a midnight swim, so she picked out a conservative but colorful swimsuit. She then paired it with a matching wrap skirt and open blouse creating a flattering summer dress. A new pair of white sandals from Toby's completed her outfit. With everything in order, she placed the vegetable tray and the map provided in the invitation on the car seat and drove toward the party.

Sadie could see her co-workers' cars parked along both sides of the street—Greg's Mercedes, Donna's BMW convertible, and Bob's black Lexus. Any bank officer who wanted a fancy car could get on the waiting list to buy repossessed loan collateral from the loan department for the balance owed. At times the loan officers would bypass the required qualifying ratios, making questionable loans to get the right cars in the bank's portfolio. Many customers never realized until it was too late that one delinquent payment meant no amount of negotiating could return the car to the original owner. Especially if the car met the description of a vehicle coveted by the powerful people at the bank.

Sadie always thought that that particular activity had to be illegal, but she never openly questioned the bank's lending practices. When Adam had offered to put her name on the list for a car, she declined.

She pulled her ten-year-old Chevy next to the curb a block and a half away and walked to the house. A string of paper lanterns hung from the trees and blinking lights outlined the curved walkway toward a gate at the side of the house. Sadie walked to the end of the path and stopped. She could hear the crowd talking and laughing around the corner and for a split second she thought about fleeing back to the refuge of her dirty-brown car. Looking at the display of vegetables on her grandmother's beautiful plate, she took a deep breath and continued. Donna stumbled toward Sadie, a pink drink in one hand and a red paper bow stuck to the top of her head.

"Look, everybody," Donna yelled back into the crowd. "It's our little Indian princess."

Sadie swallowed and waited for a moment while she reassessed her first inclination to run. Her face felt warm, partly from the angry blood rushing to her face and partly from the humidity that hung in the air. But, for some reason, she was determined to show she was stronger than her shallow-minded co-worker.

"Here, let me take that," said Donna, taking Sadie's platter of vegetables. "I'll show you where you can put your things."

People sat in clumps around tiny tables on a perfectly landscaped terrace between the pool and the patio. Individuals milled back and forth from outside into the house. A car race thundered across a big-screen TV set up at one end of the pool where most of the men stood drinking beer. Sadie followed Donna through a maze of people, through an open set of patio doors that led into the combined kitchen and dining area. The women had congregated in two locations—the den and the kitchen. A game of Trivial Pursuit was going on in the den. The kitchen was full of food. Sadie hated games so she opted for the food.

A long table, decked in a white lace tablecloth, held an eclectic group of food concoctions placed precariously around a crystal bowl brimming with something pink. Donna's drink of choice, she presumed. Sadie plucked at fruit balls brimming out of a watermelon that had been hollowed out in the shape of a basket. Then she added miniature egg rolls and cocktail wieners to her red, white, and blue paper plate. She made her way completely around the long table, fetched a cream puff to balance on the corner of her sagging cardboard dish, and realized her vegetables were nowhere to be seen. There must not be enough room for all the food here, she thought, and made a mental note to check the other rooms for the rest of the food.

The doorbell rang, announcing more arrivals at the front door, and Sadie wondered if she had mistakenly entered the party through the wrong door. One of the voices belonged to Adam, but she did not recognize the other. Sadie bit into a cream puff and white powdered sugar sifted onto the colorful stretchy material that lay on top of her shapely breasts.

"Damn it," she mumbled.

Sadie put her plate down on the edge of the table and reached for a napkin. She leaned over and attempted to knock the powder onto the floor before it sank into the fabric.

"Need some help?" Adam stood in the doorway holding two twelve-packs of imported beer. Sadie thought she could hear the old friendship they'd once had returning to his voice.

"Oh, Adam," she said. "I am such a klutz." Sadie's face flushed as she continued to dab until she successfully dissipated the remaining powder.

"Heard you were up for a new position, Sadie. You got my vote, you know."

"I bet." Sadie didn't try to hide the sarcasm in her voice.

Adam opened the refrigerator and began to rearrange wine bottles until he could cram in the last of his beer.

"Be nice now," he said. "By the way, do you remember my friend Jaycee?" Turning, Adam nodded toward the doorway. "Jaycee, Sadie's going to be the new security officer at the bank."

"Oh, really?" said Sadie to a confident Adam and then shifted her attention to his friend.

Jaycee spoke first. "Actually, we already know each other."

"Really? I don't remember you," Sadie lied and then smiled with electric blue eyes.

"I remember you," he teased. "You looked like you were overcome by the loss of your hair." He threw his head back and ran his fingers through make-believe locks of hair.

"Oh?"

"Ever hear about Samson?" he asked.

"Samson?"

"He lost his strength when Delilah cut his hair."

"And you think that's going to happen to me?"

"No, you're too pretty for that. And I must say it is a pleasure to see you again."

Jaycee took her hand and Sadie found herself unthinkingly staring at his fingertips. Adam dismissed the couple and retreated through the doors to the patio.

"Anybody need a beer . . ." Adam's voice trailed off into the party.

"It really is nice to see you again," said Jaycee. He continued to hold her hand in both of his and stare directly into her face. His penetrating eyes reminded her of how handsome she thought he was the first time she saw him.

"You'd better be careful." Sadie pulled her hand free. "How do you know you can trust me not to blow your cover?"

A frown covered his face. "What cover is that, may I ask?" The tone of his voice went flat.

Continuing the tease, Sadie added, "I'll tell them where you have your nails done."

They both burst into laughter and Adam reappeared at the doorway. "Hey, man, are you going to jabber all night? You're going to miss all the fun."

"In a minute." Jaycee waved Adam away. "I want to hear more about your ranch," he said, returning his attention to Sadie. "You really live on a ranch?"

"No," she laughed. "I live in a farmhouse." Then after a moment, she added, "With a dog in the yard and a horse in the barn." ·

"And a husband?"

"No, not anymore, and you don't want to go there," Sadie warned. Then seizing the opportunity to reciprocate, "What about you?" Her eyes had not detected any sign of a wedding ring earlier.

"No, not me. I'm free as a bird," he assured her. "Say, I'd love to see your ranch."

Adam stuck his head around the corner again, this time with a short stubby cigar dangling from the corner of his mouth. "Jaycee, you got to help me out here. They're ganging up on me in this poker game. Did you bring any money?"

"Duty calls," Jaycee said, making a slow retreat toward the door. "I may have to referee the betting out here. Maybe we can talk later?" And with that he was gone.

Suddenly, the kitchen seemed cold and empty. Sadie strolled first outside and around the pool, then back inside to the kitchen. As usual, she appeared to be the only person with skin color there. She felt like a puppy who had wandered into a wolf den, realizing they all had four legs and fur but that the similarities ended there. Except for Jaycee, who would look up from the poker table from time to time and smile, her presence seemed to be totally unnoticed. That is, until she stepped on someone lying on the floor or tried to squeeze through the hallway en route to the sanctuary of the bathroom.

Eyeing a quiet corner in the den, she staked claim to an easy chair and began to wonder why she was there. She knew she didn't fit in and figured she never would. She had run into Officer Lance Smith earlier in the week and he had invited her to a Memorial Day stomp dance. She had been flattered at the invitation, but having already committed to the party, she declined.

Going to a stomp dance was kind of like going to church, Cherokee style. She had been raised in the Baptist church and her family rarely attended stomp dances. But she'd heard about the ceremony, held entirely in the Cherokee language, where the participants danced around the sacred fire. It had almost been lost after the Cherokees moved to Indian Territory but had been revived in an effort to preserve the old ways. Sadie's dad used to remind her to never forget where her people came from. Now, she wished she had gone with Lance. But, she rationalized, that path would have caused her to miss seeing Jaycee.

The men continued to play cards and channel-surf from one sports event to another, whooping and hollering until the night skies flickered and dumped a rainshower all over everything. In a matter of seconds, the party moved inside, big-screen TV and all.

The night wore on and after several trips through the maze of the house, she decided she'd had enough fun for one night. The only friendly people were Adam and Jaycee, and they both seemed to be busy. Deciding an exit could be deemed reasonable, she looked around for Donna or Cindy to say goodnight. Suddenly, she remembered her grandmother's plate.

"Donna, what did you do with the plate I brought?"

"I don't know," she said. "I gave it to Cindy."

Sadie looked down the hallway where she had last seen Cindy. The first door was closed, but she could hear a group sending up what sounded like cheers every few minutes. She opened the door and stood there unnoticed while her eyes adjusted to the darkness. A tall, slender girl in a fluorescent-green string bikini leaned over a mirror-topped coffee table. She held a dollar bill rolled in the shape of a short straw between her thumb and first finger. The girl grasped her long, straight blond hair and held it while she placed one end of the bill to her nose and the other end to the mirror. With a sucking noise, she drew the makeshift straw down a line of white powder, snorting the substance into her nose. Another cheer rose from the crowded room. The blond, still clutching the money straw in her hand, fell backward on the bed.

Sadie cringed and fought a flood of nightmarish memories, expertly repressed but not yet evicted from her mind. "Damn," she said.

"Hey, close the door," came a voice from the darkness.

"Either get in or get out," another faceless voice demanded.

"Oh . . . sorry . . . just looking for Cindy," she said, trying to crawfish, physically and mentally.

"Try next door."

Sadie wasn't sure she wanted to try the next door, but she did. Sure enough, she found Cindy and Adam, working their way around the corner of the bed. Just as Cindy tossed her underwear toward the ceiling with her big toe, Sadie backed out and closed the door.

"That's it," she said in a loud voice as she walked back down the hall.

The kitchen was empty. She thought about getting her plate later and then reconsidered. "No, I'm not going to leave Grandmother's plate," she said aloud. She opened the refrigerator. Nothing there but wine and beer. The countertop was strewn with discarded paper plates, empty glasses, and wads of aluminum foil that hadn't quite made it to the trash. Suddenly, Jaycee appeared out of nowhere.

"You're not leaving, are you?" he asked.

"Yes, I need to go . . . but I brought a tray of vegetables and I can't seem to find my plate. Have you seen any lost broccoli lately?" Her voice reflected her irritation.

"No, but I'll help you look."

Sadie's eyes moved down the counter and came to rest on two overflowing trash cans. Behind the first, the lid was tilted just enough on the second container for Sadie to see the edge of her grandmother's plate sticking out from under a broken wine bottle. The blood drained from her head and she almost stumbled as she ran across the floor.

"Oh, no," she whimpered. "Please don't let my plate be broken." Sadie threw off the lid and picked at the top layer of trash, letting it fall where it may. Her beautiful plate of vegetables lay there with the plastic wrap still in place.

"What?" asked Jaycee. "Someone threw it away? Plate and all? I can't believe it."

Sadie loosened the covering, allowing the entire contents of the plate to bounce across the floor. Her heart raced as she desperately touched the plate, searching for cracks.

"Is it all right?" Jaycee seemed to be genuinely concerned.

"I think so. I've got to go."

The screen door slammed behind her as she escaped out a side door. Cool, summer rain mixed with angry tears as she ran up the street to her car.

Jaycee's instincts told him to follow Sadie and he reached for the door. He wanted to catch her, take her in his arms, hold her, and tell her everything would be all right. As he opened the door, he felt a set of sharp fingernails in his side.

"You're not going anywhere, are you, honey?" The words came from behind him and were accompanied by a warm breath and nibble on his ear. "The party's just getting started." Donna rubbed her breasts against his arm as she pushed the door closed.

Chapter 10

The windshield wipers flopped from side to side with an irritating squeak as Sadie drove on autopilot, taking an extra circle around the lake. Her mind churned and replayed the party. She wished she could hide her schoolgirl feelings about Jaycee. Then she began to think about her grandmother's plate. The fillings in her teeth ached and she realized her jaw was as tight as a vise. She tried to relax.

What is wrong with those people?

The scene of the cocaine gang resurfaced, propelling her thoughts to Michael. She lowered the window, hoping the fresh air would clear her head.

As she turned up the lane toward the house, Sonny's eyes reflected in the headlights for a moment before the automatic sensor caught the movement of the car and flicked on the pole light. Sadie slipped off her new sandals and fumbled for an old pair of sneakers she kept under the car seat. With a second thought, she decided to go barefoot. After all, she was dressed for water. Holding her grandmother's plate next to her chest and her shoes in her hand, she dodged mud puddles all the way to the door.

Once inside the safe haven of the enclosed back porch, Sadie squeezed the excess water from her hair, wiped her feet on an old rug, and stood dripping. Sonny stuck his head through his custom-made doggy door, pushing the rubber flap up with his nose. As if judging the situation under control, he slid through the opening. He looked at Sadie, then shook water from his entire body, starting at his nose and ending with the tip of his tail.

"Nice rain, Sonny?" Sadie smiled and ran her hand up his long nose and over the top of his wet head as he nuzzled her fingers. Silently, he asked if he could come inside. "Oh, okay. Come on," Sadie gave in and then rationalized, "I'll let you back out in a little while."

Inside the kitchen, she placed the rescued plate gingerly on the table and picked up a towel. Sonny stood perfectly still while she wiped his face, ears, and back, then raised one foot at a time so she could dry the bottom of his feet. Her mind continued to grind and she began to talk to Sonny as if he were a person. "Guess I'll think twice before I do something like that again," she said. "I don't know what on earth I was thinking. I will never fit in with those people . . . and I don't know why in the world I try."

The antique clock above the living-room fireplace chimed one time. Simultaneously, the shriek of the phone in the quiet house caused Sadie to jump. Instantly, thoughts of bad news or an emergency swirled in her head. When she picked up the receiver, she noticed the tiny red light on the answering machine blinking erratically as if sending out Morse code.

"Hello?"

"Hello there." Sadie's heart skipped a beat when she heard Jaycee's voice. "Sorry to bother you so late, but I left a message earlier and I was worried."

"Worried?"

"Did you have trouble getting home in the storm?"

"Storm?"

"Isn't it raining at your house? It's a flood here."

"Where are you?" she asked.

"Back at my place . . . about halfway between Sycamore Springs and Tulsa."

"Oh, you're already back there? No, we just have rain. Not enough for a flood I don't think."

"I was concerned about you when you left. You were so upset. I couldn't believe we found your plate in the trash. Are you all right?"

Sadie touched the edge of the plate with her fingertips. "Yes, I'm okay. It's just that—"

"How far from Sycamore Springs are you, anyway? I've got to go to an estate sale near there in the morning and I thought you said you lived—"

"Oh, the Burgess auction?"

"And since I'm going to be up there, I thought maybe you could show me around that part of the country. That is, if you're not busy."

"I'd love to," she gushed. "Actually, I had planned to stop by that auction myself. You know, always looking for a bargain."

"Good." Jaycee sounded excited. "Then it's a date? I'll look for you. It's supposed to start at ten and I thought I'd get there a little early, say around nine-thirty if I can find the place. I hope it's not raining."

"Okay then, I'll look for you, too."

"The party got pretty boring after you left."

"Oh, really?" The conversation idled for a moment. Sadie had no plans to share her opinion of the party with Adam's friend. Not yet, anyway. "By the way, how did you get my number?"

"I beat it out of Adam," he laughed. "Say, can you give me directions? It says on this flyer six miles east . . ."

Sadie gave him directions, pausing periodically while he slowly repeated her words as if he were taking notes.

"Hey, thanks. I think I can find it now. If I get lost, I'll call you and you can send out a search party."

Sadie chuckled, wondering how he was going to call her. Telephone satellite signals had a tendency to bounce a lot between the valleys and ridges in northeastern Oklahoma causing the reception on most cell phone conversations to be short-lived. Knowing that, she had never invested in a wireless phone.

"I'll talk to you in the morning then," he said. "Sleep tight."

Sadie held the phone receiver against her chest for a moment before she replaced it gently on the hook. *Wow, things are looking up . . . a date . . . with a hunk . . . I don't believe it.* She pushed her shoulders back and smiled while she ran her fingers through her wet hair. Then she pushed the button on her answering machine and listened to the voice on the tape.

"Hi, this is Jaycee Jones. Just checking to see if you're all right . . . Uh . . . I'll call you back later. Bye now."

She pushed the rewind button and played the message back three times. It said the same thing all three times. After the third replay, she left the machine to automatically reset itself and, to her surprise and disgust, discovered a second message.

"Hey squaw, this is Mike. You know, your ex-con husband. Kind of rhymes, don't it? Uh, just thought you might want to know . . . I've been out since March and I'm keeping my nose clean . . . and we need to talk. I came by to see you and that damned dog of yours almost bit my leg off. Oh, hell, never mind." Clunk.

Sadie stood frozen, breathlessly staring at the phone. The hair on the back of her neck involuntarily stood on end. She didn't know what on earth she had done to deserve to be dogged by this lowlife. She had made one mistake in her life. It was gigantic and it was Michael. And before it was over he had latched on to her and nearly sucked the very soul out of her body before she could rid herself of him.

"Why can't you go the hell away from me and stay there?" Sadie rolled her eyes and spoke at the answering machine as if expecting it to talk back. She opened the closet door, picked up a Browning double-barreled 12-gauge, and popped it open. Satisfied it was ready for action, she carried it into the bedroom and slipped it under the foot of her bed. She really had no desire to use the weapon on anything, human or not, but she knew how and would not hesitate if the time and the need arose. Michael was the need; she just hoped the time never came.

She retrieved a towel from the hall closet and wrapped it around her head. Then she climbed onto the bed, sat with her back against the wall, and pulled a quilt up around her to chase away the chill. The heavy weight of the covers gave her a secure feeling. She fingered the wedding ring design of the quilt her grandmother had given her when she got married. Her mind reeled from the events of the party, then faded back and forth to recollections of a past with Michael. It seemed like a lifetime ago.

She had been so young, so vulnerable, when she met Michael. And now some fifteen years later, she could honestly look back and see she wasn't ever in love with him. He was simply a way for her to get away from her mother.

Barely eighteen, Sadie had just graduated from high school when they got married. They had rented a small place in Eucha and Sadie started to work full time at the drugstore. Michael had been working at a horse ranch near the lake, but two weeks after they were married he quit or got fired. Sadie never really knew which.

He started drinking and meeting with a lot of out-of-town strangers. Then, every other weekend, Sadie and Michael would drive south through Texas and across the Mexican border. Michael would meet with a man and exchange briefcases. Then they would turn around and drive all the way back to northeastern Oklahoma while Sadie slept in the back seat. It was a business deal, he explained to Sadie.

With his new plan he would never have to work for anyone else again, he told her, promising they would someday have their own ranch. Sadie blindly believed in her new husband and never questioned him.

Things began to get tight. The bills outnumbered her small paycheck at the end of every month. So, she took a second job, working nights at the local beer joint. Often when she came home after the bar closed at midnight, she would find strangers in the house. They would be sprawled on the couch or on the floor and the house would be littered with beer bottles and overflowing ashtrays. Too tired to argue, she would wake them up, kick them out, and drag Michael to bed. The next morning, he would promise never to let it happen again, and she would come home a few nights later only to find the same mess.

They had been married barely six months when Sadie returned home to find Michael in bed with another woman. Anger turned into shouting, and shouting turned into shoves. For the first time in her life, Sadie began to realize her life was out of control. She prayed for mercy and cried until she had no more tears.

A week later, an early-morning argument turned into a brawl and Sadie became ill. The time for her monthly period had passed and Sadie faced the awful proposition that she might be pregnant. When she showed up late for work, limping and with a bruise on her right cheek, the owner of the drugstore called Sadie's mother.

Cathryn Walela came and picked up her daughter and took her to the Indian hospital in Sycamore Springs. While they drove, her mother talked and Sadie was silent.

"I don't know what you did to make him hit you like that, Sadie. But you've got to learn that you've got to take a lot when you get married. You're not a kid anymore. You can't just run home every time you get in a disagreement with your husband." Cathryn looked at Sadie with a pretentious smile. "I don't suppose you know if you're pregnant, do you?"

When they arrived at the hospital, they had to wait for over three hours before she could even catch a glimpse of a doctor. After the examination, Sadie stared out the window while the doctor and her mother talked. She could hear the doctor talking in the distance as if she was either not present or too young to understand.

"Nothing's broken. She's just bruised," he said. "The pregnancy test is negative . . . probably just stress induced . . . living in . . ." The doctor's voice faded from Sadie's ears as tears of relief rolled down her face.

Convinced Sadie would be all right, her mother drove her home where they found a note on the kitchen table next to a pile of dirty dishes. It read: *Be back in the morning. Clean the house. Mike.*

"Sadie, this place is a pigpen. You can't stay here." Her mother's voice was laced with I-told-you-so, entangled with a pinch of genuine concern as she looked at the messy apartment. "Why don't you come home for a few days? Just until Michael gets back and you two can get things worked out."

Sadie reluctantly agreed to stay with her parents. Mostly she agreed to let her grandmother, Rosa, fuss over her. Michael never called and neither Sadie nor her parents ever mentioned his name. It was as if he never existed. The sadness and confusion left Sadie overwhelmed.

Five days later, Sheriff Henry Sapp rolled up the lane in his old, creaky truck.

"*'Siyo.*" Sadie's father greeted his old friend with a wave and walked out to meet him. The two men shook hands.

"Bird, I don't know exactly how to tell you this." Henry put his boot on the back bumper of the truck and spit at the nearby row of weeds tangled in the bottom of the fence. "Looks like the girl's husband, there . . . uh, have you seen him lately?"

Henry Sapp and Bird Walela had gone to a one-room school together when they were youngsters. Henry was a mixed-blood with fair skin and brown, curly hair. Bird was a fullblood with brown skin and black, straight hair. But as kids growing up in Eucha, they were all just Indians.

"No." Bird removed his ball cap with a local feed store logo on it and scratched his head. "She's been kind of sickly and her mother and granny have been taking care of her since last Friday, I guess it was." He placed the cap back on his head, leaving the bill at a slight upward tilt.

"Well, he's missing, and we found an old boy dead over at his place this morning. He'd been there all night . . . looks like." Henry shook his head and spit again. "Shot in the back . . . looks like," he added. "One of my boys, he went in the house and found a bunch of drugs in there." Henry gazed off into the distance, spit a third time, and returned his attention to Sadie's dad. "I'm sorry, Bird, we need to talk to the girl and see if she knows anything."

Bird invited Henry inside and everyone gathered around the kitchen table. Sadie sat next to her grandmother and listened to Henry Sapp relate the story of drugs, death, and missing husband.

"Is there anything you can tell us, Sadie, that might shed some light on all this?" asked Henry.

"I don't know," said Sadie. "He changed. He changed really fast. He's not the same person I married. There's this man named Juan . . ."

For the next few hours, Sadie revealed the story of her life for the last six months, including the trips to Mexico, the business dealings with Juan, the promises of a horse ranch of their own. She explained her absence from the house, her two jobs, and the strangers she would periodically find on her living-room floor.

"Do you know where he might be, Sadie?" asked Henry.

"No, not really," said Sadie. "The last time I saw him, we fought, then I got sick . . ." Tears began to fill her eyes.

"That's okay, Sadie. Would you call me if you hear from him?"

"I suppose he went back to Mexico," offered Sadie. "I just don't know. And I don't really care."

After Henry Sapp left, Rosa took Sadie's hand and said, "I think we need some fresh air." The old woman led Sadie out past the barn and toward the creek. The two women sat on the hillside overlooking the stream for a long time. Sadie listened with great reverence when her grandmother finally talked.

"Sadie, everybody makes mistakes. Sometimes we just don't know about people. But, that's okay, we go on. We are a strong people. Your ancestors came a long way on the Trail of Tears. Many people died. But they never gave up. My grandfather—your great-great-grandfather—he was a warrior in the Civil War. Fought with Stand Watie and the Cherokee Volunteers. Right or wrong, we have always stood up for what we believed was right. You will get over this thing and move on with your life. You are a Walela."

"Only half," she whispered. The words came out with a long sigh as if that were a reason for her failures thus far in life.

"You are a Walela," her grandmother repeated. "In the old days, you were either Cherokee or not. Identified by your clan. None of this half or quarter stuff."

"I don't have a clan." Sadie's words sounded bitter. She knew the story well. Cherokees were identified by their mother's clan. Her mother was white. Therefore, she had no clan.

Rosa ignored Sadie's comment about her clan. "Who do you think one of our finest leaders was?"

Sadie was silent.

Her grandmother continued, "John Ross, that's who. Of course him and Stand Watie, and probably Grandpap if the truth were known, were at odds most of the time. But that's okay. They lived the way they believed was right. John Ross was a great chief. But, he was no fullblood. More like an eighth or some such thing." Rosa looked toward the sky and used her hands as she spoke. "He brought us together during a time when the white people were trying to pull us apart, pushing us from our homelands back east, dumping all us Indians together in Indian Territory. And then that wasn't good enough. They took the land and cut it up into little pieces and assigned everyone their own plot so they could take what was left over and give it to the white settlers. Indians didn't create blood quantum, Sadie, *aniyonegas* did. It's the white people's way of controlling us." Then she looked back at Sadie. "*Hi tsalagi.* You are Cherokee. You are a Walela."

Just then, a hummingbird came and frantically fluttered his wings right in front of Sadie's face. It flew backward, circled above, and returned. Sadie sat still as it appeared once again in front of her as if suspended on a thin string. The tiny bird flew close to her face, nearer and nearer to her bruised cheek. Then, as quickly as it appeared, the hummingbird vanished. Sadie's pain was gone, withdrawn by the hummingbird, along with the heavy weight from her heart.

The two women sat in silence, Sadie in awe, until finally her grandmother spoke again. "Fly like a hummingbird, Sadie," she said. "Fly like a hummingbird." And with that the old woman got up and headed back to the house, leaving Sadie where she sat.

"Thank you, Gramma," Sadie whispered. Looking into the clear blue sky she added, "Thank you, *walela.*" Then she rose and followed her grandmother's footsteps back to the house.

The next day, Sadie went to a judge and had her marriage annulled. Then she drove to Tahlequah and enrolled in Northeastern State University. She easily qualified for grants and scholarships through both the University and the Cherokee Nation. When she graduated with honors and a degree in business three years later,

Mercury Savings Bank hired her immediately as a management trainee.

A lawman eventually picked up Michael in south Texas on an outstanding warrant. He was brought back to Delaware County and charged with murder. Sadie did not appear at the trial except for the afternoon when she had to testify. From a distance, Michael sneered and threatened to kill her as soon as he got out. She refused to look at him. When the jury found him guilty and sentenced him to prison, Sadie slammed the door on that awful page of her life. And now, against her wishes, the demon had reared its ugly head.

A flash of lightning flickered through the bedroom window and Sadie instinctively counted until the rumble of thunder ended—a childhood game used to determine the distance of the lightning. She got up and tiptoed into the dark kitchen. Quickly, she double-checked the locks on every door and window in the house. Sonny, curled up by the back door, raised his head and questioningly wrinkled his forehead.

"Come on, boy. I need some company tonight."

When Sadie patted the top of the quilt, Sonny reluctantly jumped on the corner of the bed. She stuck her feet under the covers and wiggled her toes under his heavy body.

"And by the way, Sonny, you have my permission to attack first and ask questions later."

Sonny laid his head on his front forelegs and closed his eyes. Exhaustion, mental and physical, overtook Sadie and before long she was dreaming. She dreamed she was dancing with a handsome man in the rain.

Chapter 11

The stormy night gave way to a morning filled with skies the color of robins' eggs. As she drove north toward Eucha, Sadie lowered the car window, taking in the fresh smell of damp soil. Growing up in rural Oklahoma had given her an appreciation for the simple things in life—clean air and land around her. She drove through Eucha's lonely three-way stop sign and turned toward the highway that would take her east to the Burgess place.

Hank Burgess had been a good friend to her father and she hated to see his things sold to the highest bidder. But she guessed that's what happens when you die and there's no one left to take care of it for you.

Her mind wandered to her own situation. At thirty-four, the tick of her biological clock had become deafening at times, then, after long conversations with herself, it would just fade into the distance. She had been unlucky in love so far in her life, and somehow she felt that her short stint with Michael had jinxed her chances of living the life of her childhood fantasy—a husband, two kids, and the proverbial house with a white picket fence. She never dreamed her dad would already be dead and she would be living alone on the farm. For now, she had resigned herself to the pursuit of career instead of family.

By the time Sadie arrived at the auction, parked cars clung to both shoulders of the road in front of the Burgess house. Lance Smith stood in the middle of the highway directing traffic. He smiled and nodded to her as he guided her to a spot behind a rental car. She set the parking brake and checked her watch: 9:23, right on time. Her car door opened magically and she realized Lance had left the traffic to move on its own while he helped her out of her car.

"Aren't you out of your jurisdiction?" she teased.

"Yeah," he said. "But I knew they were going to need some help out here so I volunteered my services." He walked with her across the highway to the entrance to the farm.

Sadie shaded her eyes with her hand and tried to look inconspicuous as she searched the crowd for Jaycee.

"By the way, are you going to the hog fry tonight?" asked Lance. "It's at the Sixkiller place between here and Sycamore."

"Didn't know about it."

"It's being held in honor of Wanda Sixkiller. It's been a year since she passed on, you know. All the kids are getting together for it, probably already cooking the pig. Gospel singing, all night long."

Sadie returned her attention to Lance. He had a twinkle in his eyes that looked like he had just gotten away with a juvenile prank of some sort and his sheepish grin softened the rugged features of his face. "I'll think about it," she said. But before she could finish her sentence, the sound of screeching tires and blaring horns sent Lance running back to the middle of the road, waving his arms and taking control of a near mishap. Not wanting to be late for her rendezvous with Jaycee, she dismissed Lance and his hog fry from her mind and walked up the lane toward the farm.

People milled in and out of the buildings looking for potential bargains, waiting for the sale to begin. Sadie could see Jaycee from a distance talking to Bud Carter, the auctioneer. Jaycee, neatly dressed in an open-collared shirt, slacks, and dress shoes, looked out of place among the crowd of old men in bibbed overalls and ball caps. Looks like a banker to me, she thought. She looked down at her own attire—tight jeans and cowboy boots topped with a plain white shirt. She hadn't dressed to impress, had just worn her usual Saturday duds.

Since Jaycee was busy, she decided to walk through the house. The furniture, antique by some people's standards, was just old to Sadie. She wandered into the dining room where a china cabinet caught her eye. To Sadie's delight, she discovered a water pitcher on the top shelf, the same pattern as her grandmother's plate. It was out of her reach, so she visually searched for the identifying tag, hoping when the number was called she could make a successful bid. Suddenly, she felt someone's presence and smelled a familiar fragrance.

"It's about time," he said and handed her a Hershey's chocolate kiss. "I've been lost for hours."

"Oh, you have not." Sadie unwrapped the candy and popped it into her mouth. "I saw you out there talking to Bud." Then returning her attention to the china cabinet she asked, "Can you reach the tag on that pitcher?"

Jaycee stood on his tiptoes and flipped over the paper tag attached to the handle. "Sold," he said.

"How can they do that?" she whined.

"I don't know. I guess they have privileged buyers who get to pick out things ahead of time."

They walked through the rest of the house for a few moments and then found a place next to the front porch to wait. Finally, the auctioneer pounded his gavel on a wooden block to get the sale under way, then projected his voice into a jabber of excited words and numbers.

Sadie watched while farmers she knew to have spoken only five words in the last year became aggressive bidders on everything from furniture and dishes to tractors and plows to mystery boxes that appeared to be full of nothing but junk. From time to time, Jaycee would take a folded piece of paper from his pocket, make a note on it, and then put it back.

During a lull in the action, Sadie turned to Jaycee and asked the question she had been dying to ask ever since she got there. "Now, why is it exactly that you needed to come to this sale?"

"Money, my dear," he answered matter-of-factly. Then seeing the question on her face, he continued. "The trust officer handling this estate didn't want to come. Thought it was too far up here in the sticks. And since I wasn't too far away, I volunteered to come for him. It's not a big deal. We work with the auctioneer and handle the paperwork and get a percentage of the revenue."

The gavel crashed against the block again and the sale continued. Within three and a half hours the entire contents of the house and barn were sold.

"If you will wait for me, I've got to sign a few papers and then we can go grab a bite to eat," said Jaycee.

"Okay, I'll be right here. I've grown kind of attached to this seat," she said, leaning back against the chair.

Jaycee disappeared into the crowd and Sadie decided to see if the bathroom was still in working order. When she came out of the bathroom, she was amazed to see the entire contents of the house being carried out piece by piece. She looked for the china cabinet. It and all of its contents were gone.

When she reappeared on the empty porch, a man walked up from behind her and grabbed her shoulder. It was Michael. Sadie jumped backward and almost lost her balance.

"Don't touch me," she yelled.

"Hey, what's wrong with you?" he asked. "I told you the other day on the phone, we need to talk."

"I don't have anything to say to you. I don't want to see you . . . and I want you to leave me alone." Sadie defensively crossed her arms in front of her and held on to her shoulders. "What are you doing here, anyway?" She looked toward the highway, hoping somehow she could get Lance's attention. "By the way, I know a police officer that's here."

"Let's just say, I'm keeping my eye on you. Besides, is that any way to talk to your husband after all this time?" The high-pitched tone of his voice made Sadie sick.

"You are *not* my . . ."

Jaycee appeared from nowhere and handed Sadie a box. He then strode past her to Michael and stuck out a confident hand. "I'm Jaycee Jones. I don't think we've met." Jaycee sounded like a used car salesman getting ready to go for the big sale. Then, before anyone could say anything, Jaycee put his arm around Michael's shoulders and escorted him off the porch away from Sadie and into the yard.

Sadie watched in quiet amazement as Jaycee continued to talk to Michael, just out of earshot. From her view, Sadie could see Michael's face as it appeared to fill with fear. The expression on Jaycee's face never varied from the artificial, salesman-like grin. Michael shook his head as if saying first yes and then no. Jaycee let go of his shoulders and Michael raised his hands up in front of him as if ridding himself of the entire situation. Michael then turned, walked out the gate, and crossed the highway. Jaycee climbed back on the porch, smiling as if he were seeing her for the first time.

"I'm at a loss for words," she stammered.

"I'm not. I'm hungry. Let's go find some grub." He took Sadie's hand and they walked straight to her car. "Say, what's in the box?" he asked.

"It's the box you just gave me," she reminded him.

"Well, what's in it?" Jaycee had a mischievous look on his face.

Sadie carefully opened the box. She couldn't believe her eyes.

There was the water pitcher she had seen earlier, the one marked as sold.

"How did you . . . ?"

"You got to be the early bird . . . say, if you want to follow me I know where there's a great little barbecue place."

Sadie could only nod her head and say, "Okay."

Chapter 12

Both of Sadie's old vehicles sat between the farmhouse and the barn, proof that she must be home. As Jaycee crossed the cattle guard and drove up the lane toward Sadie's house, he realized how enamored he had become of this woman. He had known a lot of women in his time, but Sadie was different. She affected him in an uncomfortable way, almost as if she had him under a magic spell.

He opened the door of his rental car and waited. Sonny had instilled a serious case of cautiousness in him a few weeks back, so he waited to see if anyone showed up to greet him before approaching the house.

After deciding it was safe, he knocked at the door and peeked through the kitchen window. But he could raise neither woman nor dog, so he strode across the yard to check the barn. The rusty hinges creaked when he pushed the door open and a barn swallow flew from its nest. Jaycee jumped. Other than the birds, the barn was empty, which meant Sadie and her two companions, Sonny and Joe, must be together. Hopefully, not far away. Maybe the favorite spot Sadie had told him about. He wondered if he could find it on his own. After a few minutes, he decided to give it a try.

He returned to his car, retrieved a green camera bag from the back seat, and threw it over his shoulder. The bag contained his new toy, a digital camera. It was the latest model available, and expensive to boot, and he was anxious to try his hand at taking pictures with it. The new contraption had more buttons and knobs than he had ever seen, but the young clerk who had sold it to him assured him even a monkey could make it work. He had taken her unspoken challenge and paid cash for it on the spot.

The main reason for the purchase had been his desire to capture Sadie's timeless beauty. In all his forty years he had never cared to carry around a picture of a woman, but he guessed that was about to change. He let himself through the gate and started walking through the pasture.

Summer had definitely arrived. By the time he reached the creek, the relentless Oklahoma sun pounded on his head and sweat began to stream down his back. Looking for a place to rest, he finally found one at the edge of a clear stream. He knelt and splashed cold water on his face, then sat down in the shade of a tall red-oak tree. As he surveyed his surroundings, he began to question his decision to track down Sadie. After all, how would he find her on an 80-acre tract of land where hills and valleys rose and fell indiscriminately, with each ridge merging into an endless maze of treetops?

Sunlight shimmered through the leaves of a gigantic sycamore and long-legged insects danced a bug ballet on top of the water. A crow called out a warning to another, reminding the city dweller of Hollywood westerns that depicted Indians as savages, making coded animal sounds just before they attacked the white settlers. He had never realized how degrading those images were and how tainted his impressions of Indians were before he met Sadie. He wanted to make sure she knew he didn't feel that way.

Periodically, a slight breeze would rustle the leaves in the trees and the birds would chatter at a gray squirrel as it played hopscotch in the trees above, bending the limbs to their maximum flexibility before jumping to another. The beauty of this place enveloped Jaycee and his thoughts returned to Sadie. She was a rich woman, he thought, but her wealth had nothing to do with the price of rocky, red dirt in northeastern Oklahoma. She had a beautiful spirit, and this land, along with Sonny and Joe, supplied the nourishment. For a moment, Jaycee surrendered to sadness. He knew he would never experience that degree of happiness.

Jaycee left his shady spot near the water and walked alongside the stream until he reached an oasis in the middle of nowhere—a deep, blue pool fed by a nearby spring. Crystal-clear water trickled from the mouth of a cave and down the side of a steep bank. Sadie had described the cave where she had played fearlessly as a child. Unfortunately, she had confessed, the opening was now too small for her to venture in, so she resorted to just sitting and watching the miniature waterfall making endless circles on top of the water before it splashed headlong into the stream below. It was her favorite place to meditate, she had told him.

But Sadie was not there. Disappointed, Jaycee decided to make the best of the situation and take a few photos before heading back. With camera in hand, he squinted one eye and looked through the viewfinder with the other. He angled the lens up and down, crouched and stood on tiptoe, looking for that perfect frame—that perfect stolen second to imprint on a piece of paper. Jaycee beamed, delighted with himself. He would capture Sadie's favorite place, frame it, and present it to her as a gift—a special gift.

He placed his camera bag on the ground and squatted next to it to change his lens to get a wider shot. Suddenly, he heard Sonny bark. He jumped to his feet and when he did, the rocks under his feet gave way, causing him to fall backward into a thick and thorny bush. He threw his hand back to break his fall and his shiny new camera crashed to the ground. In the commotion, he failed to hear the warning—the tiny rattles, just before the young diamondback coiled and struck. Two needle-like fangs punctured the skin on the fatty part of Jaycee's palm. Then, as quickly as he could jerk his hand away, the rattler deposited its deadly venom and disappeared into the bush.

He looked at the two tiny holes in the palm of his hand, felt the pain mushroom, and wondered how long it would take to die. Before he had a chance to yell for help, Sonny found him, barking with excitement as if he had found a prize. Sadie and Joe rounded the big sycamore at the bottom of the hill and Jaycee found himself thanking a God he didn't know for the sight of a woman and her horse.

"You okay? What are you doing up here?" asked Sadie.

"Looking for you," he said. "But that damned dog of yours about scared me to death. Fell into that bush and a snake got me." Jaycee held out his left hand, already beginning to swell.

"Where is it?" Sadie jumped down and fished for a knife in the front pocket of her tight jeans.

"Here, my hand."

"I see your hand. Where's the snake? Did you kill it?

"Didn't have time."

"Good," she said. "What did it look like? Was it in the water?" Sadie already knew from the size of the two pinholes in his hand it was either a copperhead or a rattlesnake, unless he had gotten hold of a cottonmouth near the water. She also knew that very young snakes, lacking the experience, failed to hold back venom for another possible strike. Instead, when they bit, they gave all the venom they had, making the situation worse for the victim.

"What do you mean, 'good'?" he asked.

"Talk to me, Jaycee. What did it look like?"

"I don't know. Kind of brown."

"Brown like a copper-brown? Or brown like a gray-brown?"

"More gray, I think. In the bushes there . . ." Jaycee pointed to the spot where he had fallen.

"Did you hear a rattle? Was it a rattlesnake? How big was it?"

"Hell, I don't know. He bit me and was gone before I . . ."

"That's okay. Don't get excited. It only pumps the poison to your heart faster. Sit down."

"Oh, great."

Sadie opened her pocketknife and pulled his hand between her knees as if shoeing a horse and slashed both holes, allowing the blood to flow freely.

"Ouch! What the hell are you doing . . ."

"Get up."

"I think I'm going to be sick . . ."

"Get up!" Sadie guided the wounded man to a boulder at the edge of the stream. She dipped her hands in the cold water and splashed his face. "You'll be okay, Jaycee. Sit on this rock, rest your elbow on your knee and let your hand bleed. I'll be right back."

"Where are you going? You can't leave me . . ."

"Do as I say," she demanded in a loud voice. "Keep your hand below your heart and let it bleed." Sadie backed up, stuck her boot in the stirrup, and mounted Joe in a fast and fluid movement. She squeezed the stallion with her knees, dug her heels into his flanks, and gave a click with her tongue. With that command, Joe wheeled and they raced down the hill and across the meadow with the grace and speed of champion barrel racers. Sonny ran alongside, barking with excitement.

Jaycee sat at the edge of the stream holding his hand over the water. He doused his face again and wondered how long it would take for his whole life to drain out through those two tiny holes in his hand. He could see schools of small fish swimming back and forth in the clear water and he became dizzy. He suspiciously watched the grassy area around the pool, half expecting the snake to return to finish him off, but before he could conclude his thoughts about life after death, Sadie returned and knelt beside him holding a green plant.

"Chew this up," she commanded. "Swallow the juice, just the juice, then spit it out into my hand."

"Are you crazy?"

"Just do it."

Jaycee followed Sadie's instructions with hesitation and began pushing the leafy plant into his mouth. He realized, as badly as he didn't want to, that he was going to have to trust his life to somebody besides himself.

"Joe, come." The stallion lowered his head, grumbled, and walked up to Sadie.

"Just the juice, Jaycee. Spit the rest in my hand." Sadie took the chewed plant and placed the poultice on Jaycee's wound. She pulled a white handkerchief from her shirt pocket and tied it snugly around his hand.

"Get up, Jaycee, you've got to get on Joe. Try to keep your hand lower than your heart."

"I can't feel anything in my hand. I think I'm going to throw up."

"You're going to live, if I can just get you on this horse."

Joe stood perfectly still while Sadie pushed Jaycee into the saddle.

"Good boy, Joe." Sadie placed her hand on the stallion's strong neck while Jaycee pulled himself up. "Hold on to the saddle horn, Jaycee. That's it. Now, take your foot out of the stirrups and lean forward." Sadie mounted the horse and sat behind Jaycee, holding him in the saddle. From a saddlebag, she produced more of the bitter weed and thrust it in Jaycee's face. "More snakeweed, please." Her request sounded as if she were ordering more tea at lunch.

"You know, this stuff tastes like . . ."

"Yeah, I know." Sadie pulled the knotted reins off the saddle horn, held them with her left hand, and nudged Joe with her heels. "Let's go, Joe. Easy does it . . . that's it, slow and easy . . . just swallow the juice."

In a matter of minutes, with Sonny leading, they returned to the barn. Sadie jumped off the back of Joe and helped Jaycee slide down. His knees buckled and he fell.

"Come on, Jaycee," she said. "You can do it." She left Joe saddled in the corral and helped Jaycee to her car.

"Oh, Sadie, I left my new camera . . ."

"That's okay, I'll get it later. Let's go."

Sadie delivered her snakebite victim to Eucha Memorial Hospital in a few short minutes and helped him through the emergency room door.

"Do you have an insurance card?" the young girl sitting at the emergency reception desk asked. She wore a red-and-white stick-on badge that read IN TRAINING.

"Yeah, in my wallet—"

"He's got a snakebite," interrupted Sadie. "I'll stand good for him. Can we get that information in a minute? I promise he won't die until he signs."

Sadie's frivolous attempt at humor about death in the emergency room went unnoticed, but when the registered nurse on duty, Eileen Summers, overheard the word "snakebite," she dropped the file she was holding, placed Jaycee in a wheelchair, and rolled him down the hall.

"Rattlesnake, I think," said Sadie.

Her voice echoed in her head and she retreated to the waiting room and collapsed into a large lounge chair in the corner. She closed her eyes and laid her head back on the lumpy chair. Her mind swam. *What was he doing there . . . good thing I circled back around . . . must have been a rattler . . . could have been a copperhead . . .*

Sadie's thoughts faded into a fitful dream.

An old Indian woman leaned on her walking stick, wiped sweat from her face with her sleeve, and gazed into a clearing. She shaded her eyes with a shaky hand and scanned the hillside. Then she caught a glimpse of a green plant. A storm cloud approached; lightning flashed and thunder rumbled. Quickly, the old woman harvested the plant, preserving the roots, so she could replant it later near her house.

A young child ran to meet the old woman. "Where ya been, Gran'ma? What ya got?"

"Snakeweed, my child. You never know when you might need some," answered the old woman. "The plant is powerful against the bite of the snake."

A white woman appeared, took the plants from the Indian, and threw them on the ground. When the child looked down, the ground was covered with snakes. Snakes intertwined in a massive conglomeration. A gleaming snake in the center rose up and transformed into a man. The young girl looked up at her grandmother's brown wrinkled face. "Gran'ma?"

"No, I'm not your grandma," said Eileen as she gently touched Sadie's shoulder. "Are you okay, Sadie?"

Awakened with a start, Sadie bolted from the chair, heart pounding, trying to recognize her surroundings. When she saw Eileen's plump face, her white uniform and nurse's cap, she remembered Jaycee.

"Jaycee? Is he all right?"

Eileen smiled and touched Sadie's forearm. "I thought that poultice looked like it might be your handiwork."

"Is he okay?"

"He's fine," she said. "We've already given him several shots of antivenin. He's probably going to need more, but we have to watch him for a while first to make sure he doesn't have a reaction. You can see him if you want."

Sadie followed Eileen down the hall and into a room where she found Jaycee propped up in a hospital bed, his tanned face and arms a stark contrast to the white sheets. His wounded hand lay at his side, wrapped in a bandage. Sadie could see that the swelling had reached and passed his elbow. He cradled a plastic, kidney-shaped bowl against his side with his other hand.

"You okay?" asked Sadie.

"How can you live where snakes come out of nowhere and try to kill you?" he asked. "And by the way, what was that comment about your being glad I didn't kill it?"

Sadie thought for a moment before explaining. "To make the story short, the old ones used to say if you killed a rattlesnake, his family would come back, hunt you down, and kill you."

"And you believe that?"

"Well, not really. But you never know. Indians are smarter than most white people give them credit for. I've lived around here all my life and I've never been bitten. I've seen plenty, but I just leave them alone . . . give them a wide berth. You know, they don't like you any more than you like them. After all, you were in his blackberry bush."

"I can't believe you're taking sides with the snake."

Sadie laughed.

"You don't see me laughing, do you?

"I'm sorry." Sadie took the plastic bowl and placed it on the bedstand, clearing a place for her to sit on the edge of his bed. She fussed with his pillow and offered him a wet washcloth.

"The nurse says you're going to make it," she said. "What did the doc say?"

"He said it could have been a lot worse but I don't know how. I guess the little devil gave me a pretty good dose. The doctor said I might have black marks on my hand for a long time—even after it's healed. That is, if the swelling ever goes down. And I can't say I'm too crazy about the initials you carved in my hand even if they did work wonders. Along with whatever that . . . he and the nurse were both carrying on about my homemade remedy. They actually think it may have helped."

"It's been known to save the life of more than one good Indian—including my great-grandfather. You could at least thank me for that."

"You're right. Thank you, Sadie." Jaycee stuck out his chin begging for a kiss and Sadie obliged. "Thank you for saving my life," he said. "It wasn't very smart for me to be sniffing around in the woods without my guide." Jaycee smiled and squeezed her hand. "And if it hadn't been for you . . . you are amazing."

"The pleasure was all mine, I'm sure." Sadie ran her hand across his forehead.

"What was that awful stuff?" Jaycee screwed up his face and gently licked his lips as if he could still taste the plant.

"Snakeweed," she said. "I've never tasted it personally, but my grandmother—"

"Man, that was awful."

"Well, you're alive. So quit complaining."

"Oh, okay. Can I buy you dinner for saving my life? You turned out to be a knight in shining armor, and I'm jealous because I wanted that scene."

"I'll take a rain check." Sadie stood and combed the top of her hair with her fingers. "I've got to go. Daylight's burning."

"Why?"

"Poor Joe's still got a saddle attached to his back. And I thought I'd see if I could find your camera."

"No. Please, forget it, Sadie. I can get another one."

"We'll see. Talk to you later."

And with that, Sadie slipped through the door and disappeared.

The hospital hallway bustled with activity and as Sadie headed for the front doors, she thought she heard someone call her name. She turned and saw Soda Pop and her mother sitting against the wall in the waiting room.

"Hi, Sadie," said the little girl as she waved her hand at her friend.

"My goodness," said Sadie as she moved to join the two. "What are you doing here?"

Soda Pop's mother spoke up first. "She had a reaction to some new medicine and about scared me to death. I rushed her down here and now she seems to be fine." Mrs. Andover shook her head. "We're just waiting a few minutes to make sure she's okay."

"Why are you here?" asked Soda Pop. "Are you sick, too?"

"Oh, no. Nothing like that," said Sadie. "Joe and I had to rescue a friend of mine who got in an argument with a rattlesnake and lost."

"Oh, my. That's terrible," said Soda Pop's mother.

"I hate snakes," said Soda Pop and then added, "Who is Joe?"

"Joe is my horse. He's my buddy, too."

"Can I ride your horse?" asked Soda Pop.

"Agatha Gertrude," scolded her mother. "It's not polite to ask for things like that. And it is 'may I,' not 'can I.'"

Sadie laughed. "Of course you may. In fact, he's already saddled up if you want to follow me home."

"We had better pass today," answered Mrs. Andover. "Maybe we can come some other day."

"Call me anytime," said Sadie. "Or you can always find me at the bank."

"We'll see you at the bank then."

Mrs. Andover and Soda Pop waved as Sadie left the hospital.

Chapter 13

Sadie felt strangely uncomfortable in her new office. She fingered the supple arms of the mahogany leather chair and studied her surroundings. A thick pane of glass topped the immense, dark-cherry desktop. Two armchairs, covered in brocade fabric, burgundy and navy paisley designs, stared at her from the other side of the desk. The hutch above the credenza stood against the wall, a trail of green silk ivy spilling off the top. On the wall behind her, a large painting burst with pink, purple, red, and green dollops of color in an abstract bouquet of flowers.

Looking through the office window, she could see down three stories to the covered parking provided for the senior officers of the bank. The Sycamore Springs Parkway ran diagonally on the east side of the building and Sadie could see tiny sailboats as they floated in the distance on Blue Lake.

So, this was it, Sadie thought. This was her reward for twelve years of hard and loyal service to the bank. She'd heard rumors that her promotion had come about in part to help meet the bank's requirements for a certain percentage of minority officers. The fact that Sadie was not just a woman but an Indian woman provided a double credit for the minority-employee numbers.

She also had her own theory regarding her sudden promotion. The words had come from Stan himself as he and Adam exited the elevator one day: " . . . Give her enough rope and she'll hang herself. Hell, it's all just a game." Even though Stan had not reprimanded Sadie formally after the robbery, he had openly criticized her, blaming her for Gordy's death. Now she believed her promotion was his way of setting her up so he could turn around and tear her down. He could withhold management support from her in her new position and then blame her for the first thing that went wrong. Down the corporate ladder she would fall. She had seen him do it to other employees before.

But she refused to be distracted by anything right now. With a new title and a new office, her workload had more than doubled. Her new title of security training officer made her responsible for instructing personnel in six branches about security procedures, which was going to be quite a feat since she had so little in the way of written guidelines to work with. She would have to start from the ground up, do the research, write the procedures, and create and implement the program.

Old Mr. Clarke had stammered when he presented her with the promotion. "We chose you for this position, Sadie, because you know what it feels like to be robbed."

Frail, with deteriorating health, Mr. Clarke served mostly as a figurehead for the bank. He left all the operational issues to the younger, more aggressive Stan Blackton. The older man kept a bottle of gin in a brown paper sack hidden in his bottom drawer, bringing it out from time to time when he thought no one could see him take a swig.

The poor man hadn't even realized the inappropriateness of his comment to Sadie. Thelma, representing the personnel department, had quickly offered her congratulations, stating she knew how hard Sadie had worked for the promotion and pointing out the dire need for security training. Sadie had acknowledged Thelma's comments with a smile and a nod.

Sadie agreed it was none too soon to start worrying about security at Mercury Savings. A few months after her own branch had been robbed, the Farmers Bank branch down the street had been hit. It had been horrific. Two young men, customers of the bank, had returned to the bank after being turned down for a loan and killed five people. Earlier, they had overheard one of the young tellers make what they mistakenly thought were derogatory comments about them. The two men went home, loaded three shotguns, and returned to the bank. In a crazed frenzy, they shot as many people as they could, including customers—a farmer standing in line to cash a social security check, a young woman pregnant with her first child, and an elderly man who could barely hear.

It had all happened so fast, no one even got a chance to set off the alarm. The killers had emptied the cash drawers into their pockets and made a quick getaway, leaving the victims to be discovered by the next customer who walked in on the bloody mess. Shortly thereafter, the two assassins ended up in a suicide shoot-out with police, bringing a violent end to everything. Sadie was thankful those robbers had not been customers of Mercury.

And although everyone agreed security was a good thing, Sadie just wished she had a little more experience in that area. In her estimation, being caught off-guard, watching her co-worker be killed, and then being tied up on the floor didn't exactly qualify her for the position. But she wasn't going to argue. It didn't matter how she got the job; she would make a difference and be successful doing it. She knew no other way.

Her first project, she decided, would be to push for armed guards at all of the branches. She didn't think guards were the only answer, but the employees might feel safer opening the branches if they were escorted by someone wearing a uniform and carrying a gun. Stan had already told her expensive perimeter alarms were out of the question. The budget simply would not allow it.

She called Sergeant McCord and asked him to help her compile a few statistics. Charlie was happy to help Sadie and together they submitted a ten-page report demonstrating the need for armed security. The request met with surprisingly little opposition, except when it came to the cost of hiring off-duty police officers. In typical fashion, Blackton substituted a cheaper alternative, and the bank was stuck with rent-a-cops.

Sadie always tried to look at the positive side of everything, and believing something was better than nothing, she withheld judgment until she could meet security guard Melvin Crump. He was being sent out by the Safety First Security Company to work in Sadie's old branch. Eager to meet him, Sadie left her new office and headed toward the Harvest Street branch.

As she drove through Collier Circle and turned south toward the branch on MLK, she felt good about her first accomplishment as security officer of the bank. She visualized a tall, young man in a starched uniform standing at the front door of every Mercury branch. For a moment, she wondered if Gordy would still be alive if they had hired guards in the past, but it was too late to wonder about that now.

She parked in her old parking space, walked across the lot, and entered through the south doors. When she first saw Melvin, she could hardly believe her eyes and struggled between feelings of disgust and outright laughter. He looked to be a little past his prime, at least mid-sixties, maybe early seventies. An obvious toupee sat on his wrinkled forehead. It looked like it might slide off at any moment. He wore high-water pants, a pair of brand-new black tennis shoes, and a .38-caliber Smith and Wesson low on his left hip. Sadie walked past Melvin and straight into Tom Duncan's office. She let the door close behind her before she slid weakly into a chair. Tom stood leaning against a wall, holding a cup of coffee in his hand. They both looked at each other and broke out in hysterical laughter.

"What on earth will he do if he comes face-to-face with a real robber?" asked Sadie between howls.

Tom continued to chuckle as he sat down across from Sadie. "I don't know," he said. "I'm actually afraid he may be more of a liability than an asset."

They sat for a few minutes, both weighing the pros and cons of the situation in silence.

"Well, I guess it's worth it just to have someone else check out the building before the employees have to go in," said Sadie, remembering her own situation. "At least he'll get killed instead of one of us."

"Sadie, you're awful."

Sadie balanced her elbow on the corner of Tom's desk and rubbed her forehead with her fingers while she thought. "Seriously, Tom, what if some robber comes blaring in here in the middle of the day and this guy gets somebody killed?"

Tom raised his eyebrows and wrinkled his forehead in a don't-ask-me look.

"Surely," Sadie continued, "they wouldn't give him a gun if he wasn't officially certified or something."

"With my luck, it's probably the 'something,'" said Tom. "I thought you were getting us real cops. What happened to that?"

"Stan nixed it. Cost too much," said Sadie. "If we spend too much money on guards, the execs might not have enough extra dough to keep their memberships going at the country club." Sadie's voice dripped with sarcasm. "We wouldn't want that to happen, now would we?"

"Yeah, all you guys are sitting over there in your ivory tower on the parkway while the rest of us peons are out here on the front lines like sitting ducks. Did you hear about those maniacs over at Farmers?"

"Yeah, I know."

"I wouldn't have given you that promotion if I didn't think you could do us some good," said Tom and then winked at Sadie. They both knew he had nothing to do with her becoming the security officer of the bank.

"Okay," she said. "Give me some time. I'll see what I can do. But I wouldn't hold my breath if I were you. I'm new at this officer game-playing crap."

"Okay, so what do we do for now?" asked Tom. "And don't forget, I'm leaving early today."

Sadie let out a long sigh and looked at the door. "For right now?" she asked. "I guess we go meet him . . . and show him around." Laughter contained, she opened the door, strode across the lobby, and offered her hand to security guard Crump.

A man sat in the front corner booth of the Blue Dumpling Café sipping coffee and thumbing through the *Sycamore Springs Gazette*. From his seat, he could look past the top of his paper and have an unobstructed view of the bank across the street. He chewed on a plastic coffee stirrer and watched as Sadie and Tom directed Melvin Crump around the outside of the branch. He could see Sadie and the two men disappear and then reappear by the ATM as they encircled the entire building.

The man rolled up his paper, stuck it under his arm, and laid a dollar bill on the table before walking outside.

"That's what I like," he muttered to himself. "A woman who can take charge. Makes life more interesting."

After showing Melvin Crump around, Sadie decided to stay at the branch for a while in an effort to get him off on the right foot. Somehow, she thought if she got to know him better, she would discover he had numerous marksmanship trophies somewhere at home in his closet. Or even better, maybe he was retired from the military or some foreign legion. She secretly hoped to find out he purposely dressed in his eccentric manner to confuse any would-be robber. As hard as she could, she scratched for a simple straw of hope. By the end of the day, she had found none.

Excited customers flocked to Sadie's side when they saw her standing near her old desk and Sadie received each one with a handshake or a light hug. Although many begged her to return to the branch permanently, she assured them she was in a better position and welcomed their congratulations.

The best part of the day came when Soda Pop arrived. Tom had called Soda Pop's mother and told her Sadie was in the branch. Soda Pop came in all dressed up, wearing her new wig created from Sadie's hair, and surprised Sadie. The little girl sported her trademark slicked-down bangs, with the rest of her hair falling to just above her shoulders.

"Look," said Soda Pop as she approached Sadie. She held out her hair on each side of her head and smiled. "I have hair like yours now."

Sadie swallowed hard and kneeled down for a hug. "And it is beautiful, Soda Pop, just beautiful." Sadie couldn't help but notice that the child seemed to be even more frail than the last time she had seen her. Tom handed Sadie a balloon and she blew it up for Soda Pop and gave it to her. She had a sinking feeling there wouldn't be too many more balloons for Soda Pop.

As Soda Pop and her mother left, the last of the procrastinators made a mad dash for the door before closing time. Sadie waved as the little girl and her mother drove off. Just then, an old gray Chevrolet with dark tinted windows turned and crept into the parking lot. The unusual movement of the car gave Sadie an uneasy feeling, and she glanced at Melvin standing in the middle of the lobby, feet apart, at parade rest. He faced the teller line, guarding it as if he thought it might get away.

The car parked near the front door and sat motionless. Realizing Tom had already left for the day, Sadie looked at her watch and counted the minutes until the doors would be locked. *Only two more minutes . . . maybe I should call the police . . . that's stupid, what am I going to say—there's a car in the parking lot . . . who would just sit there like that . . . damn, why couldn't we get real police officers . . .*

Sadie picked up the new set of keys she had been saving to present to Melvin and walked toward the door. The passenger-side door of the car opened and a man got out. He wore army fatigue pants, a black T-shirt, and black tennis shoes. There was something familiar about the man and Sadie hesitated before walking through the first set of double doors. *Oh, please don't let it be him.* Her mounting fears were realized when he turned and looked straight at her.

"Melvin, you had better come here."

Melvin Crump almost tripped on the carpet when he heard his name called, but caught his balance and hurried to Sadie's side.

"Melvin, I don't know what this man wants, but I want you to stand here while I talk to him."

Melvin didn't say a word. He threw his shoulders back, stuck out his lower lip, and gave Sadie an affirmative nod, as if they had some unknown understanding. Sadie felt queasy and her hands shook a little as she pushed through the double set of doors. "What do you want, Michael?" She bluffed her nonexistent confidence. "We're closed."

"I just came by to say hello, Sadie," he said. "Aren't you glad to see me?"

"Not particularly."

"Who's your pal there?" Michael nodded at Melvin.

Sadie ignored the question, standing her ground. Melvin looked at Sadie, unsure of what to say or do.

"We just thought we'd do a little business, that's all." Michael looked at the driver of the car and smiled. "Where's your big-bad-protector boyfriend?"

"I want you to stay away from here and leave me alone," said Sadie.

"You better move along," said Melvin with the deepest voice it sounded like he could muster. "Bank's closed."

Then through a stroke of luck, or perhaps an answered prayer, Sergeant McCord pulled his black-and-white police cruiser into the parking lot. Before Sadie could say another word, Michael jumped back into the car and it roared off, disappearing into five o'clock traffic.

Charlie parked and rolled out of his car, looked at Sadie and Melvin, and then looked behind him and around the parking lot twice trying to figure out what they were staring at. "Did I miss something?" he asked.

"Yes, but if you come here I'll give you a kiss."

"No sir, no problem," blurted Crump. "We've got everything under control here."

Charlie stood with one foot on the curb and looked at the unlikely pair, trying to comprehend the contradiction. "I was just trying to dodge the afternoon car wars and thought I recognized your car parked over there. Want to have a cup of coffee?"

"I'd love to," she said. "But I've got to get home. Thanks for showing up when you did, though. Looks like my ex-husband is going to be a pain in the ass now that he's out of jail."

Charlie and Melvin both looked at Sadie with equal expressions of surprise.

Sadie tossed the keys to Melvin. "Here's your keys to the bank," she said. "You can lock up, can't you?"

Melvin smiled, nodded, and walked back into the branch with a self-assured stride. Charlie looked at Sadie and waited for an explanation.

"Who was that?" asked Charlie.

"Our new protection," said Sadie. "Why is it, you suppose, I don't feel very safe?"

"No, who was that in the car that just drove off?"

"I told you. My ex."

"What was he in for, Sadie?"

"Murder."

"You want to help me out here?" asked Charlie. "Maybe fill in some of the holes. I think I missed something."

They both climbed into Charlie's cruiser, sat in the bank parking lot, and Sadie recited her life story against the background noise of Charlie's radio.

"I was young," she said quietly. "What else can I say?"

Charlie listened silently.

"He was so good-looking and I'm such a sucker for a handsome man. I didn't really love him. Just infatuation, I guess. Or if you want the real truth, I just wanted to get away from my mother." Sadie stopped for a moment and then continued. "You know how it is when you're young. I was working at the drugstore . . . the summer I turned sixteen. That's when he came to town, to Eucha. Anyway, my mother hated him and that just made me want to be with him all that much more."

Charlie's radio crackled and Sadie looked out the side window of the squad car. Charlie adjusted the volume and sat back in his seat, waiting for Sadie to continue.

"We ran off to Arkansas and got married. My mother about died. She was so mad when we came home I thought she was going to kill me. My dad didn't like it, but he didn't say much. That's the way he was." Sadie chuckled fondly at thoughts of her father. "I guess he thought I'd figure it out on my own. And sure enough I did."

Sadie stopped talking while she watched the employees leave the bank in a group through the side door with Melvin bringing up the rear. Sadie lowered the car window and shouted at the new guard, "Everything locked up, Melvin?" Melvin nodded his head and waved at Sadie.

"I'd better double-check," she said as she started to open the car door.

"Stay there," said Charlie. "I'll check for you."

Before she knew it, he had bounded out of the car and disappeared around the side of the building. She closed the car door and relaxed, inhaling the delicate aroma of honeysuckle as the gentle summer breeze carried it through the car window. After a few minutes, Charlie climbed back into the cruiser and Sadie continued to tell her story. "We had a lot of dreams," she said and turned her head toward Charlie. "He promised me a horse ranch—a ranch and a white picket fence around a big, blue ranch house."

Charlie's eyes followed the movement of traffic as it snaked down the nearby boulevard.

"You know what I got?" asked Sadie.

Charlie returned his attention to Sadie and she continued. "I got a rundown apartment, a full-time job at the drugstore, and a part-time job at the Eucha Bar. He started drinking and then every time I'd come home, the apartment would be full of drunks . . . people I didn't even know. And then every other weekend or so he'd take me to Mexico so he could trade briefcases with some man. Guess he thought it looked better traveling with a woman." Sadie ran her fingers through her bangs and straight back across the top of her head. "Damn, I was so naive."

"So, he was a drug dealer?"

"I guess. Hell, I don't really know what he was." Sadie squirmed in her seat and looked at Charlie. "You know, Charlie, nothing is ever what it seems to be, is it?"

"I thought you said something about murder. "

"I wasn't there when it happened. He hit me. No, he knocked me down. So I went running home to Momma and Daddy to lick my wounds. Then the sheriff showed up one morning and said they found some dead guy in front of our apartment. They finally found Michael somewhere in Texas. I never spoke to him again. He was real mouthy because I testified against him." Sadie looked at Charlie and smiled. "And you know what? I had almost, just almost, forgot about him and that part of my life . . . until a few days ago, that is."

"So the car that drove off as I came in was him?"

"Yeah, looks like he's out. Killed a man and out of jail in fifteen years. Is that all a man's life is worth? Fifteen years?" Charlie didn't answer and she continued. "I guess he thinks we can just pick up where we left off. My uncle said he saw him snooping around my place. And then we had a run-in at an auction."

"Are you still married to him?"

"Nope, got it annulled."

"If you want, I can get you some protection, Sadie. Hell, I'll do it myself or if you want I'll get Lance Smith to do it. He's always asking about you, anyhow."

"Really? Thanks, but I'll be all right. I don't think he'd actually hurt me."

A garbled message came across the radio waves. Charlie picked up the transmitter, answered, listened some more.

"Looks like some unhappy driver has managed to make a mess down at Collier Circle. Want to ride with me for a while? I'm pulling a double shift today. Looks like the rest of the folks have left. Do you have to go back inside the bank?"

"Nope, I'm through here. Left my purse in the car and got my keys in my pocket."

"You be careful and give me a call if you need anything." Charlie waited until Sadie got into her car and locked the door, then he followed her out of the parking lot and into the evening traffic.

Chapter 14

Sadie woke up exhausted, her sheets clutched in a wad next to her stomach. Her dream had turned into a nightmare when a faceless man chased her into a giant cardboard box. The dream had repeated itself periodically since the robbery and each time Sadie would wake up before she could see his face. Today was no different.

The disturbing images usually faded once she busied herself with her morning routine. She finished her chores and headed to work. The morning drive to Sycamore Springs gave Sadie a chance to prepare, organizing the day's agenda in her head. She did not plan to visit the Mercury branch again any time soon, so she would need to call Tom Duncan and tell him about Michael's unexpected visit. Also, she would need to check on Melvin Crump's disposition after his first day on the job.

Sadie liked to get into the office early, giving herself enough time for an extra cup of coffee before the start of the day. But today she seemed to move in slow motion and arrived just as a large herd of employees funneled through the back door, poking time slips one by one into an ancient, mechanical time clock.

She made her way past the group into her office, set her coffee on a coaster next to her computer, and turned her attention to the corner of her desk. Thirteen red roses stood at attention in a silver vase in the shape of a large Hershey's candy kiss tied with a red bow on one side. The flowers had arrived yesterday while she was at the branch. Try as she might, she could not convince a soul to confess the unknown source, much less explain the meaning of the thirteenth rose. The candy-shaped vase represented a significant clue, she was sure. Jaycee always seemed to be eating the small morsels of chocolate every time she saw him.

Just as Sadie sat down at her desk, Stan Blackton and Adam

Cruthers ran into her office in a panic and started yelling, both at the same time.

"They killed him!"

"We've been robbed!"

"What?" Sadie could not believe what she was hearing. "Killed who? Who's been robbed?"

Stan stood at Sadie's window, hands on hips, staring into space. He removed his glasses, ran his hand over his face, and then jammed his glasses back against his eyebrows. Adam walked around in a small circle, wringing his hands. Sadie stood up and Stan started talking again.

"They found that new security guard you hired with a bullet in his head this morning. Right in the head . . ." Stan's voice trailed off and then he turned to Sadie and emphasized the rest of his sentence: "inside the branch!" His face had turned a blazing shade of red and a vein popped out on his neck. He repeated the routine with his glasses and then started talking again. "We're trying to run a bank here. This shit is costing us a lot of money. Not to mention the bad publicity. What are the customers going to think?"

Sadie picked up her purse and keys and headed for the door.

"Where do you think you're going?" Blackton's voice had hit a high pitch.

"I've got to go—"

"Oh, no you don't." Beads of perspiration broke out across Stan's forehead, his face still beet red, as he turned his wrath toward Sadie. "I'm beginning to think you're in cahoots with somebody in this robbery business."

"What?" Sadie took a step backward.

"Right before he died, the guard told somebody the door was unlocked," stammered Stan. "How the hell was the door left unlocked, Sadie? Weren't you there all day yesterday? Couldn't you even get the doors locked?"

"No, no, no," said Sadie. "I gave Melvin the keys. He locked up." Sadie's head began to swirl. *I didn't actually see Melvin lock the doors. I was too damn busy talking about my personal problems. But Charlie double-checked for me.* Suddenly, she remembered Michael again. "Oh, God," she said and sat down in one of the chairs in front of her desk.

Stan was still talking: ". . . fingerprints on the dye pack from that last robbery and they said you were friends with that homeless man who robbed us last time. I'm afraid we can't keep you if this is the way you are."

"What do you mean . . . the way I am?"

Adam stood still for the first time, looked at Stan and said, "I think I'm going to be sick." And with that announcement, he disappeared down the hall.

"Wait a minute," said Sadie. "Who else was there? How did they get the vault open?"

"You tell me, Sadie. You're the one in charge of security."

"There's no way—"

"Somebody's going to have to pay for all this," said Stan, "and I've decided it's going to be you. You hired him, he's dead, so you're fired."

"What? You can't do this."

"Oh, yeah? Watch me. Be gone by the time I get back or I'll throw you out this window myself. I've got to go talk to the damn television reporters again."

Stan stormed out the door and Sadie stood frozen, trying to comprehend what had just taken place. Her mind felt like mush; her thoughts bounced around like shock waves inside her head. *I'm fired? He can't really mean that . . . Melvin's dead? . . .* Sadie looked at the flowers on her desk and wished with all her might that she had the ability to turn back time. Suddenly, Adam reappeared at her door, his tie loosened. His shirt had a large wet spot on the right side of his chest.

"I'm sorry, Sadie." His words sounded genuine.

"He fired me," she said weakly. "He didn't really mean that, did he?" Sadie grasped for a glimmer of hope.

"I'm afraid so. He sent me back down here to make sure you didn't take anything that wasn't yours."

"Oh, really?" Sadie's shock began to shift into anger. She picked up her purse and started toward the door. Then she stopped, returned to her desk, scooped up the flowers, and stormed past Adam and out the door.

Sadie took her time driving home and decided to go by the branch. From a distance she could see two police cars and one media van parked near the front door. She recognized Lance Smith but didn't see Charlie anywhere. Several onlookers stood in the back of the parking lot near the honeysuckle bush and a young child, oblivious to the morning's event, rode his tricycle up and down the sidewalk.

Sadie wanted to stop. Her head was swimming with questions. Was someone already inside like before? If so, how did they get in? All of the branch employees had keys to the branch. Could one of them be involved or perhaps have misplaced their keys? Or maybe someone ambushed Melvin outside and forced him to unlock the door. Even so, how did they get the vault open? Melvin didn't have the combination. Was it the same man who robbed her? Or, worse yet, could it have been Michael? Or were they one and the same? Nothing made sense.

When she reached the driveway of the bank, her foot would not move to touch the brake. She simply drove north until she reached the ramp of the expressway and turned onto the highway that would carry her out of Sycamore Springs and back to Eucha.

The drive home was a blur. When she got inside the house, she placed the roses on the kitchen table and dropped into a chair. The phone rang and she jumped.

"Hello?"

"Are you all right?" asked Jaycee.

"Yes, I'm fine," she said quietly, and then added, "I guess."

"I was just about to leave town when I heard about the robbery. Called your office and they said you were gone and not coming back— ever. I was afraid something might have happened to you. Then I called Adam and he said they had let you go. What happened?"

"I don't know. You probably know more than I do."

"I just thought you might want to talk. Can I come by?"

"Oh, I don't think so. I need to get some of this sorted out in my head."

"Are you sure? I would really like to see you again even though I wish the circumstances were different. I was hoping to call you today to thank you for saving me from rattlesnake death."

"Oh, you're welcome for the hundredth time. How is your hand?"

"Marked for life, but other than that, not too bad. How did you like the roses?"

"I thought that might have been you." Her mood shifted as she gazed happily at the bouquet.

"The florist didn't snitch on me, did they?"

"No, nobody snitched. But the vase was a dead giveaway."

"It was?"

"Every time I see you, you're eating candy kisses." Sadie surprised herself when she giggled like a young girl.

"I knew I had some bad habits that were going to catch up with me one day, but I didn't know eating chocolate candy was going to get me in trouble."

"They are beautiful. I don't really know what to say."

"Beautiful flowers for a beautiful lady."

"Thank you." Embarrassed, Sadie could feel warmth rising in her face. "Thanks for the compliment . . . and for the roses."

"You're welcome, my dear."

The conversation waned and Sadie shifted her weight from one foot to the other. She wanted to beg him to come over, to hold her and tell her everything was going to be all right. She wanted to tell him what a jerk Blackton was, how they had accused her of being involved in the robberies and fired her for no good reason. She wanted to tell him Michael came to the bank and she was scared. But the words twisted in an endless circle in her head, unable to make a connection with her voice.

"Okay, then," he said. "If you insist, I'm going to head back to Dallas. I'll be back in a few weeks. Around the last week of July. How about a date on that Friday evening? Say around seven. Okay? I'll bring you some candy kisses."

"That would be nice." The words gushed before Sadie had a chance to think.

"I'll call you before then. Bye now."

Sadie heard the line go dead, then the buzz of the dial tone before she hung up. Realizing the conversation was over and having shot down any hopes of seeing Jaycee, she felt empty. Why did she have to be so independent? If he would just call back, she would tell him to come. But it was too late now. He was gone.

In the meantime, she was going to have to figure out how to dig herself out of this hole on her own. Somehow, she believed that Happy must hold the key. Where did he get the robber's jacket? Why were the dye packs at his box? Why wouldn't he talk? Why hadn't somebody found all this out by now? Why wasn't somebody trying to solve her bank robbery? They had to be all connected. Couldn't somebody else see that besides her?

She decided to find her own answers. Why were the doors unlocked? She made a mental note to call Sergeant McCord. After that, her next stop would be to see Happy.

Chapter 15

Charlie finished his fourth cup of strong coffee and tossed the stained Styrofoam cup in the trash. He leaned back in his chair and contemplated the papers that lay in two orderly stacks in front of him, then opened the top desk drawer and picked up a roll of antacids. Since the new cook at the Waffle House had started, his occasional indigestion seemed to be turning into a routine.

He picked at the tightly wrapped cylinder with his big fingers, which only resulted in more frustration. He muttered several words of disgust and pulled his reading glasses out of his shirt pocket. After close inspection of the situation, he leaned to one side and fished in his left pocket for his favorite knife—the one he had been carrying since he was a young boy more than forty years ago. He opened the blade, laid the roll of antacid tablets on the edge of his desk, and carefully sliced it in two. A tiny piece fell to the floor. Charlie rolled back in his chair and visually searched. Unsuccessful at finding the elusive sliver, he returned his concentration to accessing the rest of the chalky-white tablets of relief.

Federal Agent Victor Robinson appeared at the doorway, walked right in, and dropped a brown envelope in the middle of Charlie's desk.

"I don't know why you asked for this report, McCord. But in any case, here it is."

Charlie extracted an antacid and popped it into his mouth before glancing over his reading glasses at the agent. "Thanks, son." Using the same blade, he sliced open the sealed edge of the envelope before snapping the knife closed. Once more, the big man stretched and leaned to one side as he dropped his knife back into his pants pocket. Then he looked at his watch and threw his glasses on the desk.

"You're out early, Robinson. You want to stick around for the seven o'clock roll call? You can witness some real action out on the streets today with some of my troops, if you'd like."

"I think I'll pass," said Robinson, ignoring Charlie's jab. "By the way, since you're so interested, you ought to know we're putting the Mercury Bank robberies on hold temporarily. I'm on my way to Oklahoma City right now. We've got a rash of threatening rumors floating around with Tinker Air Force Base mentioned as a possible target of some kind. I've got orders to leave these penny-ante robberies to you local law dogs to figure out. Anyway, I think this homeless guy is looney. And until someone finds where he hid the money, there isn't much else to go on. Makes no difference to me whether he's locked up in jail or in a crazy house. It's all about the same. From what I can tell, he's going to be staring at the walls of Eastern State for a while."

Charlie thumbed through the contents of the envelope, a stack of reports from the hospital. "I guess your higher-ups don't care that two people were murdered?"

"Why do you care about this case, anyway?" asked Robinson.

"It's personal," said McCord. "That particular bank happens to be my bank." Charlie put the emphasis on the word *my*. "You know, that money he took could have been some of my piggy-bank money, not to mention he killed a kid . . . and a security guard." Charlie shoved the papers back inside the envelope and looked straight at the agent. "Besides that, just in case you care, I think you feds have got the wrong man."

"Is that so?"

"Yeah, and I thought in my spare time I might help you boys out by catching the real robber."

"Great," said Robinson. "Now that you got your chance, McCord, go for it." Robinson rolled his eyes, turned on his heels, and disappeared out the door.

Charlie placed the remainder of the antacids in his shirt pocket along with his reading glasses, stuck the envelope under his arm, and headed down the hall.

Charlie had studied the FBI agent's hospital reports for several days and had finally come to the conclusion he needed to see someone in person. There was a lot to be said for looking at a person face-to-face when you talked to him, Charlie thought. After eighteen years as a cop, experience had proven that a lot of information could be gleaned from one's eye. So he had decided it would be worth spending a personal day to get some answers and it would give him a chance to get away. Picking up Highway 69 at Adair, Charlie drove north through Big Cabin toward Eastern State Hospital in Vinita. He turned down a tree-lined street on the edge of town that led to a complex of large brick buildings. The grounds were well maintained, simple landscaping with large oak and maple trees providing an abundance of peaceful shade. As he drove in front of the main building, he could feel unseen eyes watching him through the metal-screen-covered windows. He parked in a visitor's space, placed his gun under the front seat of his truck, and approached the front door. When he entered the building, he questioned his decision to wear casual clothes instead of his customary uniform.

He had felt uncomfortable about the case being placed in a permanent pending status. Although he came in no official capacity, he thought there were answers here—if he could just figure out how to get them.

Once inside, he asked a young woman at the reception desk for Dr. R. M. Graham, who turned out to be Dr. Rachel Marlene Graham, a petite woman with shoulder-length, caramel-colored hair. She wore octagonal-shaped, rimless glasses that looked like they belonged on the face of someone's grandmother. A white doctor's coat swallowed her tiny frame by at least two sizes. She radiated a youthful appearance, which Charlie thought must contradict her age. He knew she had been head psychiatrist at Eastern State Hospital for several years. The sergeant shook her hand, careful not to squeeze too hard for fear he might break her delicate fingers.

She directed him to her office. It was decorated in several shades of blue and reminded Charlie of a living room in someone's elegant home. Fresh-cut daisies graced the coffee table centered between a cushy, blue-striped sofa and two comfortable armchairs covered with pink, yellow, and blue print fabric. The doctor chose one of the armchairs and Charlie took the other.

"So, Sergeant McCord, you're here about one of our patients?" she asked. "Yes, ma'am," answered Charlie. "I have a few questions about John Doe. He was sent here from Sycamore Springs by a judge for evaluation a few months ago. I've got the report you sent right here, but—"

"Oh, yes, that would be Rob."

"Rob?" Charlie turned his head and looked at the doctor with an apparent question on his face. "You know his name?" he asked.

"No," the doctor laughed. "He hasn't exactly told us his name—or anything else, for that matter. I'm kind of embarrassed to tell you this." She looked down at the floor. "The first night he was admitted, we read his chart and found out he had been arrested for robbing a bank. One of the night orderlies started calling him 'robber' and then it got shortened to Rob. It stuck." She looked at Charlie and smiled. "It's better than calling him John Doe or Number XYZ, don't you think?"

"I see. Yes, I guess so." Charlie shook his head and wondered what it must be like to work with mental patients day and night. "Look, Doc," Charlie began. "I don't want to take up too much of your time. It's just that I've been reading these reports and I was wondering if you could just tell me a little about him. He's tied to a robbery case where a young man was murdered. And . . . well, these reports just don't . . . well, I guess I just don't understand the jargon."

"I'll be glad to fill in the blanks for you."

"Good." Charlie sounded hopeful. "Do you think he's ever going to be able to talk again?"

Dr. Graham looked past Charlie and stared through the window into space for a moment and then returned her attention to the sergeant. "Psychiatry is not an exact science, Sergeant McCord," she explained. "So, I guess a short answer to your question would be . . . I don't know, or at best, I hope so. It is our goal to administer the right combination of medication and therapy to improve the mental state of the patient. He's been here less than six months. Not a very long period of time to expect a miraculous recovery in a patient like Rob." The doctor walked over to a corner table and poured a cup of coffee, then held the pot in the air gesturing an offer to Charlie. "Black?" she asked.

Charlie nodded and rose to take the cup from the doctor.

"I can tell you nothing more than what is already in the report sent to the judge and the FBI," she continued. "In my opinion, Rob has had a psychotic break, a break with reality. He is delusional. We are not sure, at this point, what brought on this psychotic break. It could be the result of a trauma, a psychotic depression, or post-traumatic stress disorder. We are not going to know that for sure until he makes enough progress to talk to us. And even then, he could be amnesic. Right now he seems to be living in the moment, with no conscious connection with his emotions and feelings."

"Amnesic?"

"He might have amnesia," she explained. "Could have lost his memory and not remember who he is or—"

"Or what he's done." Charlie finished the doctor's sentence for her.

"Yes, that's right," the doctor agreed. "He is definitely experiencing a repression from the conscious knowledge of who he is, and I get the feeling he's not sure life is worth living right now. However, I think we should be optimistic. He still has the basic instincts of survival. He was securing food for himself and staying out of the elements, even if it was in a box." The doctor smiled.

"Do you think this man could have calculated entering a bank, waiting out a time lock, and killing someone if necessary to make off with enough money to buy him boxes from now till kingdom come?"

"I'm afraid he's the only one who can tell us that, Sergeant McCord." The doctor placed her half-empty cup on the coffee table and rose, signaling the end to their meeting. "You can look in on him if you want," she added.

Charlie followed Dr. Graham out of her peaceful office and back into the sterile world of long halls and double-locked doorways. After Charlie thought he had walked at least three miles, Dr. Graham suddenly stopped in front of a closed door and gestured toward a small window.

Charlie had to duck his head to peer through the glass. The small room appeared to be about the size of a single jail cell, Charlie thought, except nicer. The bed looked like an army cot with sheets tucked in tight, blanket folded and draped over the foot of the bed. The toilet and lavatory were in full view. No mirror. Nothing that could be used to hurt oneself.

The homeless man Sadie called Happy, the perpetrator Charlie identified as John Doe, the patient Dr. Graham referred to as Rob, the lonely man who could not speak, all one and the same, sat on the bed staring out the window of his hospital room. His back rested against the wall, knees bent, bare feet on the edge of the bed. He was dressed in clean, hospital-green pajamas. His hair had been washed and cut, his beard trimmed short. A pair of slippers sat neatly on the floor next to a small dresser.

Charlie returned his gaze to the brightly lit hallway and Dr. Graham.

"That's about all there is to see," she said.

"Thanks, Doc," said Charlie as he pulled a business card from his shirt pocket. "If he ever gets around to saying anything, would you mind calling me?"

"I'll be glad to," she said.

The doctor followed Charlie to the front door and swiped a card-like device through a scanner. The front doors magically opened.

Charlie walked to his truck, got in, and slammed the door. Silently, he thanked God that he was not crazy. He rolled down the window and breathed in the fresh autumn air. The breeze smelled like football weather and for a moment he let his mind wander to memories of earlier years when, as a defensive lineman, the most important thing in life had been winning that week's varsity game. The oncoming colder weather would inevitably reignite the pain of arthritis in his knee caused from the absence of cartilage—a souvenir from the last game he ever played.

As he reached to turn the key in the ignition, a car sped into the parking lot, drove past his parked truck, and nosed into a space near the sidewalk. Charlie recognized the car immediately, even before he saw the driver get out. He had seen it a hundred times parked at the bank. The car belonged to Sadie Walela.

Charlie sat still and tried to blend in with the upholstery. He didn't want Sadie to see him just yet. And he hoped she wouldn't recognize his old truck. He watched as Sadie got out of her car and walked straight to the building and entered. Charlie shook his head and spoke aloud to himself.

"What in the . . . ?"

After a few minutes had passed, Charlie couldn't stand it any longer. He jumped out of his truck, marched back into the building, and ran headlong into Dr. Graham.

"Back so soon?" Dr. Graham smiled.

"Did you see a woman come through here a few minutes ago?" he asked. "She has black hair. An Indian woman."

"Yes," she said. "Yes, I did." The doctor offered no additional information.

"Where did she go?"

"I believe she is visiting one of our patients. Is there a problem, Sergeant?"

"I'm not sure yet." Charlie rubbed his forehead. "Exactly which patient is she visiting?" Charlie knew the answer before the doctor spoke.

Dr. Graham walked over to the check-in station, picked up the sign-in book, and looked back at Charlie. "It looks like she's visiting with the same man you were asking about. What do you call him? John Doe?"

Charlie shifted his weight and placed his right hand on his hip, an unconscious habit he had of resting his hand near his gun. Only today, there was no gun. "I don't suppose you could tell me if she's been here before?" Charlie found it hard to hide his aggravation.

The doctor looked at Charlie for a moment as if trying to decide whether she wanted to share that information. Then she ran her finger up and down the last few pages of the book she was still holding. "Once before, about a week ago."

"Why didn't you tell me he had been having a visitor?"

"You didn't ask." The doctor handed the book back to the nurse sitting at the desk. "Is there anything else I can help you with to-day?"

"Is she the only one that's been here to see him?"

"As far as I know," she said. "You two are the only people interested in him."

Charlie thanked the doctor and returned to his truck to wait. As it turned out, he didn't have to wait too long.

When Sadie turned the key in her car door, Charlie appeared out of nowhere at her elbow.

"Hello, Sadie."

"Damn!" she yelled before she recognized Charlie. "Don't ever do that to me." She caught her breath and leaned against the car. "What are you doing here?"

"I was about to ask you the same thing."

"I came here to see Happy," she said.

"Sadie, if you are in cahoots with this man and he is faking his inability to talk, I'm going to wring your neck and put both of you away for the rest of your lives."

Sadie stared at Charlie in disbelief. "Please, you can't turn on me, too," Sadie pleaded.

"Then come clean with me, Sadie."

"There's nothing to come clean about."

"Then why are you here?"

"To clear my name."

"Of what?" Charlie began to sound impatient.

"They fired me, Charlie. They fired me and accused me of somehow being connected to the robberies. They blamed me for Gordy, Melvin Crump, everything. You know, I take responsibility for going into the bank alone that day. I thought, under the circumstances, it was the right decision. Obviously, it wasn't. But they seem to have forgotten I'm the one who got robbed. Now, I have to clear my name. And if nobody will help me, well then, I'll do it myself." Sadie wiped a tear from her cheek with the palm of her hand. "I have plenty of extra time now, anyway." It felt good to hear her thoughts and feelings finally take form, expressed in words for the rest of the world to share. Suddenly, she stopped and looked at Charlie. "I know I've already asked you this, but are you sure those doors were locked that day?"

Charlie frowned and rubbed his chin. "Yes," he said. "I'm sure. But I can't vouch for the next morning." Charlie put his hand on her shoulder and turned her body so that she had to look straight at him. "Can you?"

"I didn't do it, Charlie," she whispered.

"Okay, that's settled," he said. "I didn't think you did, anyway." He smiled and Sadie smiled back. "Let's work on one thing at a time," he said. "Did you see Happy while you were in there?"

"Oh, yes. I did. He seems to be really sad, doesn't he?"

"Will he talk to you?"

"No. Not yet. But he will. I know he will. He looks at me and I think he wants to talk." Sadie pursed her lips. "He has the answers, Charlie. If he could just tell us where he got the sweatshirt . . . the dye pack. He's the only one that can help me. I just have to figure out how to get it out of him."

They stood in silence for a while. A gust of wind caught Sadie's hair, pulling it across her face. As she swept the strands behind her ear she looked back at the hospital. Yellow and crimson leaves fell from a nearby sugar maple tree and landed near her feet. "What do we do now?" she asked.

"Let's go home," said Charlie as he opened her car door for her. "We can't do any more here today."

Chapter 16

The aroma of fried chicken welcomed Charlie McCord when he walked through the front door. It was the end of what he thought would be an endless day, and a good meal sounded good. He had spent all afternoon writing paperwork on two juveniles who had been wreaking havoc on the owner of a small grocery store. One would distract the old man while the other would squeeze all the soft tomatoes he could, squirting scarlet juice and tiny yellow seeds all over the wall behind the produce counter. Then, when the old man went to clean up the mess, they would grab as much beer as they could carry and run.

Charlie had collared the culprits and delivered them to juvenile hall, where he was sure they would be out on the street tomorrow with renewed vigor. At which time, he would consider taking the two brats out behind the store and applying his own custom-made form of punishment. Some kids, Charlie thought, needed an attention-getter they could remember before any learning could take place. He and Lilly had never had any children of their own and Charlie didn't really like dealing with kids on the street. But, in all likelihood, the big man would follow the book and keep hauling the young hoodlums in again and again.

Charlie could see Lilly standing in the kitchen dredging chicken parts, first in a mixture of milk and eggs, then in a mountain of flour, before carefully placing them, piece by piece, into the hot grease. Silky blond tresses looked like they were trying to escape the tiny bun held in place by a blue rubber band on top of her head. White flour smudged the end of her pale pug nose where she must have absentmindedly rubbed the back of her hand to stifle a sneeze or quell a tickle.

He thought Lilly was still a beautiful woman. He knew she had been a product of a cultured upbringing, born with a proverbial silver spoon in her mouth. She had never learned to cook until they got married. Her outspoken mother had warned Lilly in front of the entire family one evening at dinner that she was making a big mistake. You should marry into money like you were bred to do, her mother had said. But Lilly and Charlie had fallen fast in love and at the senior prom, in an act of rebellion more than anything else, Lilly had spurred Charlie into marriage by telling him she was pregnant.

Of course, not long after the shotgun ceremony, the truth came out. Even though Charlie loved Lilly, he could never bring himself to trust her again. He had thought about leaving her right then and there, wedding gifts and all, but she had wrapped her arms and legs around him and convinced him to postpone the separation. That was twenty years ago. Now they stayed together as a matter of convenience. They had grown accustomed to and accepted each other's habits, good and bad. Sadly, any passion Charlie once had for Lilly had perished years ago. They had an unspoken, congenial agreement. He paid the bills and she took care of the house.

Lilly greeted Charlie with an obligatory peck on the cheek. "Dinner will be ready in ten," she said. Then she backed away from the stove as grease splattered on her apron.

Charlie picked up the stack of mail from the edge of the kitchen table and shuffled through it. He had two credit card companies promising the lowest rates in town, the electric bill, and an envelope addressed to him from the Oklahoma State Game and Wildlife Commission. The last envelope made him smile.

Charlie didn't splurge very often, but he had this time. He had sprung for a $550 lifetime hunting and fishing license. One of the few things Charlie really enjoyed in life was getting away from the asphalt and concrete and disappearing into the blue-green tranquillity of the lakes and the countryside of eastern Oklahoma. He pulled out his billfold, placed his new license in its special place, and announced, "I'm going to the shooting range tomorrow."

"What?" said Lilly as she poked at the chicken with a long fork. "It's Saturday. I thought we were going to work in the yard. You know we are going to have to trim that tree in the back or it's going to ruin the fence. And the shrub in the front looks terrible. It's going to frost any day . . ."

"Call somebody," he said. "Have somebody come out here and take care of it. I'm not going to."

Charlie hated yard work. It wasn't that it was beneath him, it was just that he had better things to do with his spare time and wanted to do them while he still could. Lilly made a smirk with the right side of her mouth and placed her right hand on her hip. "Fine," she said. "We'll never get any money put back if we keep spending it on trivial stuff like this."

Charlie knew Lilly had never really adjusted to not having a large amount of money in the bank, evident by her clawing at every extra dime. It was a trait she had inherited from her father. He had been very successful at compiling more than a modest nest egg and she thought everyone else should do the same. Her father had invested in oil when he was young, struck it rich, and got out before the bottom fell out of everything. Never one to rest on his laurels, he had bought himself an influential position in the banking community when he became a director on the board of Mercury Savings Bank.

Lilly's father had offered her a job more than once, trying to convince her to get out of the house. Nepotism was not allowed at the bank, but board members had a bad habit of breaking the rules if and when it suited their agenda. It was no secret, though, that Lilly had no aptitude for numbers, and Charlie doubted she could balance a cash drawer if her life depended on it. Fortunately she knew it, too. So she declined her father's offers in order to save face for him. After the robbery at their own branch, they were all glad she hadn't taken the job. Charlie didn't know what all the fuss was about anyway since she would inherit the family fortune when her father died, but she acted like she was forever stuck in a middle-class quagmire. He just didn't care about money the way Lilly did.

"I make enough to put a roof over your head, don't I?" Charlie retorted. "And it doesn't look like either one of us has missed too many meals."

They ate in silence. Lilly cleared the dishes and Charlie buried his nose in the newspaper while the television blared in the background. Before long, he was snoring on the couch.

Lilly lay in a fetal position on the right side of the bed with her back to Charlie as the digital clock radio silently flicked another digit in front of Charlie's eyes. It read 5:55 A.M. and he knew in another five minutes those tiny tin speakers would erupt in sound, stealing the luxury of silence.

Lilly did not stir as he reached over her and slid the alarm button into the "off" position. He skipped shaving, savoring the opportunity to bear a five o'clock shadow all day long. Then he quietly dressed and left the house before she missed his presence on the other side of the bed. He placed his rifle behind the seat of his truck and headed for the Waffle House for some grub.

When he drove into the diner's parking lot, he was glad to see it wasn't too busy for a Saturday morning. He knew Gladys would be surprised to see the old truck drive up. When he let the door of the restaurant slam behind him, he could see her straightening her cap and checking for debris decorating the front of her uniform. She grabbed a paper napkin, wet it with the end of her tongue, and dabbed at a bright yellow spot right below the top button where cleavage sprang from her tight uniform, her breasts like two warm dinner rolls rising over the edge of a pan.

"Hey, Red, what's cooking for Saturday morning?"

Gladys always made Charlie smile. "We got anything your little heart desires, darling," she said, scrunching up her nose and shaking her red head in the air. "And I think you know the menu by heart now." Gladys stretched the word *heart* like a piece of elastic and laughed as she served his usual hot coffee and ice water. "What on earth are you doing out this early on Saturday morning?" she asked.

"Well, you know, Red, I'm going down to the shooting range this fine morning and tune in the sights on my 30.06. Deer season's just around the corner and I got my gen-u-ine lifetime hunting license in the mail yesterday."

"Whoa, look at you go," Gladys teased. "Sugar, you don't really like to shoot those poor little innocent things, do you?" she added in a melodramatic voice. "Those big black eyes and everything. You could be shooting somebody's momma."

Charlie smiled and shook his head as Gladys slapped the top of the counter and burst out laughing.

"Mommas don't have antlers, Red," Charlie responded, "and the antlers are the prize. No point in shooting at a deer unless you get to keep a souvenir, is there? How about some biscuits and gravy?"

Charlie spent about an hour at the Waffle House laughing and joking with Gladys before Lance Smith walked in and joined him at the counter.

"You making this your home away from home?" asked Lance as he threw a handful of coins on the counter.

"Want yours black, too, honey?" asked Gladys as she plopped a mug in front of Lance and started pouring the steamy hot liquid.

Lance nodded.

"Headed down to the Buck-n-Bear. Want to join me? Thought it wouldn't be too crowded this early."

"Sounds like a deal to me." Lance swallowed less than half of his coffee before following Charlie out the door.

"You'd think they could air this place out a little, wouldn't you?" muttered Charlie as he held the door open for Lance. The darkness inside the gun club gave Charlie a skewed feeling, as if he were entering one of the east-side nightclubs he used to work as a beat cop. The musty, dark green carpet, saturated with stale cigarette smoke, released its own brand of perfume to everyone who entered.

"Nah. It'd lose its appeal to the seedier side of life," remarked Lance. "Whatever happened to target shooting in the woods, anyway?"

The lack of windows in the dank building created a false sense of security and reminded Charlie of some secret-society assembly hall. Actually, anyone could enter, pay their money, and shoot their firearms at a whole array of paper targets ranging from small circles to large silhouettes, including B-n-B's trademark targets—bucks and bears.

"It's not the target shooting I need," said Charlie. "It's the gunsmith."

A huge white sign shouted in red letters: "NO LOADED FIRE-ARMS ALLOWED IN THE LOBBY." Inside, it was Rodney Turner's job to inspect all weapons as they entered the building, making sure everyone observed the rules until the shooters passed through one of two sets of doors into either the indoor or outdoor range. Charlie pulled his Remington 30.06 rifle from its brown suede, zippered tote, careful of the barrel's heading, and handed it to Rodney.

"Hey, Charlie. Lance. How you boys doing? Haven't seen either one of you in a while."

Lance nodded a silent greeting.

"Oh, don't mind him," said Charlie. "He's just along for the ride." He grinned and then added, "Indians don't need to target-practice. It's in their blood."

Lance rolled his eyes. It hadn't taken him long to figure out that Charlie only picked on people he liked.

Rodney handed the rifle back to Charlie without even checking the magazine. He wasn't worried about Charlie's safety habits. He knew the sergeant would be wearing his service revolver in a high-rise holster under his jacket and he knew it would be loaded. It always was and always would be. Charlie was always prepared and he assumed the same about Lance. Rodney respected that.

Rodney had known Charlie since the gun club had opened some seventeen years earlier when Charlie was a junior officer. Rodney had watched in amazement as the big man honed his skills with his Model 65 Smith and Wesson 357. From day one, Charlie never even had to cock his revolver. He had bobbed the hammer so it never got in his way, never slowed him down.

As a recruit, Charlie had started out as a sharpshooter. He had smoothed and tuned the action of his gun and made it strictly a double-action weapon. After reaching the coveted title of a distinguished master on the police pistol team, Charlie basked in the glory of holding some of the highest scores in the department's history.

Now, years later, the new recruits referred to Charlie as a dinosaur, a man unwilling to give up his revolver for one of the new high-powered, semiautomatic weapons. Charlie accepted the ribbing with a good nature, because he knew as well as they did that, if he wanted, he could leave them in the dirt when it came to hitting a target.

Charlie used to visit the gun club at least once a month. He'd pick up a bucket of wadcutter bullets and tear through the paper targets. Even in later years following his stint as a competition shooter, Charlie had always been a ten-ring man, a perfectionist, accepting no less.

The center of each silhouette target contained an oblong circle, two inches by three inches—the ten-ring. The ten-ring contained an even smaller one-inch by two-inch circle—the X-ring. When Charlie qualified with his service revolver each year, he continued to maintain his hits inside the ten-ring and usually obliterated the X-ring. Extra practice sessions had ceased a long time ago for the veteran cop, but he still enjoyed his visits to the Buck-n-Bear with his personal long guns.

Charlie offered Rodney a dollar bill for two rifle sight-targets. Rodney handed him a handful of targets and pushed Charlie's dollar back across the counter. Then, out of habit, Rodney plopped down two pairs of ear protectors. They reminded Charlie of the stereo headphones he'd had back in college.

"Thanks, I've got my own," said Charlie as he slid one set of headphones back toward Rodney.

Lance reluctantly pulled the other pair off the counter and held them behind his back.

"Is Bennie in this morning?" asked Charlie. "I've got a new scope I'd like to have bore-sighted. That is, if he's got time."

"Yeah, sure, go on in. He'll be glad to see you."

Rodney motioned with his head toward a fishbowl work area in the corner of the lobby where a bearded man, dressed in a red-and-blue flannel shirt and jeans, worked at a bench, filing a piece of metal.

Bennie Holt was a gunsmith. The best there was, in Charlie's opinion, and he looked forward to talking guns for the next ten minutes or so while Bennie fondled the new scope, placed it on his contraption, and expertly adjusted the sight to the bore of the rifle. As Bennie worked, he never stopped talking, comparing firearms and commending Charlie's choice of weapon.

"That ought to do it, Charlie," said Bennie. "Take it out back and see how it works."

"That's where I'm headed, Bennie," Charlie replied. "Thanks a lot." Charlie paid Bennie for his services and carried the Remington through the doorway that led to the outdoor range. Lance followed him out into the crisp morning air. The frost had already disappeared from the Bermuda grass along the path, but the men could see their breath as the chilled air floated skyward like smoke. The sugar maple trees lining the far edge of the range sang a last hurrah, dressed in leaves of amber and red. Soon they would turn bronze, then brown, before retiring for the winter.

"You know," said Charlie, "I don't know how I'd ever have made it all these years if I'd been tied to some desk job."

Lance pursed his lips and nodded in agreement. It took a special kind of person to be a lawman. One who liked being on the move twenty-four hours a day.

Charlie attached his targets at both 100 yards and 300 yards.

Then he fished in his coat pocket for a handful of cartridges and popped five into the internal magazine of the bolt-action rifle and slammed one into the chamber. In less than fifteen seconds he had wiped out the two-inch center X-rings of both targets in grand style.

"Sure don't take you long, does it?" said Lance.

Charlie reloaded the rifle and handed it to Lance. Then he stood back while Lance tried his hand at a different target. His results rivaled Charlie's.

"See there," said Charlie. "That proves it. Anybody can hit a deer with the right weapon."

"Yeah, but I've got an advantage," teased Lance. "It's in my blood, remember?" Lance handed the rifle back to his friend and they both laughed.

"Yeah, right," said Charlie.

Pleased by the performance of the new scope, Charlie placed the rifle back into the suede carrier and the two men returned to the indoor lobby of the gun club.

The traffic inside the B-n-B had begun to pick up. Sounds of someone target-shooting came from the indoor range while Rodney explained the safety rules to a young couple at the counter. Charlie stood outside Bennie's work area and let his eyes adjust from the bright sunlight.

"Hey, Charlie," said Bennie. "How'd it work?"

"Like a champ, Bennie."

"That's what I like to hear. How about a cup of joe? I've been at it since six this morning and I could use a good excuse for a break."

"You got it, my man. The first cup's on me."

The two officers and the old-timer walked across the lobby and into the lounge area. The coffee machine took up one end of the counter, alongside a mountain of white Styrofoam cups, a box of sugar cubes, and a jar of powdered coffee creamer. A rubber mat lay on the floor in front of the machine, soaking up as many spills as possible. The swinging door on top of the trash container hung open, exposing yesterday's trash.

They chose a small table in the viewing area, designed to allow customers a comfortable vantage point to observe the shooters in the indoor range. The three men made small talk while absentmindedly gazing through the thick bullet-resistant glass at a lone shooter. The man would shoot first with one hand and then the other. Then he would flick the switch on the clothesline-type contraption that carried the targets to the desired distance and back again.

As the man inspected his targets time and time again, Charlie couldn't help but notice something out of the ordinary. As a veteran cop, Charlie had developed a keen ability to pick up on things out of place, and this man piqued Charlie's interest. The shooter stood, aimed, and shot with complete confidence. A damn good shooter, Charlie thought, and wondered if he were a competition man.

"Who is that character out there?" asked Charlie.

Lance turned in his chair to get a better look and took another sip of coffee.

"Can't say as I know him," said Bennie. "I saw his weapon, though. It was a Colt .45. The other's a wheel gun. A 357, I think." A wheel gun meant it was a revolver, a term used by those who appreciated the weapon's simple mechanics. "One of yours?" asked Bennie, referring to perhaps a past collar for one of the lawmen.

"Not mine," said Lance as he lost interest and turned back to the table.

"No, I don't think so," said Charlie. He continued to observe the shooter.

As the man shot, he stood with one sneaker slightly behind the other and leaned somewhat forward on the balls of his feet, with the appearance of someone who was about to run. The man practiced with both hands.

"Ambidextrous," commented Charlie.

"Oh, yeah?" Lance turned again and watched the shooter for a moment.

The man was clean-shaven and wore a baseball cap over short, dark hair. Not too tall, maybe five-foot-ten or five-foot-eleven, muscular build, about 175 pounds. Charlie couldn't tell for sure, because of a thick, heavy jacket. That was common, though, as the range ventilation unit piped in cold, outside air to help disperse the gun smoke. The shooter seemed to be pretty average-looking to Charlie, nothing outstanding—except for his shooting.

"Say," asked Bennie, uninterested in the shooter. "How's Lilly doing?"

"Oh, fine. About the same," said Charlie. A simple answer to a complex question.

After a while, the men rose and shook hands.

"Don't be such a stranger around here," said Bennie.

The two officers offered empty promises to be back soon as they left the gun club, then headed in separate directions.

As the breeze flew through the open window of the truck, the big man whistled along with a Garth Brooks song coming from the small, tinny speakers of the truck radio.

Images of the shooter in the range came back to him. Something about him I missed, he thought. He dismissed the man from his thoughts as he drove up to the house. He had hoped Lilly would already be on her way to her parents for her weekly visit. He was in luck. She was gone.

Back at the range, the shooter picked up the brass that lay strewn on the floor and packed up his guns. Both in fine working order and ready for action.

Chapter 17

Johnny parked his car behind a trash Dumpster on the corner of Ross and Hudson. Across the busy intersection, a branch of Mid-State Bank bustled with late-afternoon traffic. Through his small, powerful binoculars Johnny could clearly see both north and west sides of the bank. It was a brown rock building with several huge windows.

"Bankers sure do like their glass," he muttered to himself.

Each time the front door of the bank opened, it winked at the thief with a flash of reflection from the western sun. The ground floor of the small building seemed to house the entire branch operations. The second floor, smaller than the first, created the visual image of an off-centered, two-tier cake. Two large windows on the second story revealed what appeared to be a break room for the employees. A massive air conditioning unit sat on the roof of the lopsided structure, next to the break room.

Johnny turned and drove south on Hudson, past West County Memorial Hospital, pulled into a convenience-store parking lot, and got out. He purchased two bottles of water and a newspaper, then sat in his car thinking for a few minutes before driving back north to the bank.

Inside the first set of double glass doors, Johnny observed to his right a large metal door. From the layout of the building, he guessed it led to the stairs.

A small, pale, dishwater blond sat at the first desk just inside the second set of glass doors. She was the younger of the two employees available in the lobby. Johnny carried the newspaper under his arm and a bottle of water in his hand as he approached her station.

"May I help you, sir?" she asked.

"Yes, I was just noticing here in the paper that your competition is offering a really low rate on car loans. What do you offer?"

While the young girl searched through her desk for information, Johnny sat and surveyed the bank. There was one camera mounted above the door through which he had just entered, pointing toward the tellers. He could see no motion detectors, no video cameras, and no armed guard. The busy tellers, from time to time, carried money back and forth through a door behind the teller area. Obviously, the location of the vault, he thought.

"Here we are. Depending on what kind of car . . ." The young girl launched into a well-rehearsed speech, more irritating than a phone solicitor selling insurance. Johnny listened politely until she finished.

"Great. Now all I have to do is go pick out a car. Can you give me a copy of that?"

"Sure."

Sensing a chance to increase her loan numbers for the month, the young woman jumped up and hurried to the teller area to make a copy for her new prospective customer. Johnny followed her across the lobby, waiting for his copy and absorbing as many details as possible.

A college-aged teller stood holding the door open to the vault room with his foot, a bundle of money in each hand, talking nonchalantly to a woman inside he addressed as Bonnie. Johnny could see it was the same industrious woman he had watched arriving early and leaving late from the branch every day for the last three weeks. Perched on a stool, Bonnie stacked money in front of her while the currency counter whirred in short bursts. The keypad to the alarm system hung on the outside wall, left of the vault door.

Johnny thanked the young girl for the copy and started to walk away. Then he stopped and turned, dangling the empty plastic water bottle in his hand. "By the way, do you have a restroom I can use?" Johnny smiled.

"Of course. It's upstairs. I'll unlock the stairway for you." The young girl retrieved a set of keys from one of the tellers and returned to open the locked door for him.

Johnny thanked her, put the empty water bottle in the pocket of his jacket, and let the door close behind him before ascending the short flight of stairs. He had been right. The deserted second story housed a small kitchen for the employees.

Dirty dishes were piled high in the sink right below a sign that

read: "YOUR MOTHER DOESN'T LIVE HERE, CLEAN UP AF-
TER YOURSELF." A table sat in front of the window facing the
street. A short hallway contained three doors—two restrooms and
one unknown.

Johnny pulled the shirttail out of his jeans and used it to try the
knob on the unmarked door. It was unlocked. He pushed the door
open with his shoulder, unleashing a rush of noise from an old, belch-
ing heat pump. Johnny quickly slipped inside, careful not to let the
door slam, and let his eyes adjust to the darkness. An outside vent
provided just enough light to allow Johnny to move farther into the
room. The outdated unit consumed a large area, causing Johnny to
be careful not to come away marked with a hefty layer of dust. A
built-in ladder hugged the opposite wall, leading to an opening in the
ceiling. Johnny pulled a pair of leather gloves out of his pocket, put
them on, and scaled the short ladder, discovering an access door to
the roof. He could see no alarm contacts and a disconnected padlock
inside the portal dangled to one side. Pushing up on the hatch, Johnny
could see the flat, tar-and-gravel roof with a brick ledge. This was
going to be easy.

Johnny quickly slipped from the room and returned to the stair-
well. A second check revealed no motion detectors. As he left through
the door at the bottom of the stairs, he could see the dishwater blond
staring at her computer screen.

At home, Johnny pulled his car into the garage, next to the van. Inside the house, he removed two new gym bags from the closet and
checked their contents. One held gym shorts and T-shirt, a black
hooded sweatsuit, running shoes, a trash sack, and his special vest.
The other bag held two zippered gun bags, gloves, ski mask, mirrored sunglasses, tape, and a rope with a rubber-coated grappling
hook attached to one end.

Johnny pulled out the double-lined canvas vest, unzipped it, and
ran his hand in the secret compartments that would hold the money.
The vest, a souvenir brought back from Vietnam by one of his dad's
buddies, would not be serving as protection tonight. Instead, where
it was originally designed to hold bulletproof armor, the modified
vest would now house Johnny's loot. The former owner of this army
invention, a helicopter gunner, used to sit on it to protect his bottom

from enemy fire. It had served that veteran well, and now it would become a handy tool for Johnny.

He replaced the vest and placed both bags next to the back door, sat on the couch, and flicked on the television. Before long, he had dozed to the drone of the six o'clock newscaster.

At straight up 10 P.M., Johnny awoke as if an alarm clock had gone off in his head. He splashed his face before filling a plastic container with cold water and pouring it into the top of the coffee maker. The appliance gurgled and hissed before sending a stream of fresh coffee into the pot below. The aroma gave Johnny renewed energy. Opening the refrigerator, he foraged for something to eat. A white Styrofoam container held the remainder of a block of lasagna, last night's carryout. He placed it in the microwave and watched the box ride around on the glass carousel. Just before the greasy tomato sauce began to disintegrate the vessel, he popped the door and pulled out dinner. He ate directly from the container before washing the last bite down with a slug of coffee. He poured the remaining coffee into a thermos.

He placed all of the things he had gathered into the back of his van and drove toward the expressway. He exited onto Jenkins Avenue and made his way toward Dawes Street. Twenty minutes shy of midnight, he turned into the shopping area that housed the Day-In Day-Out Fitness Center. The neon light above the front door buzzed "Open 24 Hrs a Day."

When he entered the gym, a muscular woman with bleached hair and unnaturally large biceps looked up from a well-worn paperback book she was reading.

"Hey, man, how's it going tonight?" she asked as Johnny signed the check-in sheet.

"When are you going to get a real job, Margot?"

Ignoring his comment, she sat tall in her seat, hit a key on a nearby computer keyboard, and waited for the screen to come to life.

"If you don't quit reading that trash your mind's going to turn to mush," he muttered. "Not to mention the unsavory effects the steroids are having on your body."

"Hey, it's good to see you, too." Margot leaned back in the chair, raised her chin, and flexed the muscles in her right arm by squeezing a tennis ball in her hand. "Working out kind of late, aren't you?" she asked.

Johnny didn't answer as he looked through the glass wall behind her into the empty weight room.

The blond looked at the clock above the door. "I'm out of here in ten minutes . . . in case you're interested."

"I'm not."

Having already lost interest in the late customer, Margot returned her attention to her book.

Johnny carried his gym bag to the men's locker room where he changed into shorts and T-shirt, grabbed a towel from a stack by the door, and headed to the treadmill. After a slow ten-minute jog, Johnny returned to the locker room, showered, and dressed in his special vest and black sweats. He placed his jeans and shirt inside the gym bag, along with the shorts and tee, and left the fitness center through the side door. Once inside the van, he placed the gym bag in its place under the seat.

Johnny drove to the hospital parking lot and parked in the southeast corner, backing against tall, dense shrubbery. He climbed into the back of the van, removed the guns, and placed the zippered bags in the empty tool chest. Mechanically, he punched the release button on the Colt .45 with his right thumb and dropped the magazine into his left hand, checking for a full load. A flick of the wrist on the wheel of the Smith and Wesson 357 produced the same results. Both guns went inside the waistband of his tight underwear—the Colt in the front, the 357 in the small of his back. A police-band radio, smaller than Johnny's hand, rested in an inside T-shirt pocket. The earpiece, positioned snugly in his ear, remained hidden from view under his hood. A slender, collapsible grappling hook and rope fit comfortably in the hand-warmer pocket of his sweatshirt next to a small roll of duct tape.

He checked the time and sipped coffee, careful not to drink too much. He didn't want to be distracted later by a full bladder. It was 2:45 A.M., time to go.

Quietly, he walked the short distance to the shrubbery at the outer edge of the bank parking lot and waited in the moonless night for the police cruiser to make its nightly drive-through. Johnny knew the burglary shift ended at 4 A.M., and the car assigned to this area made its rounds routinely at 3:30 A.M.

The black-and-white Ford Crown Vic turned into the driveway

right on time, the young officer sitting low in the seat, steering the wheel with his right hand and aiming the spotlight in and around the bank with his left. The velocity of the vehicle never fluctuated until it moved back onto Hudson and headed downtown.

Ski mask in place, Johnny positioned himself at the inner corner of the odd-shaped building with the movement of a sleek cat stalking prey. He removed the grappling hook and soft rope from his pocket. With the first toss, the small rubber-coated hook landed silently in perfect position. Johnny pulled on the rope, testing its hold. In less than fifteen seconds he scaled the side of the building, using the nubby, round rocks of the structure as footholds.

Once on the roof, Johnny lay on his stomach and checked the ground for movement. Detecting none, he wound the thin rope around the collapsed hook and replaced it in his pocket. From his location next to the air conditioning unit he waited once more until he decided it was safe to move. Within seconds, he had scaled to the second level, opened the roof hatch, and lowered himself inside. A quick check of the time revealed four o'clock. Now all he had to do was go to the vault room and wait.

A few minutes after 6 A.M., Bonnie arrived just like Johnny had watched her do every morning for weeks. He waited in the darkness as she punched in the code on the alarm pad next to the vault.

"Okay, sweetheart. Keep it cool and nobody will get hurt." The intruder's voice was calm, yet forceful enough to convince Bonnie he meant business.

Startled, she screamed and fell backward, turning her ankle, keys and papers flying toward the ceiling. Johnny quickly grabbed her from behind, muffling her voice with his leather glove and holding the Colt to her right temple.

"Shut up or you're going to die. Understand?"

Bonnie made no sound but agreed with a nod of her head and he loosened his grip. Then she began to plead, "Please don't kill me. Oh, God, I'm going to die. Oh, please, I don't want to die."

"I said shut up. Do you understand?" He could feel her body trembling as he retightened his hold around her neck.

"Yes . . . okay," she said weakly. "Please, don't shoot me."

"Open the vault," he said and let her go.

With shaky hands, Bonnie inserted the key and rotated the combination. When she grasped the handle, the door would not budge.

"Try again and pay attention this time," Johnny calmly commanded.

Bonnie took a deep breath and spun the dial back and forth once more. This time the door cooperated.

"Open them." Johnny motioned toward the cash drawers with his Colt.

Bonnie opened two drawers that were marked on the outside in capital letters: "VAULT CASH."

"That's good. Get on the floor."

"Please, please, don't kill me," Bonnie begged. "If I get on the floor, you'll kill me like an animal."

Johnny ordered her again: "I said, get on the floor."

Bonnie obeyed and Johnny pulled out the duct tape, which he used to blindfold, bind, and gag her. He pulled off his sweatshirt, removed his special vest, and began to fill it with large bills—first hundreds, fifties, then twenties. When it would hold no more money, he put it back on, zipped it, and pulled the hooded sweatshirt back over his head. He wanted to leave the building by 6:45 A.M., right when the regular mob of sleepy cops would be heading to the station for shift change like a herd of cattle on their way to the barn.

He was right on schedule. It was 6:33 A.M., and if the rest of the bank's employees stuck to their usual routine, they wouldn't be here for over an hour.

"Be quiet and lay right there. I'm going to go out here and wait for my ride. If you try to get up, I'll come back in here and kill you. Got it?"

Johnny didn't really expect an answer and walked away from his victim toward the back of the bank. She hadn't made a sound or moved for quite a while. With my luck, she'll probably strangle on her own vomit, he thought.

With the alarms off in the building, Johnny stood by the back entrance and listened. He pocketed his gloves, ski mask, and sunglasses, left his hood in place, and slipped out the door. Jogging slowly toward the hospital in plain sight, he listened in his earpiece to a police officer trying to make a date with the dispatcher on the radio.

When he reached the van, he climbed inside and quickly disrobed. He placed the money vest and guns inside the empty tool chest;

the sweats, gloves, ski mask, sunglasses, and running shoes went in the trash bag. He couldn't chance keeping the shoes, just in case he had left footprints on the roof. He donned his jeans and shirt from under the seat and drove to the other side of the hospital, pitching the trash sack in the huge trash container. He parked, entered the front door of the hospital, and walked straight to the busy cafeteria.

At this time of the morning, the cafeteria buzzed with an eclectic group of people—doctors and nurses, hospital staff, family members keeping vigil for their sick loved ones. Johnny picked up a newspaper, filled his tray, sat down, and ate a hearty breakfast.

Charlie turned the nose of his black-and-white cruiser into the Waffle House parking lot. When he walked through the door, Gladys hit the button on the front of the coffee brewer. The old coffee machine let out a shriek and dwindled into a purr as fresh coffee streamed into an empty pot.

Charlie took off his cap, sat at the counter, and never said a word as Gladys worked the busy diner. She winked at him as she whizzed by balancing three plates of eggs, grits, and waffles on her left arm and a half-empty coffee pot in the other. After serving the customers at the booth, she returned to the coffee machine and switched the coffee pots with lightning speed, spilling not a drop as the coffee continued to drip. With the precision of an expert, she poured a cup of fresh brew for Charlie and placed it in front of him along with a glass of ice water. He spooned ice from the water into his coffee, because, as always, it was too hot to drink.

"How about a sticky cinnamon, Big Mac?" asked Gladys. "They're fresh out of the oven and I know you can make room for just one." Gladys didn't wait for an answer as she sashayed through the swinging door into the kitchen with an armload of dirty dishes.

About that time, Charlie's radio began to crackle and spurt. Charlie had an uncanny ability to decipher the garbled messages streaming from the small speaker, even while in the midst of conversation and surrounded by dishes clanging and babies wailing. He got up off his stool and threw a dollar on the counter for the free coffee. Yelling at Gladys through the kitchen window, he headed for the door. "Forget it, Gladys," he said. "Some fool's gone and robbed another bank."

Chapter 18

Sadie sat in a booth next to the soda fountain in the Eucha Hilltop Drug Store and cruised the help-wanted ads in two newspapers—the *Sycamore Springs Gazette* and the *Eucha News Press*. The Sycamore Springs paper usually listed a few general job openings; the *News Press* rarely had any.

She pushed her hair behind her ear with a pencil and then pressed the eraser against her temple while she read, periodically stopping to sip Dr Pepper through a straw. Her hair had grown fast in the last few months, already dividing over the tops of her shoulders.

A young Indian girl who had waited on Sadie earlier was busy decorating the soda fountain with colorful fall leaves, gourds, and miniature pumpkins. Thanksgiving was only a week away, and its arrival would signal the end of another jobless month for Sadie.

Sadie finished circling a lone advertisement and parked her pencil behind her ear. The Colonial Grocery Store on the other side of Sycamore Springs was looking for a cashier. Sadie put the paper down for a moment and thought about her situation.

She had already used up half of her savings, which meant she was going to have to turn up the heat on the job search. To no avail, she had called every bank in Sycamore Springs, following up with a résumé to each one. She had not received a single call. She knew Mercury Bank—Blackton, to be more specific—had already put the word out that she had been fired, the kiss of death for another banking job.

If she dwelled on Blackton too long, her anger would take over and she would never get anything accomplished. She reached into her purse and pulled out an envelope she had picked up earlier from her mailbox. She had been saving it, so she could savor the ceremony of opening and reading it again.

It was one of those romantic cards where the words were so gooey they almost slipped off the page, the kind of card the newly-in-love shared with each other. Jaycee had taken an ink pen and underlined some of the words. She skipped from phrase to phrase, imagining the words coming from her lover's lips: *You are the air I breathe, a kiss of sunshine on a cold day. Your touch is music in the still of the night. Your words, nourishment for my soul. Your presence brings joy to my heart, meaning to my life. All I want to do is share my life with you. You are my true love, today and forever.*

He had signed it *With Love, Jaycee.* Sadie returned the card to its envelope and held it to her chest. Overwhelmed with affection for this man, she took it back out and read it again. Their passion, it seemed, grew more intense with each card, letter, and phone call. She anticipated his visits like a child waiting for Christmas morning.

Jaycee came to Oklahoma the last week of every month, calling on customers for Powerhouse Investments. He never returned home without seeing his new love, Sadie. They had become a familiar two-some, seen at movie theaters and nice restaurants all over Sycamore Springs.

The weeks they spent apart seemed to intensify the days they spent together. When Jaycee returned to Texas each month, Sadie's mailbox would fill to capacity with cards and letters, each full of warm expressions of infatuation. Sadie found herself surrendering to this man, leaving silly messages on his voice mail almost every day, something totally out of character. It was the real thing. This time she was truly falling in love.

Jaycee threw his bag in the trunk of a rental car at the Tulsa airport and headed straight toward Sycamore Springs. There, he reported to his good friend Adam Cruthers at Mercury Savings. The bank's account with Powerhouse Investments outperformed every other investment Mercury had.

"Jaycee, I don't know how you do it." Adam shook his head and rubbed his chin while he reviewed the portfolio numbers.

Jaycee smiled, clasped his hands behind his head, and leaned back in his chair. Through the high-rise window he could see sailboats floating in the distance on Blue Lake.

"Talent, my friend, pure talent," he said.

"I hope so," said Adam. "I hope this isn't just a fluke. I talked the board into approving the transfer of another one-point-two million to your firm this week. If these funds don't perform like I told them they would, my ass will be on the line."

"Good job, my man." Jaycee rose from his chair and leaned over the cluttered desk to shake Adam's hand. "Good job. And, don't worry," he added. "You know as well as I do I wouldn't be in this business if I wasn't good. No, make that the best." Jaycee picked up his briefcase and turned before he reached the door of Adam's office. "Remember," he said, "if you don't make money, I don't make money . . ." Then, in a raspy voice, he added, "And I like money."

Eli sat perfectly still under a tall oak tree while his small herd of horses grazed nearby. Nothing in the world delighted Eli more than being outdoors. His horses were used to him sitting in the pasture among them while they ate grass or rolled in the dirt to scratch their backs. Being there gave him a rich feeling of life.

He had often commented that he had been born a century too late, that he really belonged on the bare back of a horse, riding for days on end with no fences to stand in his way. He knew before he got out of the army and came back to Eucha that he could never work at anything else. Having inherited the uncanny ability to understand and communicate with horses, he had been raising and selling paint horses all of his life. Just like his daddy before him, he had eked out a meager living for himself and his wife. Lucky for him, Mary had the gift to make money and food stretch beyond belief. It had been an enjoyable existence.

Sonny joined Eli, sat next to him, and patiently waited for a pat on the head. Eli stroked the wolf-dog's shoulders and talked to him. He missed Little Wolf, who was still on chicken-house duty for Mary's sister.

Together, they watched from the upper pasture as an old Chevy slowed to a stop before crossing the cattle guard at the entrance to Sadie's place. Sonny sensed the intrusion a quarter mile away before Eli did. He stood tall on all four feet, his ears at attention, then raised his nose in the air and sniffed.

Michael lowered the car window. "Don't drive in, you idiot," he barked at the driver. "Someone will see us." Michael reached below the seat and found the baseball bat he had brought along and slid out through the passenger door. He stuck his head back into the car and said, "Just pick me up by the lake road after dark."

"Who you calling an idiot? Looks to me like you're going to be back in the slammer before me." The driver backed off the cattle guard and checked the rearview mirror. Then he jammed his foot on the accelerator, throwing gravel with the back tire as he climbed onto the pavement and blazed off down the road.

Michael marched the short distance to the house, the bat riding high on his right shoulder. If he had estimated right, Sadie wouldn't be home for several hours. He should have plenty of time to let himself into her house undetected and wait for her return. As far as he was concerned, she was still his wife and he planned to get what was his. All he had to do was get past that dog of hers, and he figured the bat would take care of him. If that didn't work, he always had his Saturday Night Special in his boot. So far he was in luck. No dog in sight.

With the bat propped against the side of the house, he pulled a plastic credit card from his back pocket and slid it down the door-jamb in an effort to open the locked door. "Damn it," he said. He dug in his other back pocket, producing two jailhouse-forged tools. The first one would serve as a tension wrench, allowing the second tool, which resembled a flat crochet hook, to spring the lock. He glanced at the highway for a moment and then proceeded to work the dead bolt with experienced precision.

"Since when did women—" A click inside the mechanism inter-rupted him in mid-thought. "All right," he said and backed up to replace the utensils in his pocket and pick up his bat.

When Sonny attacked, Michael heard no bark, no growl, only the crunching sound of teeth against the back and side of his neck. He fell backward, losing his grip on the bat. He tried to scream, but the wolf-dog's powerful grip on his throat made it impossible. They wrestled on the ground and Michael tried in vain to pry himself loose. He could feel the bat with his leg, so he grabbed it and hit Sonny as hard as he could. Sonny let go of Michael's neck just long enough to get a better hold near the intruder's jugular vein. Michael lost his grip on the bat as Sonny began to drag him across the yard.

Cherokee words spewed from Eli as he rounded the corner of the house. *"Gitli! Tlesdi! Tiyohi!"* Reluctantly, Sonny obeyed and let go of his prey, remaining close enough to regain his position if needed. Eli stood poised to shoot the 12-gauge shotgun he had pointed at Michael's head and continued to speak rapidly in Cherokee asking him what he was doing: *"Gado hadvneha?"* Then he told him to get up: *"Talehvga!"* Finally, his words began to give way to broken English: ". . . or kill you where you are. Understand?"

Michael had no idea what Eli was saying, but he got the message. He tried to get up but became dizzy and fell back. He opened his eyes to a growling beast of bloodied fur, bared teeth, and foul animal breath. On the second try, he made it to a vertical position and started walking as fast as he could toward the highway dragging his bat. He thought about the gun in his boot, but dismissed the thought of trying to shoot a crazy, shotgun-toting Indian with a handgun. He wasn't that stupid. Michael held his hand firmly on the wound, where he could feel the blood trickling down his neck. He headed across the highway toward the lake road where he would wait for the rendezvous with his comrade.

As Michael worked his way through the woods, the thick underbrush slowed his pace considerably. By the time he reached the meeting place he was exhausted. He knew he had lost a lot of blood so he sat on the ground, leaned against a tree, and waited, trying to be as still as he could. When the vehicle stopped a few feet away, Michael never knew it. The driver got out and walked over to Michael. He kicked Michael's leg, checking for reflexes. Michael did not react. The driver drew a small-caliber handgun from his back pocket, pulled Michael's head forward by his hair, and emptied one bullet into the base of his skull.

Back at Sadie's house, Eli praised Sonny for a job well done and checked the dog's front leg where he had taken the blow from the baseball bat.

"Hatlv tsesdane? Where are you hurting?" asked Eli. "Not broke." The old Indian spoke softly as he felt each leg and patted the dog on his head. Then he took Sonny to the barn, hooked up the water hose used to fill the horse trough, and doused the dog with water. The cold shower removed most of the blood but not all of it.

Eli looked at Sonny and said, "I'm sorry, boy, but I'm afraid we're going to have to tell Sadie about this escapade." He picked up his shotgun and walked back toward his house to check on Mary.

Sadie came out of the Colonial Grocery Store and got into her car. She had just finished an interview with the manager, Mark Baldwin, in which he presented a job offer to her right on the spot. The store's management had decided to stay open twenty-four hours a day through the holidays, instead of their usual sixteen. He offered Sadie the position of head night cashier, working from eleven in the evening until seven each morning, with weekends off. She would be the only cashier on duty, with a stock boy who could detain customers for her when she needed to take a break or go to the bathroom. Sadie told him she would think about it.

Before she left the store, she picked up a package of frozen strawberries and a container of chocolate-almond ice cream. She expected Jaycee this evening and she knew how he loved this combination of berries and ice cream.

The farm seemed quiet when Sadie got home. The back door was unlocked and she suddenly felt vulnerable. Surely, she wasn't losing her faculties to the point of forgetting to lock the door. Nothing appeared to be out of place. She noticed the blinking red light on her answering machine, hit the message button and started putting things away while she listened.

Sadie could hear the strain in her aunt's voice as she explained how her sister, Essie, had taken a bad fall and broken her hip. She and Eli were on their way to Tahlequah to take care of her. The message ended with, "Eli said to tell you something about Sonny getting into a fight today. Said he checked him over and he's okay." Sadie could hear her uncle speaking Cherokee in the background. "Oh, he's going to have to tell you about all this later himself. We've got to go. See you soon, honey. We love you."

Sadie left the machine to rewind and went back outside. Sonny had not immediately greeted her when she got home and she wondered where he might be. She whistled first and then called his name. Joe snorted and walked around the barn.

"Hey, Joe. Where's Sonny?" she asked as if expecting the horse to answer.

A car turned into the farm and Sadie knew the rental car had to be Jaycee. Her heart pounded and a twinge of excitement raced through her body. He got out of the car and she ran to him. He embraced her and they kissed like teenagers. In the distance, Sadie could hear Sonny's playful bark. Subconsciously, she dismissed his safety

from her mind and enjoyed the moment. Jaycee wrapped his arm
around Sadie's waist as they walked into the house.

"You won't believe this," he said. "I got another account out of
Adam—over a mil."

"Really?" Sadie was pleased for Jaycee, but the mention of anything to do with Mercury Savings Bank dampened her spirits.

Jaycee immediately sensed Sadie's less-than-cheerful mood.
"Well, as a stockholder, you'll be pleased to know the value of their
stock is skyrocketing."

When Mercury had gone from a mutual to a stock company, the
employees had been required to buy a minimum number of shares
whether they wanted to or not. Sadie could still remember the speech
when Blackton told the employees that being stockholders of the
bank showed they were committed to their jobs. Sadie had taken the
obligatory number of shares, allowing Thelma to deduct the cost from
one month's paycheck.

"Stock?" she asked. "Well, if you know anybody who wants mine,
donate it to them." She walked over to a stack of papers on the edge
of the table, pulled out an envelope with the word "stock" printed on
it, and handed it to Jaycee.

"You want me to sell it for you, Sadie?"

Sadie gave Jaycee a determined look and shook her head. "No,"
she said. "No, I don't. I want you to give it away . . . give it to some
charity. I will not take any money from that . . ." Sadie searched for a
word that could describe how she felt about Mercury Savings, then
dropped it.

Jaycee took the envelope and slid it into the inside pocket of his
jacket. He took Sadie in his arms and kissed her on the forehead.
"It'll be okay, darling." When he felt her shoulders relax he patted
her on the back and added, "Come on, I'm famished and I've got
movie tickets for the seven o'clock show."

They locked the door and walked toward Jaycee's rental car just
as Sonny limped around the barn. The fur around his face and neck
had turned a ruddy brown.

"Damn it, Sonny," grumbled Sadie. "What have you been into?"

Jaycee groaned and rubbed his forehead.

Sadie dropped her purse and bent down to check Sonny's ailing
front leg. "Well, it feels all right," she said. "How in the world did
you get so dirty?" Sadie examined his face for cuts or gashes and

found none, then looked into his eyes to see if he was hurting. Convinced he was okay, Sadie looked at Sonny and said, "Stay home tonight, would you, please?" When she went inside to wash her hands, she thought about her uncle's message and realized the discoloration of his fur could be dried blood.

Jaycee picked up her purse and got into the car to wait. He wasn't going to take any chances. Sonny and Jaycee had never taken a fancy to each other and Jaycee knew the dog tolerated him only because Sadie demanded it.

When Sadie came out of the house, Jaycee got out and opened the car door for her. "Don't you think that might be blood on your dog, Sadie?" he asked.

"Oh, I don't think so," she said, not wanting to alarm Jaycee or disrupt their plans. "It's probably just red dirt . . . or mud."

He started the car then reached over and patted her hand. "Oh, I guess so," he said.

As they drove out onto the highway, Sadie gazed back at the house and wondered what had gotten in a lick good enough to make Sonny limp. Then she wondered if it had lived or died.

Chapter 19

"Merry Christmas, Sadie."

The voice on the other end of the line sounded familiar.

"Sergeant McCord, is that you?"

"Now, look. I know I haven't seen you in a while, but what happened to calling me Charlie?"

Sadie laughed. "Okay, I'm sorry," she said. "How have you been?"

"I have a Christmas gift for you."

"What? Christmas is almost a month away . . . and why . . ."

"I just got off the phone with one of those federal boys, Agent Robinson, and I thought you might like to hear what he had to say. And since I doubt seriously he's going to call you up himself, I thought I'd do the honors."

The mention of the FBI agent's name gave Sadie a chill. "Why would he want to call me?"

"Well, I'm sure you've heard about the robbery a while back over at Mid-State Bank. You know, the branch up on Hudson?"

Sadie swallowed hard. "Yes, I read about it in the paper. That poor woman, choking to death like that."

"Sadie, I'm sure, and what's more important so is the FBI, that the guy who robbed Mid-State is the same one who robbed you. I'm guessing he's the one who killed Crump, too."

Charlie's words hung in the phone receiver for a moment, then rolled around in Sadie's head searching for a place to land. "I was afraid you were going to say something like that," she said. "He's back, killing again. What's it going to take to stop all this madness, Charlie?"

"The good news is your name has been taken off the suspect list, as far as having anything to do with the robbery, and so has John Doe's."

"You mean they cleared Happy?"

"Well, it would be pretty hard to rob a bank and kill a woman when you're locked in a hospital room in Vinita, wouldn't you think?"

"I told them . . ."

"Yeah, I know. I just thought you'd be glad to hear that it is official."

Sadie let out a heavy sigh of relief. "You have no idea."

"That's about all I had to say."

"Charlie, I still say Happy has the key to all this . . . if he could tell us where he got the sweatshirt and stuff . . ."

"Probably so, Sadie, and with him it will most likely stay."

The day after her conversation with Charlie, Sadie decided to take the job at Colonial Grocery. It would bring in just enough money to help her squeak by without using what was left in her savings account. She figured she could survive until after the holidays, at which time she felt sure the job situation would get better, especially now that public opinion had shifted away from her as having any possible connection with the bank robberies.

Sadie didn't particularly like working nights, but it left her days open to think first about Jaycee, and then about Happy. In fact, she had become obsessed, thinking about Happy. She drove back to Sycamore Springs twice, to the place she used to deliver food to his makeshift shelter. The wind and rain had taken its toll. The wet box had collapsed and begun to disintegrate. Sadie poked around under the cardboard shell but could find nothing that would give her any answers.

As she drove home she worked through all the filing cabinets in her brain, trying to make sense of her situation. Then late one night, a tiny angel walked through the front door of the grocery store and answered Sadie's prayers.

Candy was all dressed up as a Christmas angel. Her white dress and tights were a little worse for wear with smudged knees and elbows. Her left wing drooped unmercifully, creating the saddest-looking angel Sadie had ever seen. Christine followed the little angel into the store, holding a cigarette between her lips, teetering on red spiked heels.

"My, what a beautiful angel you are," said Sadie, kneeling down to the little girl's level. "Do you remember me? I met you one time . . ."

"Leave the lady alone, Candy. Leroy's in a hurry for this beer."

Christine hoisted a twenty-four-pack of beer onto the checkout counter. "Do I know you?" she asked.

Sadie slid the beer across the scanner. "I met you in the lobby of the Sycamore Springs police station . . . a while back."

"Oh."

"Actually, I'm glad I've run into you," said Sadie. Before Sadie could think, she launched into a myriad of questions she had wondered about ever since Charlie had told her about Candy's encounter with Happy.

"I don't know nothing about that man," said Christine. "And neither does my little girl. He was just weird."

"Listen, I get off at seven o'clock. Can I buy you and Candy some breakfast? I'd like to talk to you some more about this."

"And Leroy?"

"Bring Leroy, too. I'll buy all you can eat if you'll help me out."

Christine looked at Candy, then back at Sadie. "I guess."

"Be back at seven, okay?"

Christine agreed to return as she left the grocery store, toting the beer in one hand and dragging the little angel with the other.

A few hours later, Sadie was sitting in a corner booth at the Waffle House with Christine, Candy, and Leroy. Her three guests ate like they were starving, giving Sadie some satisfaction that what she was doing was right.

The redheaded waitress kept oohing and ahhing over how cute Candy was in her angel outfit, each time she swished by to refill someone's coffee. Suddenly, the waitress looked up and saw a car pull in the parking lot. She stopped dead in her tracks and rushed behind the counter to start a new pot of coffee.

Sadie watched the woman in amusement as first she straightened her uniform, then tried to finger-comb her hair using the window of the kitchen door as a makeshift mirror. Sadie was sure every customer in the diner had disappeared as far as this waitress was concerned.

The door opened and the waitress's face glowed and her voice took on a musical flair. "Hey, Big Mac, got a fresh pot brewing . . . just for you."

"Why, thank you, Gladys," he replied as he nonchalantly took a seat at the counter.

Sadie watched quietly while Gladys fussed over the big man.
She felt like she was intruding on Charlie's personal life and wished
she could become invisible, or somehow grow small and shrink under the table.

He spooned ice into his coffee and stirred, casually looking in
Sadie's direction.

Christine and Leroy reluctantly agreed to help Sadie and waddled
out of the Waffle House, each with a full belly. Sadie handed Gladys
a credit card at the front register and chewed on a toothpick, waiting
for the transaction to process. When she walked out into the cool air
of the morning, somehow she knew who was following close behind.

"Come on, Sadie, get in the cruiser before I catch my death of
cold." Charlie sounded irritated.

Sadie opened the passenger side of the police car and climbed in
beside an assortment of electronic gear. One contraption looked like
a space-age mini-computer.

Charlie started the car and turned the heater on low. "Let's hear
it," he said.

"Hear what?" Sadie tried to sound innocent.

Charlie propped his elbow on the steering wheel, placed his hand
on his forehead, and rubbed his eyebrows. "What in the world are
you doing having breakfast with one of our most frequent customers
at the county jail and his lady-of-the-evening friend?"

"Charlie, I have a great idea . . . well, maybe a crazy idea . . . but
if it works, it'll pay off real big . . . and I could really use your help,
too . . . tomorrow . . . it's Saturday."

"I'm listening."

Sadie's eyes shined with excitement as she explained to Charlie
how she planned to take Candy to visit Happy. The little girl was the
only person who had stirred something deep inside the poor man to
make him want to talk. However, under the circumstances, he had
never gotten the opportunity. Sadie wanted to give him that chance.
Once he started talking, Sadie felt sure Happy would shed some light
on the bank robber.

"Charlie, will you help me?" she asked.

"Sadie, I think you're crazy." Charlie stopped long enough to
listen as his radio began to gurgle, then he reached over and turned
the volume down. "But I'll go with you."

Sadie almost jumped in her seat. "Oh, thanks, Charlie. You don't know . . ."

"Go on, now. I've got work to do. Just remember one thing . . ."

Sadie opened the car door to get out and then turned and looked back at Charlie.

"I wouldn't do this for just anybody," he said.

The next morning, Charlie and Sadie, with Christine and Candy in tow, arrived at the state hospital. Leroy had opted to stay at home and drink the free beer Sadie had provided. The north wind began to deliver the first cold blast of the season, adding a sense of excitement to the air. Two cedar shrubs that flanked the front door twinkled with tiny white lights, a reminder that Christmas was not far away.

Dr. Graham met the group at the front desk and asked them to assemble in a small meeting room to discuss Sadie's proposal again. She had been reluctant on the phone, but finally agreed to let Sadie and Candy meet with the patient. The doctor decided that since Happy was accustomed to Sadie's visits, she might have a calming effect on the situation. The rest of the party would have to wait where they were.

The doctor explained to Candy that she was going to meet a man who couldn't talk, a man she had seen before at the police station. And that he might become upset, but she would be safe, that he could not hurt her. The little girl seemed to understand.

Sadie took Candy's hand and they followed Dr. Graham down the long hallway to Happy's room. The two visitors waited outside the room while the doctor went inside and talked to Happy. After a few minutes, the door opened and Dr. Graham invited the two inside.

At first, Happy sat on his bed and stared out the window. Finally, he turned and looked at Sadie and laughed. Then he turned his gaze to Candy, who stood at Sadie's side, partly hidden behind her leg.

"Hello," said Candy.

Happy's laugh fell into a painful smile, his face filled with grief, and tears spilled off his cheek. He slid from the bed to the floor, pulled his knees to his chest, and began to sob into his hands.

Tears began to fill Sadie's eyes. "Oh, I don't want to make him cry."

Candy let go of Sadie's hand and walked over to Happy and

began to stroke his shoulder. "Please don't cry, Mister. Please don't cry," she pleaded.

Dr. Graham moved quickly to the child's side, gently separating her from Happy. After a few moments, Happy raised his head and spoke calmly to the little girl. "Alicia? Where have you been? I thought you were dead."

The sound of his voice came as such a shock to Sadie and Dr. Graham that they both froze like statues, suspended in time. Sadie's eyes began to tear as she whispered to herself, "It worked . . . it worked . . . it worked."

Still stunned, Dr. Graham shifted Candy behind her, motioned for Sadie to take charge of the child, then said, "It sure did."

Charlie could hear Sadie and Candy coming down the hall and rose to meet them. "That didn't take long," he said.

As Candy headed for her mother's lap, Sadie fell against Charlie's chest and sobbed. When she'd had a good cry, Charlie handed her his handkerchief and they sat down.

"Charlie, it worked," she said. "He thought Candy was his little girl. I guess something happened to her. I think she may be dead." Sadie let out a deep breath.

"Did he remember anything else?" asked Charlie.

"Oh, I don't know. The doctor asked us to leave while she talked to him." Sadie then turned to Charlie and asked, "Did you know they have been gradually taking him off of all his medication because they can't keep him here any longer? And if we had come a few weeks ago, he might not have responded because of the medication?"

"Oh?" Charlie tried to look surprised.

"The doctor told me about it while we were walking to his room. She said they can only keep them so long and his time was running out. They are going to stick him back out on the street and let him fend for himself again . . . now that the FBI doesn't want him anymore."

Charlie was well aware of the state hospital's policy on patients like Happy. If they were not a danger to themselves or anyone else, they just turned them out on the street. Then, when they got in trouble, they ended up in jail.

"So, did he know his name?" asked Charlie.

"I don't know. But he knew his little girl's name was Alicia."

Dr. Graham walked up to Sadie and offered her hand. "Congratulations. It looks like we've had a major breakthrough with your friend," she said.

"Can we ask him some questions?" asked Charlie.

"No, I think he's had enough excitement for one day. I'd like to spend some time with him first. If you want to check back with me in a few days, I'll let you know where we are." Dr. Graham then turned and disappeared down the hall.

Unaware of the whole situation, Candy amused herself by dismantling a magazine. Christine's eyes looked like they were propped open with invisible toothpicks. "So, do I get something extra for this 'breakthrough'?" she asked.

Sadie started to speak, but Charlie broke in: "No. Let's go home."

Chapter 20

Two weeks later, Charlie found himself once again using his own time to make a trip to the state hospital in Vinita. Only this time he would be picking up a passenger. After a lengthy discussion with Dr. Graham, Charlie had agreed to pick up the homeless man the FBI had tagged John Doe and left there almost eight months ago. Since that time, John Doe had silently answered to the names of Happy and Rob, neither of which came close to his real name—Jules Hebert.

"He pronounces it like *A-bare*," the doctor had told Charlie and then added in the same breath, "Do you suppose he's part French?"

"Does it matter?" asked Charlie.

"Well, no. I guess not," she said. "It's just that I assumed he was Afro-American."

Charlie had no idea where Jules Hebert or his name came from and so indicated with dead silence. The doctor continued.

"You know the hospital can't keep him any longer," she said. "And now that he has regained a limited ability to speak I think he'll be fine. Keep in mind, he's not at a hundred percent yet. It's going to take some time. My main concern at this point is how he's going to stay out of the elements, you know, where he's going to live during the next few months. The weather in January and February can be mild in Oklahoma, but it can also turn brutal with a mere shift in the wind. You know that."

Charlie had agreed with the doctor and offered to transport Jules Hebert to the Sycamore Springs Shelter of Grace, where he could stay warm while he continued to progress. Charlie even offered to keep an eye on him, and be available to take him back to see the doctor, if needed. All this because he had an ulterior motive. He knew it would take a few days of bureaucratic paperwork for the FBI to catch up and he wanted to have first crack at questioning Jules. Mainly, Charlie wanted to know if he could remember anything about the sweatshirt that he was wearing when he was arrested. Not to mention the dye pack the agents found in the cheery little box he called home.

Last, out of curiosity Charlie wanted to know why no one had been looking for Jules Hebert. Everybody has to have a someone who cares, Charlie thought.

When the clean-shaven man got into Charlie's truck, Charlie almost didn't recognize him. All except for the far-off look in his eyes, Jules looked like a different person. He wore a new pair of jeans and sneakers, along with a starched blue-denim shirt—all courtesy of Dr. Graham, he found out later. Before they started their journey to Sycamore Springs, Charlie reached across the seat and offered Jules his hand. Jules looked at the outstretched hand for a minute as if trying to decide what to do. Finally, he shook hands with Charlie and laughed. After a few minutes of riding quietly, he began to talk. "Who are you?" he asked. "Are you going to take me back to jail?"

"Name's Charlie McCord. I'm a police officer and I'm here to help you."

"Why are you taking me away?" asked Jules.

"I've come to take you back to Sycamore Springs. That's where you were living before you came here to the hospital."

Jules made a frown, as if thinking made his head hurt.

"Do you remember anything about where you were living before you came here?" asked Charlie.

"Some," he said.

"Do you remember why you couldn't talk?"

"Just couldn't. It's like somebody flipped a switch and turned off my voice. Didn't want to talk and didn't want to live." He watched the scenery go by for several miles, then turned to Charlie and said, "Thank you for helping me."

"Just part of the job," said Charlie. "If you want to thank someone, you'd better look up Sadie Walela and thank her. She's the one that wouldn't give up on you."

"Sadie?" Jules looked thoughtfully into the distance. "She's the one who brought me food, isn't she?"

"She not only brought you food, she brought the little girl that got you to talking."

Jules sat for a moment as if he had difficulty organizing his thoughts before speaking. "I was a dead man," he said. "For all practical purposes, I was a dead man."

Charlie drove and listened.

"And then there she was, standing there looking at me. I thought she was Alicia." Jules put his head down and looked at his hands in his lap. Then he turned and looked at Charlie. "Alicia was my little girl, my little angel. She died. I killed her."

Charlie frowned. Maybe there was a little more to this character than he first thought. "How'd you kill her?"

"I dropped her doll. I was carrying her across the street. It was raining real hard. Put her down on the sidewalk and before I knew it she ran back into the street for her doll. The woman that hit her never had a chance to even touch the brakes." Jules looked forward again and watched the road as it slowly curled around the foothills of the Ozarks. Tears rolled down his cheeks and spilled onto his new shirt.

Charlie shifted in his seat trying to find an easy spot. Finally, Jules began to speak again.

"I ran into the street and picked her up. I fell on my knees and asked God to bring her back to me. But I guess He couldn't. When they took her away from me and buried her in the ground, I swore I'd never talk again. And sure enough, it was just like God took my words away. I think it was punishment for what I did. I wanted to die."

"When did all this happen?"

"I don't really know." Jules shook his head. "Lost track of time. I guess a part of me really did die."

"What about her mother?" asked Charlie. "Where was she?"

"I don't rightly know. She took off. She called me a murderer. I don't know where she went."

The two rode in silence for a few miles. Charlie couldn't remember any accidents in the area that fit with Jules's story. Finally, Charlie's desire for more information surfaced. "Where did all this happen?"

"Chalmette."

"Never heard of it."

"Chalmette, Louisiana." Jules's pronunciation of *Louisiana* reminded Charlie of a Cajun friend and he grinned.

"So, that's where you got your French name."

"Yes, sir." Jules's face brightened. "My momma said my daddy was the handsomest black French man in the state. I never knew him, but at least he gave me his name. My momma was a proud woman, came from someplace in Oklahoma. She told me we were black Indians. Our ancestors lived with the Seminole Indians. They called us 'freedmen.' She said we was part of their tribe. But I never quite understood that. She's been dead for years, since I was a teen-ager. Maybe I was trying to reconnect with some of my momma's people by coming north."

"Maybe," said Charlie.

"I caught a ride with a truck driver in New Orleans. After a couple hundred miles he decided I was crazy. Dumped me out on the other side of the state line in Arkansas, just before he headed into Missouri to unload. I hitchhiked until I found Sycamore Springs and was too tired to go on any farther. Found me a warm place to sleep in back of the big Wal-Mart store. I guess you know the rest."

"Not exactly," said Charlie. "How did you get mixed up with this bank robbery business? And, end up with some of the goods? And, get yourself arrested?"

Jules leaned back and slid down in the seat. "I never robbed no bank," he stated defensively.

"I never said you did," Charlie retorted. "But you're the one who was wearing the dude's sweatshirt and sleeping with the dye pack."

"I don't know what a dye pack is."

"Well, take it from me, you don't usually pick them up during your normal, everyday Dumpster diving."

Jules looked at Charlie and raised his eyebrows. "Yeah, I did," he said. "I really did."

"I'm listening," said Charlie as he pulled into the parking lot next to the Sycamore Springs Shelter of Grace and killed the motor.

The two men sat in the afternoon sun and Charlie learned how Jules Hebert had come to be the proud owner of the robber's dis-guise. Jules told him how he had climbed into the trash container behind the Wal-Mart Super Store that day and hid when he heard a vehicle coming around the building. He told Charlie how he'd crouched inside while the driver of the van showered him with a sack full of trash. Jules remembered how he unthinkingly laughed out loud and then feared he might have given himself away. But as luck would have it, the driver laughed too and drove off.

"As soon as the coast was clear, I took the bag and ran," he said. "The guy in the van almost ran me down when I got to the street."

"The man? Did you see him?"

"I saw the man in the van."

"What did he look like? Do you think you would recognize him?"

"I don't know. Maybe, if I saw him again."

Charlie rammed the truck into reverse and drove straight toward police headquarters. "You wanted to thank me?" he asked. "You can thank me by looking at some pictures."

"Pictures?"

"Yeah, I got books full of pictures for you to look at. And, if you find the right one, you'll win a prize."

"Oh, yeah?" Jules gave a big laugh.

"Man, am I glad you decided to quit laughing and start talking."

When Sadie got home from work, the red light on her answering machine blinked in sets of three. She wasn't used to getting that many messages all at once and quickly hit the play button. The first message from Jaycee made her heart sink.

"Sorry, hon. Can't make it up through Christmas and New Year's. Got some important clients to entertain. Promise I'll be thinking of you every moment and will call you as soon as I can get away. Promise to make it up to you the last week in January. I love you."

The next message came as a surprise. It was from Charlie McCord. He wanted to introduce her to a man named Jules Hebert. Unsure why she should meet this person, she quickly jotted down the number of the pager he left so she could call him later. Then she waited for the next message.

Sadie, this is Henry Sapp. Give me a call as soon as you can. We got kind of a mess down here at the sheriff's office and we need your help.

Due to the urgency in Henry's voice, Sadie decided to call him back first. The dispatcher said Sheriff Sapp wasn't available, but when Sadie told him who she was, he put her on hold for a moment and almost instantly Henry picked up the phone.

"Sadie? Is that you?"

"Yes, Henry. What can I do for you?" Sadie had known Henry since she was a small child and she could feel the tension in his strained voice.

"Sadie, a hunter ran into a man's body right at the edge of your property. He was in pretty bad shape. Looked like he might have been dead for a while and maybe some animal had mauled him."

Sadie felt weak as the image of a limping and dirty Sonny flashed through her mind. "Who is it, Henry?"

"We're not sure. Haven't been able to identify him yet. The FBI's on the way. Said on the phone they think it might be the man that's been robbing those banks over in Sycamore Springs. He didn't have any kind of identification on him. No wallet. But, boy, he had all kinds of money on him, in two different pockets. I mean, a lot of money."

"Oh, God."

"Sadie, I hate to tell you this, but I think it might be that boy that just got out of prison that's been hanging around here lately. You know the one. The boy you married way back there."

"Oh, God."

By the time Sadie got in touch with Charlie, he had already heard about the dead man found in Eucha. He couldn't believe he had just gotten through with one John Doe on this case and now he possibly had another. He agreed to pick Sadie up and take her to Sheriff Sapp's office to see what they could find out. That arrangement, he thought, would also give him a chance to give her the good news about Happy.

Dr. Buddy Brown, who also served as the local coroner, waited with Henry Sapp in the sheriff's office, along with FBI Agent Daniel Booker. The men sat around a small conference table, smoking cigarettes and drinking coffee, listening to Booker tell outrageous John Doe corpse stories.

When Charlie and Sadie arrived, Agent Booker leaned back in his chair and smiled. "Well, well, well. If it isn't our Indian banker woman and her sidekick, the Lone Ranger."

"Booker, if you can't get off that chair and show some respect, we'll take care of this matter without your young ass," spit Charlie. "And if you don't think I'll go over your head in a New York minute, you try me."

Henry stepped between the two men and held up his hands. "Come on, you two. This isn't necessary."

Sadie stood at the door with her mouth open.

"Tell me this, McCord," Booker continued. "Why is it every time we have a combination of dead people and missing money, your little friend there shows up with some kind of a connection?"

Henry herded Sadie out the door and down the hall. "I'm sorry, Sadie," said Henry. "I wouldn't have asked you to come if I'd known about this FBI man."

"Henry, why do they keep acting like I had something to do with all this?"

"Don't worry, Sadie," he said as he guided her into an empty office. "Stay here and I'll have Buddy bring in the photos of the dead man so you can see if you recognize him. Then you can go home." He turned on his heels and left the room.

After a few moments, Henry reappeared with Buddy at his side, photos in hand. Suddenly, Booker burst through the door behind them. "Henry, call me with what you find out. I should be able to close both bank robbery cases tomorrow as soon as I get the fingerprints run." The agent then stormed down the hall and out the front door.

Minutes later, Charlie calmly walked in and sat down beside Sadie. "You okay?" he asked.

"I'm fine," said Sadie in a defiant tone. "Let's get this over with."

Buddy slowly laid the photos on the desk in front of Sadie. At first, the person in the pictures didn't look real. Under the edge of a white sheet, the bruised neck showed puncture wounds, similar to the bite of a wolf, dog, or some other animal. The blood had been wiped away before the coroner had taken the pictures. When she looked closer, she knew it was indeed Michael.

"It's him," she said. The expression on her face never changed. "His name is Michael Jonathan Mills. He's a murderer and he went to jail for it. I'm sure his fingerprints are on file somewhere."

"We're running them right now, Sadie," said Henry. "Expect an answer back any time. You're just confirming what we already thought. Do you have any idea why he had so much money on him?"

"No, I have no idea. Last account I had he was dealing drugs."

"Sadie, do you think he's the man who robbed you?" asked Charlie.

For the first time, tears began to well in her eyes. "I don't know anymore, Charlie. I don't know." Then she began to sob.

"You can go when you're ready," said Henry.

Sadie wiped her face and walked toward the door.

"And I'm sorry about that agent Booker," added Henry. "I don't know what got into him."

Sadie rode quietly on the way back to her house while Charlie re-
lated the story of Jules Hebert. She tried to be excited about the news
of her homeless friend, but the ordeal at the sheriff's office had drained
her emotionally. She fought wave after wave of confusion. Charlie
finally managed to get her attention when he announced that Jules
had actually seen the robber and could possibly identify him.

"You're kidding." Sadie's face came back to life.

"No, I'm not. I've had him going through every book we have at
the station. Unfortunately, with no luck."

"So, he could tell us if Michael robbed me?"

Charlie pulled a photo out of his pocket and said, "We're going
to see."

Sadie laid her head against the car window. The revelation that
her quest to find the truth might be coming to an end suddenly overwhelmed her. It had started so many months ago, on April Fools'
Day, and it seemed like a lifetime ago. Could it be possible that all
the pain and suffering she had been going through was a direct result
of a teenage relationship gone bad? Had her life been turned upside
down by a monster she could not see, the result of blind juvenile
infatuation?

Charlie continued to talk, but Sadie couldn't hear him, having
lost her ability to concentrate for the moment. Her mind floated and
came to rest on Jaycee. She was lucky to have found such a wonderful, tender, loving man, she thought. She yearned for his embrace,
his kind voice, and his loving words. Why did he have to live so far
away?

". . . and the problem is there were no fingerprints left at either
bank. So, unless Booker can find some bait money in Mills's pocket
change, I don't know how he can justify closing the case without
some positive identification. But, of course, those federal boys do
show a lack of intelligence at times."

Charlie looked at Sadie and realized he was talking to himself.
Returning his attention to the highway, they rode in silence until they
reached the turnoff to Sadie's house. As usual, she could see Sonny's
eyes reflect in the headlights. Suddenly, and with an air of urgency,
Sadie turned and said, "Charlie? I need to tell you something."

Charlie pulled up next to Sadie's car and pushed the gearshift
into "park." Sonny met the car, wagged his tail cautiously, and barked
at the unfamiliar vehicle. Sadie rolled her window down and spoke

in a soft voice. "*Etlawei.*" Sonny stopped barking and chose a place to sit where he could keep a protective eye on Sadie.

"That's quite a dog you got there," remarked Charlie. "And multilingual. I didn't see him earlier."

"You only see him if he wants you to," Sadie said, and then added, "I think I know what happened to Michael."

Charlie placed his elbow on the steering wheel and rubbed his forehead. "I'm listening."

"I think Sonny killed him."

"Who in hell is Sonny?"

Sadie motioned with her head at the wolf-dog. "That's Sonny," she said.

Charlie lowered his head and looked at Sadie as if he were looking at her over imaginary spectacles and repeated her words. "You think Sonny killed him, do you?"

"Well, I don't know for sure. I didn't see it happen."

Charlie pulled the photo from his pocket and looked at the wounds on the dead man's neck. "Could have been."

"All I know is, about a week ago, he was limping and dirty, had blood all over his neck. I figured he'd been in a fight with another wolf or something. But, I don't want anything to happen to Sonny because he thought he was protecting me."

"'Another' wolf?"

"He's a half-breed, Charlie. Just like me."

Sadie's comment caught Charlie off-guard. After a few moments of contemplation he asked, "Can he shoot, too?"

"What do you mean?"

"While it's true the wolf there could have done some damage to the boy's neck, I doubt he could have put that bullet in the back of his head. However, if no one saw it happen and the wolf don't tell us he did it, I guess we'll never know, will we? And the dead man can't talk, so why can't we leave it at that."

Sadie gasped. "I didn't know he was shot."

Charlie ignored her comment. "I'm anxious to get this picture back to Hap—, I mean Jules, and see what he says. I'll call you and let you know."

Sadie reached over and touched Charlie's arm. "Thanks, Charlie."

Chapter 21

When Charlie got home, it was well past midnight. He had spent hours searching for Jules but could find him nowhere. A lady at the Shelter of Grace said she thought he had been helping someone deliver Christmas trees and didn't know when he would be back. The holiday traffic had complicated his search, slowing everything to a snail's pace in Sycamore Springs.

The dark house indicated that Lilly had already gone to bed. He took off his boots by the front door and tried to be quiet. But when he tripped over a knitting basket left in the middle of the floor, he stubbed his toe on the corner of the coffee table and scattered yarn and knitting needles everywhere. "Damn it," he growled as he fell onto the couch.

Lilly's voice startled Charlie as it calmly rose from the chair in the far corner. "You don't have to throw things just because you got caught trying to sneak in the house."

"What in the world are you doing sitting in the dark, Lilly?" asked Charlie. "I was trying to be nice and quiet so I wouldn't wake you up." His aggravation wasn't hard to detect.

"You're nice, all right," Lilly retorted. "You're nice and guilty and caught in the act. Isn't this supposed to be your day off? Someone told me they saw you driving around with that Indian woman in your car. Is she your new girlfriend?"

Lilly's voice grated against Charlie like fingernails on a chalkboard while he continued to sit in the darkness, unwilling to turn on lights for this conversation.

"What do you want, Lilly? I have been working my butt off and, no, I do not have a girlfriend," roared Charlie. "Not that it hasn't crossed my mind."

"I'll tell you what I want," she said. "No, I'll tell you what I'm going to do. I'm going to leave your sorry ass. The papers are in there on the kitchen table. I'm not going to be stuck in this nowhere marriage when my daddy's money finally comes in. It's going to be mine. All mine. I'm not going to give you half of it, nor anybody else for that matter."

"Are you expecting your daddy to die anytime soon, Lilly?"

"My daddy is lying in the hospital right now, barely holding on to life, not that I think you really care. And when he's gone, I'm not going to live like this anymore. And I'm sure as hell not going to live with you anymore. I'm sick of your running around at all hours."

Lilly's words stung like angry wasps. Charlie knew he had not been a model husband, but hadn't he provided for her all these years? And taken care of her? He knew their love had shriveled a long time ago, but they were comfortable and he had never run around on her.

"What happened to your dad?" Charlie asked with genuine concern.

"He had a heart attack. He's in intensive care. If he can regain some strength, they'll do surgery. I don't think that's going to happen." Lilly began to weep.

Charlie reached over and switched on a lamp. Lilly sat in a long, flannel nightgown, clutching her knees against her chest, rocking back and forth in the recliner. Her pale face was smudged with black eye makeup and her blond, stringy hair clung to her damp cheeks.

"Oh, Lilly, I'm so sorry."

Charlie moved to her side, kneeled by the chair, and put his arm around her shoulders. As Lilly's crying escalated into uncontrollable sobs, he could smell the odor of alcohol on her breath. A half-empty bottle of tequila sat on the table near her chair. Charlie took her delicate body in his arms and held her while her emotions spilled onto his big chest. After a few minutes, the tears subsided and Lilly came to life as if she had just awakened from a deep sleep. She flailed her arms and slung her head and Charlie instinctively tightened his grip on her.

"Let me go, you bastard," she screamed. "Don't touch me. Get away from me."

Charlie instantly let go and backed up. "Lilly, you've got to get hold of yourself. How much of that rotgut have you been drinking?"

"I don't have to do anything you say." And with that, she jumped up and stormed into the bedroom, locking the door behind her.

Charlie stood in a daze for a moment before slowly lumbering into the kitchen. He arched his back and rolled his shoulders to relieve the ache between his shoulder blades. His backside felt numb from sitting at the wheel of the police car for hours on end and his head hurt. He pulled out a chair, picked up the document, and sat down. The top of the page read "Lilly Francine McCord v. Charles Edward McCord." Everything had to be an argument. Her versus him; him versus her. This was the final dispute, he thought.

Charlie had known his marriage was doomed from the minute he uttered those famous words: "I do." Even so, he couldn't help but feel that these papers resulted from his failure. It was all his fault, he thought.

In the dim light of the kitchen, the big man thumbed through several pages of the legal document. He skipped over most of the lawyer talk and looked for the list of who got what. He didn't want Lilly's family money. He didn't really want anything.

The list was pretty short and to the point. The majority of assets were listed on Lilly's side of the page—the house, the car, and the household goods. He figured she deserved most of the property for putting up with him all these years. Charlie got the old truck and his personal items. *What the hell is a personal item in a house you've lived in for twenty years?* Charlie turned the document over and pulled back the last page where the lines were drawn for each signature. He pulled the pen out of his shirt pocket, scribbled his name in the appropriate space, and threw the pen on the table. He twisted his wedding ring, pulled it off, and dropped it on the paper. Charlie shook his head and muttered to himself, "Merry Christmas, McCord."

He walked to the bedroom door and knocked lightly. "Lilly, unlock the door. I'm bushed." His voice sounded like his feet felt—flat and tired. "Can't I at least get some of my things?" When he could hear no movement through the door, he walked down the hall and into the guest bedroom.

He undressed in the dark and climbed into bed. As his eyes adjusted to the darkness, he could make out the furnishings in the small room. It was decorated with lots of ruffles and flowers, everything in its place. He thought to himself how he didn't really know Lilly at all. And he was quite certain she didn't know the real Charlie McCord.

The next morning, Charlie rose later than usual. Strangely enough, he felt like the weight of the world had been lifted from his shoulders. If he had known he would feel this good about it, he would have come to some kind of an agreement with Lilly years ago.

The house was quiet, which was just as well. He couldn't see that rehashing last night would do anyone any good. A note stuck to the front of the divorce papers explained that his signature would have to be notarized. She would call him and tell him when and where to meet her. Charlie crumpled the note and let it fall to the floor. He had a lot to do this morning and he couldn't afford to be distracted.

Roll call at the police station turned out to be routine enough before Charlie hit the streets. A growl in his stomach reminded him that he had skipped breakfast, so he decided to wait out the traffic at the Waffle House. Maybe he could slip in a couple of eggs and some strong coffee.

Someone had painted a white snowman and two small angels on the front window of the diner. Inside, a small Christmas tree shuddered every time someone opened and closed the front door, sending silver icicles and the scent of pine floating in the air. It was two days before Christmas and Gladys's bubbly spirits lit up the inside of the diner like a shiny star. She never had much to say of any substance, but Charlie always felt better when he left there. He hoped today would be no different.

"Hey, Big Mac," Gladys called out. "Where have you been? I thought someone must have sent you to the North Pole to look for Santa and his reindeer and you got lost." She laughed and swung past him, delivering three plates of pancakes to the booth next to the door.

Charlie acted like he didn't hear her and sat down at his usual spot at the counter. She sailed down the aisle behind him and plopped a glass of ice water and a spoon in front of him before returning with a mug of steaming coffee. "You eating or just drinking?" she asked.

"Give me the works, Gladys. I'm hungry."

Charlie lifted the coffee cup with the indentation on his ring finger in full sight. Gladys caught her breath.

"What is it, Gladys?" he asked as he put his cup down.

"Oh, nothing, Mac," she said. "Just short of breath this morning. You know how it is when you get this close to Christmas, with all the excitement. By the way, what are you doing for Christmas?"

"I always volunteer to work the streets on the holidays, Red. That way the guys with little ones can be at home on Christmas morning. That's where you ought to be, I guess, with kids if you've got them." Charlie spooned several more pieces of ice into his coffee. It was at times like this he wondered if he had missed out on one of the good things in life by having no children. They appeared to be a joy when they were little, but from what he'd seen on the street, most of them turned into a pain in the butt when they hit their teen years. Of course, it was too late to backtrack now. He dismissed the thought of kids from his mind.

Gladys delivered several more plates to surrounding customers before landing one in front of Charlie. "We're going to be closed. Did you know we are cooking for the shelter that day? You're welcome to join us if you'd like."

"Why thanks, Red. I'll remember that." Charlie had never wondered if Gladys had any family. He just assumed she did.

The door opened and Jules Hebert walked in. His mood was almost as festive as Gladys's as he shook hands with Charlie and sat down beside him at the counter.

"And this is the man from the shelter," said Gladys. "He volunteered to help us serve the food. Do you all know each other?"

"Oh, yes," beamed Jules. "This man brought me back from the dead."

Gladys raised an eyebrow and grabbed a menu for another customer.

Charlie smiled, pulled the photo out of his shirt pocket, and handed it to Jules. "Does this look like the man you saw dumping trash at Wal-Mart?"

Jules eyed the picture for several seconds while the corners of his mouth turned down and his lower lip protruded. Then he scrunched up his nose. "What happened to this guy?" he finally asked.

"Not sure. Looks like he might have had a run-in with a four-legged beast that didn't take a liking to him."

Jules lowered the photo and looked at Charlie. "You all don't have werewolves in these parts, do you?"

Gladys heard Jules's remark and stretched across the counter trying to see what he was talking about.

"Well, is it him or not?" asked Charlie.

"I don't think so. People sure look weird when they're dead, don't they?"

Charlie laid down his fork, took the photo, and slipped it back into his pocket. "Was it even close?"

"Not really."

"Thanks, that's what I needed to know."

Jules started toward the door. "Bye, Gladys, I'll see you tonight."

"Okay, hon." Gladys popped her chewing gum.

As the door closed behind Jules, Charlie looked at Gladys and grinned. "You got a date, Red?"

Gladys's face began to flush. "Oh, no. We're just going to go over the details for Christmas dinner. Do you think he's eligible? I'm not sure he remembers a whole lot of things." She unconsciously glanced again toward Charlie's left hand before she casually added, "I guess he's really had a rough time of it these last several months."

Gladys had an uncanny way of prying information out of people, but it rarely worked on Charlie.

Charlie dropped his money on the counter. "Got to go, Gladys. See you later."

As Charlie drove onto the street, Gladys ran to her purse and pulled out her compact. She wanted to see exactly what Charlie and Jules had seen when they looked at her. She moaned at her pale lips and pushed her bangs up on her forehead. Then she closed the mirror and returned to the counter to clean up dirty dishes, thinking about Big Mac's empty ring finger.

With only one day left before Christmas, the Colonial Grocery buzzed with shoppers looking for last-minute bargains. Sadie had volunteered to work extra hours to help expedite the flow of customers. Staying busy kept her mind off the fact that she would not be seeing Jaycee on Christmas. If she worked hard enough, and got tired enough, she thought maybe she could sleep through it. When she finally headed toward the parking lot, her feet hurt so badly she couldn't feel her toes.

As she walked toward her car, she could feel a vehicle approaching behind her as if someone were following her. She moved to one side and waited for it to pass. The car window slowly lowered. "If you'll join us for dinner, we'll buy," offered Charlie.

Sadie smiled. She could see Happy leaning forward in the passenger's seat. "I would love to," she gushed.

Sadie, Charlie, and Jules sat in a corner booth at the Pigsicle House and ate pork ribs, barbecue beans, and corn-on-the-cob until it dripped from their chins. They laughed and talked like three old school chums at homecoming. Sadie dipped the corner of her napkin into her ice water and used it to wipe the remaining gooey sauce from her fingers.

"Well, Happy," said Sadie. "I can't begin to tell you how good it is to see you. You are like a different person."

"His name is Jules," interrupted Charlie.

"He may be Jules to you, but he will always be Happy to me," she said.

"Miss Sadie, you can call me anything you want," laughed Jules.

Suddenly Sadie became serious. "Charlie told me you couldn't find the robber in any of the photos."

"No, I'm sorry. I couldn't find him in any of them—not even the dead man."

"Oh." Sadie's voice trailed off as she thought about Michael for a moment. "That's okay, Happy. I don't think it was him, anyway."

When the Pigsicle House announced they were closing, the trio said their goodbyes, but not before Charlie and Jules made Sadie promise she would help serve Christmas dinner the next day at the Shelter of Grace.

"I'll do it for you, Happy," she said. As they walked out into the darkness, snow began to float lightly in the night air. Sadie looked up at the sky, smiled, and then added, "Merry Christmas, everybody."

Chapter 22

Sadie pulled the heavy quilts tight under her chin. Then she remembered her promise to be at the homeless shelter by eleven o'clock to help Happy and his gang dish out Christmas dinner. She thought about the falling snow the night before and decided to allow herself a few additional minutes of warm solitude.

Thoughts of Jaycee swirled in her head, and she deplored how desperately she missed him. She knew he had taken some important clients to South Padre Island for the holidays, but she felt somewhat dejected that he couldn't find the time to give her at least one call. After all, it was Christmas, and she longed for his strong embrace and lavish kisses.

She could feel Sonny's presence and knew without opening her eyes that he was trying to stare her awake. She peeked through the eyelashes of one eye and that was enough for Sonny. He knew she was awake and it was time to play. He bounced onto the bed and ran his cold nose down the side of her face while she tried to hide under the covers. Sadie let out a giggle. "Okay, okay already. You win." She grabbed the sides of his face and kissed his snout before he jumped off the bed and barked.

And then, almost as if on cue, the phone rang. Sadie grabbed the receiver and tried to overcome the sleep in her voice.

"Merry Christmas, darling." Jaycee's voice always sent a surge of excitement through Sadie's body.

"Oh, Jaycee, Merry Christmas to you, too," sang Sadie. "I wish so bad you were here. I have so many things to tell you."

"Well, I wish I was there, too," said Jaycee in hushed tones. "I don't have long to talk. I was just able to get away from all the people for a moment and I wanted to call my special sweetheart and wish her Merry Christmas."

While Jaycee talked, Sadie held the phone against her ear with her shoulder and pulled on a clean pair of slacks.

"What's on your agenda today?" he asked.

Balancing the phone with one hand, she popped a holiday sweater over her head. "I'm on my way to the Shelter of Grace," she said, "to help serve food to the homeless."

"That sounds like a fun day." The sarcastic tone in Jaycee's voice caught Sadie off-guard.

"Well, it's a long story. I'm helping my friend Happy. He's been released from Vinita . . . oh, I wish we had more time together so I could catch you up on all that's happened. I tried to call you, but all I got was your answering service. Did you get my messages?"

"Yes, but I told you I was going to be with clients." He sounded agitated. "Listen, you have fun serving dinner and I'll call you soon. Probably won't be back to Oklahoma before the last week in January, and we'll talk then. Remember, I love you, and maybe soon we won't have to be so far apart."

"Okay. I love you, too."

Sadie hung up the phone and sat back down on the bed. She had an awful gnawing in her stomach, a feeling that something wasn't right. He didn't sound like himself, so distant.

When she looked out the kitchen window she could see that a thin blanket of sparkling white covered the countryside, creating a blinding reflection of the morning sun. Opening the door for Sonny, she watched as he romped in the snow. She tried to dismiss her lonely ache for Jaycee as she went on with the day. She prepared some warm oats for Joe and delivered them to the barn. Then she brushed him for several minutes before returning to the house. Just as she walked in the door the phone rang again.

Sadie answered, but the caller said nothing. Her intuition told her someone was on the other end of the line and they just weren't saying anything. "Hello?" she said again. "Who is this? Jaycee, is that you?" Still, nothing. After a few seconds, Sadie heard the caller hang up and the line go dead. For the first time, she wished she had Caller ID. As she dismissed the call from her mind, she made a mental note to check into the cost of that service.

Sadie looked at her watch. She was going to have to hurry if she was going to deliver Uncle Eli and Aunt Mary's gifts and get to the shelter on time.

Aunt Mary wouldn't take no for an answer. First, she presented Sadie
with a scarf and hat that she had crocheted from purple yarn. Sadie
put them on and paraded around the room, then gave her aunt and
uncle their gifts—a robe and house shoes for Mary and three flannel
shirts for Eli. After admiring their gifts, they all sat down at the table
and dined on slabs of ham, fried potatoes, biscuits, and gravy. Eli
finished first and headed for the barn, leaving the women to talk over
another cup of coffee. Before long, Sadie found herself pouring out
the details of the morning phone calls.

"Just how well do you know this young man, honey?" asked her
aunt.

"Oh, I've known him for a while," said Sadie. "I'm just crazy
about him."

"If he cared anything about you, he wouldn't be off somewhere
else on Christmas."

"It's his job . . ." Sadie became painfully aware she was making
an excuse for him.

"Why can't you find a nice Indian fellow, anyway? You need a
good Indian to take care of you."

"Got any suggestions?" asked Sadie. "Besides, I don't think you
can always count on a man to take care of you, Indian or not. I know
a lot of Indian girls trying to raise kids without a husband." Sadie
picked up her plate and placed it in the sink.

Her aunt changed the subject. "You go on and get out of here. I
know your friends are waiting for you."

"Why don't you all come down to the shelter later. I'd like for
you to meet Happy."

"We'll see," said Mary. "You be careful. That snow might have
made the roads slick."

"I'll be fine. See you later." Sadie kissed her aunt on the forehead and headed out the door.

The snow had blown off the highway, and the drive to the shelter
was uneventful as there were very few drivers on the road. When she
reached the Shelter of Grace, Happy and Gladys had already arrived
with the food. They had baked six turkeys, surrounding each with
stuffing in its own throwaway aluminum pan. Equal portions of instant mashed potatoes, gravy, and green beans sat on the counter
waiting to be dished out. Sadie pulled her hair back and tied it with a

red Christmas bow she had brought, then donned the white apron and plastic gloves Gladys offered.

A crowd had already gathered and people began to drift in and out of the dining area. Happy, timid at first, seemed to loosen up as he talked with some of the regulars at the shelter. As soon as the trio got everything in its place, a line began to form and they started dishing out Christmas dinner.

Sadie had never known a homeless person before she met Happy, and the sight of so many women and children in the shelter tore at her heart. She wanted to wrap up every child, take them home, give them a warm bath, and feed them. The Indian people in her small community of Eucha seemed to take care of one another, creating no need for a homeless shelter. They might not have a lot to eat, but what little they had they were always willing to share. It was the Indian way. But here in Sycamore Springs, this shelter seemed to be filled to capacity with hungry people of every age and skin color. Sadie made an effort to ask each one their name and tell them Merry Christmas.

The day passed before she knew it and Sadie decided volunteering to help at the homeless shelter had been one of her most rewarding experiences. Happy had become a celebrity of sort and would soon be getting his fifteen minutes of fame compliments of an enterprising reporter from the *Tulsa World* newspaper. The young man had been in Sycamore Springs visiting relatives when he noticed all the commotion at the shelter. Once he struck up a conversation with Happy, the rest would soon be history. Happy's remarkable story would be featured in a human-interest article in the near future.

After Christmas, the Colonial Grocery Store started to return to normal. As the flow of customers slowed down, the store prepared to resume its pre-holiday hours. Sadie's last night to work would be New Year's Eve. Once again, she needed to seriously consider what she was going to do about her career, or lack of career, as it seemed at the moment.

The number of calls and letters from Jaycee had started to dwindle during the past week and Sadie became a master at rationalization. The end of the year had to be a busy time for the investment firm; she knew this from her own experience at the bank. Jaycee had talked about a possible promotion he had his eye on, so she assured herself everything would be okay once the end of January arrived, bringing him to town.

Sadie always enjoyed New Year's and planned to make the most of the day. She got up early and put on a pot of black-eyed peas and ham to slow-cook all day. Her grandmother had carried on the southern tradition for years, promising Sadie if she ate peas and cornbread on New Year's Day, she would have good luck all year long. Sadie didn't really believe in luck, but the ritual had stuck, anyway.

She plopped down in front of the television for a complete day of parades and football. The Oklahoma Sooners, her favorite college team, would be the last game of the day. She thought surely Jaycee would call by then to tease her about the rivalry between Oklahoma and Texas.

Sadie sat on the floor in front of the sofa and gathered an array of snacks around her with a travel mug full of Dr Pepper. She placed the phone within fingertip reach and began to surf the many cable channels.

Sonny barked an announcement of arrival. That particular high-pitched bark meant "heads up, someone turned off the highway." Sadie hit the mute button on the remote and went to the window to investigate. A large, black luxury automobile had crossed the cattle guard and rolled to a stop. Sadie didn't recognize the car and it was too far away to see the driver. For a moment, her heart sailed. It must be Jaycee coming to surprise her, she thought. When the car did not move, she decided it was probably someone out for a drive, lost and unsuccessfully trying to find Eucha on a map.

Out of habit, she went to the kitchen door and called Sonny. He trotted to the house and came inside. The closer Sonny was, the safer Sadie felt. When Sadie closed the door, the car had not moved.

The pot of black-eyed peas let out a hiss and Sadie went to the kitchen to check on them. She removed the lid and stirred a couple of times before turning the temperature on the pot to low. Suddenly, she heard a deafening blast. The living-room window shattered, covering the floor with razor-sharp slivers of broken glass where Sadie had been sitting earlier. For a moment, Sadie couldn't figure out what had happened. Then she heard another boom. This time nothing broke but she knew the sound came from a shotgun.

Sadie gasped, "What the . . . ?"

Sonny pawed at the back door, growled and then whimpered, begging to be free to face this threat head-on, whatever it may be.

"No, Sonny!" yelled Sadie. "Get down." Sadie ran to the bedroom and picked up the 12-gauge shotgun. The next thing she heard sounded like a huge thud near the barn, and then a car horn blared unmercifully. Sonny barked and scratched ruthlessly at the back door. From the kitchen window, Sadie could see that the large black automobile had T-boned one of her prize walnut trees, and the driver, a blond-headed woman, had slumped over the wheel, causing the horn to sound.

Sadie laid the shotgun down and grabbed the phonebook. In a panic she searched for the right phone number. When she found it, she hurriedly dialed the sheriff's office.

By the time Eli Walela made his way to the barn from the upper pasture, jumped into his old truck, and drove around the shortcut at the edge of the pasture to his niece's house, an ambulance and two Delaware County sheriff's cars had already arrived. Eli took one look at the car wedged against the tree and the paramedics trying to force the car door open and then began to search for Sadie. He could see her, with Sonny beside her, right in the thick of things trying to help, but mostly getting in the way.

Sheriff Henry Sapp took Sadie's arm and pulled her out of the crowd. Sonny barked when Henry touched Sadie and he immediately let go.

Eli arrived just in time to take the wolf-dog back to his truck. He opened the door, waited for Sonny to jump in, and then commanded him to stay. Appearing dejected, Sonny accepted the front seat of the truck as his temporary holding cell, but he remained at attention and watched from a distance with keen eyes.

"What happened, Sadie?" asked Henry. "Who is this woman?"

"I have no idea, Henry. I swear, I've never seen her before in my life. But she sure did a number on my window before she tried to murder my tree." Sadie pushed her hair out of her face with both hands. "They said she was barely alive. Do you think she'll be okay?"

Henry looked toward the house and then back at the car. "I don't rightly know," he said.

The medics placed the unconscious woman in the back of the ambulance while one of the deputies removed a shotgun and two handguns from the passenger's side of the vehicle.

Henry waved his hand at the deputy. "You found any identification yet?" he asked.

"No, sir," the deputy answered. "Not yet."

The ambulance carefully backed out and drove off. When it reached the highway, the driver lit up the lights and let the siren squeal as they turned toward Sycamore Springs. That meant one thing: Her injuries needed more than small-town Eucha Memorial could provide.

As several men separated the car from the tree, Sadie heard hammering and turned to find Uncle Eli on a ladder nailing boards over her broken window. He winked at her and she smiled. He always seemed to know what to do, she thought.

Sadie finished giving Sheriff Sapp what little information she had as the wrecker pulled the black car off toward the highway. "I just don't know, Henry. I can't imagine why anyone would want to shoot at me. It just doesn't make any sense. Would you mind calling me as soon as you know who she is?"

"I'll see what I can do, Sadie, as soon as I can run down the owner of the vehicle. The license plate shows up under the name of Cantor with an address in Texas."

"Cantor?"

Sadie swept up tiny pieces of glass for hours. Her mind replayed the day over and over, trying to make sense of what had happened. She spooned at a bowl of black-eyed peas, but she couldn't eat. An overwhelming feeling of violation emerged, ushering in some of the same feelings she'd had when she experienced the robbery. Why would someone want to shoot at her? Nothing made any sense.

She tried to call Jaycee and got his answering service again. Not knowing what she could say in another message that she hadn't already said, she hung up. Aimlessly, she wandered through the house. It had been almost eight hours since the unannounced visitor had arrived and now football couldn't even take her mind away. She had to know something. Finally, she picked up the Sycamore Springs phonebook and looked up the number to West County Memorial Hospital.

"I want to check on the condition of a woman who was brought into the emergency room earlier today," said Sadie. Sadie waited on hold for what seemed like an eternity.

Finally, a nurse answered and told Sadie the woman had been admitted into intensive care and Sadie would have to get information from the patient's family.

"Does she have family there?" Sadie asked. "What is her name?"

The nurse declined to give any additional information and Sadie thanked her for her help. After thinking about it for a minute, Sadie picked up her purse and headed for the car. She wanted some answers and she wanted them now.

When Sadie drove into the hospital parking lot, she could see a woman pushing a wheelchair toward the front door. Hurriedly, Sadie parked and ran to catch up with her. "Mrs. Andover? Is that you?" Sadie tried not to raise her voice close to the hospital door.

Suddenly, a tiny head popped around the corner of the wheelchair as Sadie reached them—Soda Pop and her mom. The child's gaunt face and frail arms took Sadie by surprise, but Soda Pop's beautiful brown eyes sparkled when she saw her friend.

"Hey, there, can I drive these wheels?" asked Sadie. Soda Pop's mom let Sadie take command of the wheelchair. After they entered the hospital, Sadie quickly found a place to park the chair where she could sit at eye level with the little girl. "How are you doing, Soda Pop?"

"I have to come here to get my special medicine to kill the bugs that are inside my body," said Soda Pop in an authoritative voice. "When they are all dead, then I will feel better," she added.

"You certainly will," agreed Sadie.

"And do you know what else?" asked Soda Pop.

Sadie slowly moved her head from side to side indicating a negative answer. "No, what?"

"When all the bugs are dead, my hair will grow back, too."

Fighting the lump rising in her throat, Sadie reached up and stroked the little girl's bangs. The wig made from Sadie's own hair looked remarkably natural on Soda Pop's head. "Yes, yes it will," Sadie whispered.

"Sadie?" Her voice sounded small. "You said I could ride Joe sometime. Soon?"

"You know," said Sadie with excitement, "Joe's been asking about you."

Soda Pop giggled. "Horses can't talk."

"Why, of course they can. You just have to listen."

Soda Pop giggled again. Mrs. Andover stood up and looked at her watch. "Thank you, Sadie. It's good to see her laughing. I'm glad we got to see you. Do you have a family member in the hospital?"

"Oh, no. Nothing like that. I'm glad I got to see you and Soda Pop, too. And please call me anytime you'd like to see Joe."

"We will. Thanks."

Sadie stood and watched until the young mother pushed the child's wheelchair into the elevator and disappeared, then she returned her attention to the task at hand. Across the lobby, three volunteers in pink aprons sat behind a small information desk drinking coffee and talking. Sadie decided to start there.

As she took a shortcut through the waiting area, she noticed a man sitting alone at the end of a vinyl-covered sofa. He sat with his elbows on his knees, holding his head in his hands. He looked familiar, but she tried not to stare. Suddenly, he looked up, saw Sadie, and spoke. It was Charlie McCord.

"What brings you here?" he asked. He looked tired, and his wrinkled clothes gave Sadie the feeling he'd been there awhile.

"I was just looking for someone," she said. Then, after a brief moment of silence, she asked, "Are you okay, Charlie?"

"Who are you looking for?" he asked, ignoring her question.

Sadie perched on a matching vinyl-covered chair and began to tell her story. "I swear, Charlie, I don't know who this woman is, but I'm not going to be able to sleep until I know why she was shooting at me."

"Do you want some help, Sadie?"

"I don't want to intrude on your personal time, Charlie. I can snoop around pretty well on my own."

Charlie stood up. "Actually, I'd welcome the distraction. Wait here."

He disappeared around the corner and down the hallway while Sadie contemplated the situation. She had always thought of Charlie as a police officer, hard as a rock, never imagining him as a normal human being with ordinary emotions. She suddenly realized he was as vulnerable as everyone else, and she felt sad for his apparent pain.

She wondered for the first time about his family and whose illness or misfortune might have brought him here.

After a few minutes, Charlie returned with information. "I ran into one of our officers down there. You remember Lance Smith, don't you? He said they had identified the woman and her husband showed up about an hour ago from Dallas. The woman's name is Jones—Carolyn Cantor-Jones or something like that. Does that ring any bells?"

Sadie stared at Charlie. "No, not really," she said. "There's a lot of people named Jones. In fact, I have a wonderful friend—"

About that time, Officer Smith rounded the corner and summoned Charlie. "Sergeant, I spoke with the woman's husband. She's still knocked out, but he said he'd be glad to answer any questions for you."

Sadie followed close on Charlie's heels as they approached a smaller waiting room set aside for intensive care. As Lance introduced Charlie to the man, Sadie stopped short as if she had hit an imaginary barricade and someone had clipped her behind the knees. She sank backward against the wall and tried to become invisible as she fought the pounding in her head. It was Jaycee.

Why is he here? He can't be . . .

While she listened to Charlie question Jaycee, she unconsciously shifted from one foot to the other as if the rhythmic movement might convince her legs to regain their strength. The sound waves of the men's voices drifted in and out of her ears while her mind tried to flee. She wanted to run to him, let him hold her with his strong arms while he explained away his presence. But her body would not move. For an instant she heard Jaycee's voice: ". . . my wife . . ." The words blared unmercifully before his voice dissipated into the smell of the hospital air.

Sadie began to feel dizzy and realized she was holding her breath. She tried to concentrate on inhaling and exhaling. Pieces of the puzzle began to fit. He was married. He had a family in Dallas. No wonder he couldn't be here for Christmas and only came to visit once a month. There had been no holiday client get-together. Then Sadie remembered the hang-up phone calls. His wife had uncovered the truth when he placed the call to Sadie on Christmas morning. The distraught spouse had simply tracked her down and tried to kill her.

Damn, I am such a fool.

As her anger swelled, the blood began to circulate in her limbs and the adrenaline began to flow. Sadie walked up to the men and waited. They stopped speaking and Jaycee, forced to acknowledge her presence, looked at Sadie. His haggard face took on a childlike appearance and he smiled as if he had just gotten caught stealing candy.

"Hello," he said in an apologetic tone.

Charlie started to make introductions, but Sadie stopped him. She looked straight at Jaycee and with a calm, solid voice said, "Don't ever come near me again or I will do to you what your wife tried to do to me . . . only I won't miss." She turned on her heel, stuck her head in the air, and strode back through the lobby. She could hear Jaycee calling her name as she left the hospital.

Chapter 23

Sadie hammered the last few nails around the perimeter of the new window. Her mind wandered and she missed twice, once almost hitting the glass, then nearly nailing her thumb to the shutter. The more she focused on Jaycee, the harder she pounded. Her thoughts ran on full tilt this morning after what felt like an endless night. She had finally unplugged the phone to quiet the relentless ringing.

"Come on down, Sadie, before you break something," barked Eli while he held the ladder steady.

She knew her uncle didn't know the entire story, but he seemed to be disgusted enough with the whole Jaycee business. He acted particularly protective of her after yesterday's incident, and she was sure he was willing to string up anyone, man or woman, who meant harm to her.

Sadie jumped off the ladder, stood back, and admired her handiwork. "Looks good enough to me," she said. "Thanks, Uncle Eli. I don't know what I'd do without you."

Eli said nothing. Instead, he gathered his tools and laid the ladder in the bed of his truck, then climbed in and rolled down his window. "Mary said you should come for supper. She's fixing chicken and dumplings."

"Okay." Sadie smiled and waved as he drove off. The unseasonably warm January weather beckoned to Sadie, and she lifted her face toward the bright sun hoping it would burn away her pain. She looked at the injured tree and felt the bareness where the bark had been ripped from her heart. Alone again, she began to fight the depression, struggling with the tangled mess of thoughts in her head, berating herself for falling in love with a married man. *I should have known.*

When a vehicle turned off the highway, she wiped the tears from her eyes and the hair from her face. Sonny came to her side while they waited for the old truck to roll to a stop.

"I hope you don't mind me showing up unannounced," said Charlie as he climbed out.

"What a nice surprise," said Sadie. "I'm glad you came."

"You are?"

Sadie looked at the ground and raked the dormant crabgrass with her worn boot. "I want to apologize for my behavior last night. I didn't even thank you for your help. And you were off duty." She looked back at Charlie's face. "I don't know why you were there at the hospital, but I'm glad you were."

"I was there because my father-in-law was having heart surgery," he said. "He didn't make it."

"Oh, I'm sorry, Charlie."

"Yeah, well, we never liked each other anyway," said Charlie, his face absent of emotion.

As Sadie started to echo her regrets again, Charlie cut her off.

"But," he said, "I thought you might want to know that the Jones woman never regained consciousness before she died early this morning. I was still at the hospital when they rolled her to the morgue."

"Oh, no." Sadie felt awful, willing to take full responsibility for the death of this woman she didn't even know. After all, it was her tree that had stood its ground, causing the ill-fated driver to smack her head against the windshield and cause irreparable damage to her brain when the air bag malfunctioned. "If I had only known he was married, none of this would have happened," Sadie whispered. "I would have never gone out with him if I'd known he was married. There would have been no reason for all this destruction . . . death."

"You can't blame yourself for someone else's suicide, Sadie. The doctor said her blood alcohol level well exceeded any definition of being drunk and her husband admitted finding the suicide note she left behind in Texas. Sounds as if she had plans to take you with her."

Thoughts swirled in Sadie's head again and she wrestled with overwhelming opposing sensations. It was only by the grace of God that she wasn't dead, too. She felt sorry for Jaycee losing his wife, but at the same time she hated him for his deceptions. Less than a day ago she longed for the magic touch of his fingers and now she became nauseated at the thought of him coming near her. The confusion brought tears.

Charlie put his arm around Sadie's shoulders and they walked to the front steps of the house and sat down. Alarmed, Sonny ran to Sadie's side. *"Unelagi,"* said Sadie softly. The wolf-dog relaxed.

Several moments passed before Sadie looked at Charlie. "Don't you need to be with your wife if her father just died?"

"Actually, she asked me to leave," said Charlie. "We are in the process of getting . . . what I guess you would call a friendly divorce. It's friendly, that is, as long as I'm not around."

Sadie tried to hide her surprise.

Charlie continued. "With her daddy gone, Lilly will be coming into a lot of money. So she doesn't need me around to pay the bills anymore. And it's been a long time since she needed me for anything else." He stopped talking for a moment, looked off into the distance, and then continued. "What's that old saying?" he asked. "'Money makes the world go round.' I guess that's it." He smiled. "Anyway, we started making arrangements to divorce a while back—before Christmas."

"I'm really sorry, Charlie."

"Don't be. It was long overdue." Charlie's face began to brighten. "Besides, I have some better news for you." Charlie stood up, went over to his truck, and retrieved a newspaper. "I thought you might like to see this article about Jules." He handed Sadie an inside section of the New Year's Day issue of the *Tulsa World.*

Sadie stared at the picture taken on Christmas Day of Happy carving turkey at the shelter dinner. She could see herself and others in the background. "Wow, this is neat. Long article, too."

"I thought you'd like that," said Charlie. "You can keep it and read it. Are you okay with everything else, Sadie? I know this must be hard for you. Jones explained the situation between you and him."

"Thanks, Charlie."

"Did this Jones guy ever cause you any trouble?"

"What do you mean?"

"You can't trust people like him, Sadie. He's a con."

Sadie looked off toward the Eucha hills as if she hoped to extract some answers from the air. Her heart ached for the loss of the man she loved. Desperately, she wanted to believe it was all just a big mistake, that she would wake up from this dream and Jaycee would come sweep her off her feet like he always did. He had been such a gentle lover, a pillar of support. Or had it all been some big masquerade? Who was this man that had wreaked havoc on her life? Joe wandered up to the fence near the damaged tree, raised his head, and snorted, bringing Sadie out of her daze.

Charlie shook his head and continued, "There's something about him I just can't put my finger on. I think I've seen him before. It'll come to me."

"Oh, I don't think he'd hurt anybody. He's an investment banker. Works with the bank I used to work for."

Charlie wondered if Sadie realized she was unconsciously defending the man who almost cost her her life the day before. "If he bothers you, you'll let me know?"

Sadie returned her gaze to the big lawman and smiled. "Don't worry about me," she said. "I'll be fine. *Tsitsalagi*. I'm a Cherokee . . . and a Walela."

Sadie sat at the kitchen table and reread Happy's newspaper story relating the tragedy of his daughter's death, how he came to lose his voice, and how he ended up in the state hospital. She smiled when she saw her name, her friend having given her credit for unleashing his memories, launching his recovery. Sadie felt good about Happy and his new lease on life.

Out of habit, Sadie thumbed through the remainder of the paper, and a small article caught her eye. It read: "Kansas Corporation to Acquire Sycamore Bank." Sadie skimmed the first paragraph, then slowed down and started over to make sure she didn't misread anything. It seemed her old employer was battling a hostile stock takeover by a large financial conglomerate eager to spread its holdings across state lines. The story quoted Stan Blackton as saying "Mercury Savings Bank will fight the acquisition with everything they have."

Sadie chuckled to herself. Stan Blackton had finally met his match. She knew he would never survive the more sophisticated administration of a large corporation. The good-old-boy regime at Mercury would be sent packing and she wouldn't be the only unemployed banker in Sycamore Springs. Sadie spoke aloud to the empty kitchen, "Bad karma, Stan. It'll bite you in the ass every time."

The incessant calling from Jaycee had stopped and Sadie was glad. It would be easier, she thought, if they remained on opposite sides of the Red River. Then, as if someone had turned on a faucet,

Jaycee tried everything he could think of to get Sadie to talk to him. He called; she hung up. He left messages; she erased them. He sent flowers; she refused them. He came to her house; Sonny dared him to get out of the car while she watched from behind closed doors. She methodically moved from room to room scrubbing floors, organizing closets, and throwing away everything she could find that remotely reminded her of him, as if that would help extract him from her life. Finally, as quickly as it had all started, the calls stopped and he simply disappeared.

The last week in January, Donnie Tenkiller called from the Eucha General Store. "Sadie, would you want to work at the store for a while?" he asked. "The bookkeeper had her baby early and we need someone to fill in until she comes back. I knew you had asked about a job . . ." His voice trailed off as if suddenly embarrassed for pointing out Sadie's lack of employment.

Sadie thought for a moment. It couldn't be any worse than working at the Colonial Grocery Store in Sycamore Springs. Besides, it might provide a lead on a better job. "Okay, Donnie. I'll do it," she said. "But what if she doesn't come back? You know how new mothers are."

"Then you can stay on," he suggested. "Maybe?"

Sadie could visualize the young Indian's ears turning red through the phone. "Okay, Donnie," Sadie laughed.

The next morning Sadie went into the store and accepted Donnie's offer. The job didn't pay very much, but it would keep her mind occupied. Working with numbers came easy for her, and she enjoyed visiting with the customers.

February came and dumped two more snowstorms on northeastern Oklahoma. March roared in with warmer temperatures and the first funnel cloud of the year. Sadie had spent both months enjoying the laid-back atmosphere of the Eucha General Store. Donnie Tenkiller could hardly work when he was around her. When she thought he had almost mustered enough nerve to ask her to dinner, she anticipated the question and redirected the conversation elsewhere.

It had been almost three months since the incident with Jaycee's wife, yet it lurked in the back of Sadie's mind like a bad dream and she had no desire for the company of any man. Not even Donnie.

Jules Hebert sat in a booth at the Waffle House staring first at an envelope, then extracting the contents and putting them back. He had done this three times since Sadie had arrived, having been summoned by Gladys to meet them as soon as possible for some kind of a celebration.

Gladys buzzed up and down the aisles of the diner, delivering greasy hamburgers and French fries to a crowd of rowdy kids. She smacked her gum and winked at Jules each time she passed the booth, embarrassing Jules and entertaining Sadie. Finally, Gladys untied her apron and handed it to the new waitress she had spent all afternoon training. "I think you got it, honey. If you need me, I'll be over here." And with that, she slid into the booth next to Jules and smoothed her red curls behind her ears and straightened her heart-shaped earrings. Then her eyes lit up. "Oh, look. Here comes Big Mac."

Charlie had taken most of his meals at the Waffle House for the last few months since Lilly had moved in with her mother. When he eased into the booth next to Sadie, she noticed the buttonholes on the front of his shirt struggled to hold each button in place. He placed his elbows on the table, folded his arms, and looked at Sadie. "How are you doing, Sadie?" he asked. "Haven't seen you in a while."

"Got an honest job," she answered. "Temporary bookkeeper at the Eucha Store. Why don't you come by sometime?"

"I'll do that," he said. "But first I want to know what all the hubbub is about."

Jules beamed when he had everyone's attention. "I have good news. And since you two had a lot to do with saving my life, I thought you should be the first to know."

Charlie looked at Jules, then Gladys, and finally Sadie. Sadie shrugged her shoulders. "I give up."

"You are looking at a happy man," said Jules. Then he produced a small photograph from the envelope and held it up for Sadie and Charlie to inspect. Sadie took it from Jules and held it closer so she and Charlie could look at it together.

"She's beautiful," remarked Sadie. "Look at that smile. Who is this, Happy?"

"That's Dimple. Actually, her real name is Delilah."

"Isn't that the cutest name you've ever heard?" asked Gladys, smiling ear to ear and popping her gum.

"Who is she?" Sadie repeated.

"She's my little girl," said Jules, fighting back tears. "I didn't know my wife was pregnant when Alicia was killed. And then she up and ran off. I had no idea where she went, and, well, you all know the rest of that story." Jules picked up a glass of water and gulped down half of its contents before stopping, an obvious attempt to cover the pain on his face.

"Geez, Happy, how'd you find out about her?" asked Sadie.

"Where is she?" Charlie spoke at the same time.

"Do you remember that newspaper article about me?" Jules asked. The trio affirmed.

"A Dallas newspaper picked up the story and my wife's sister, Jodeane, saw it. She couldn't believe it, because, well, they'd done given me up for dead a long time ago."

"What happened?" asked Sadie.

"When my wife had Delilah, she was—Helen was her name— she was in an awful state from what happened to Alicia and all, and she didn't know what had happened to me, either. She went to visit Jodeane, and she left the baby there." Jules dropped his head for a moment before continuing. "I guess Helen was in a terrible way. I should have been there for her. I didn't know."

"I don't think you were in much better shape yourself," piped Charlie.

"Well, no, I guess not. But they found her—they found Helen a couple of weeks later in an alley pumped full of drugs. She was dead. Her version of the easy way out, I guess. I feel awful about it, just awful. I let her down."

"What happened to Delilah?" asked Sadie in an attempt to turn the conversation.

"She's been living with Jodeane and her family. They thought I was probably dead too, so the court gave custody to them. Jodeane says if I get cleaned up, come down there, and show I can be a re-sponsible person, she will make arrangements for me to visit Delilah." Then he quickly added, "But she's got to get used to the idea first."

"That's wonderful, Happy," exclaimed Sadie.

"I hate to rain on your parade, man. But how do you know this kid is yours?" quizzed Charlie.

Sadie stuck her elbow in Charlie's side so hard he almost spilled his coffee.

"Just that Jodeane says the timing is right and that's what Helen told her." Jules looked at Gladys and smiled. "And my good friend

Gladys here is going to go with me and see if Delilah looks like me."

"Really?" Sadie looked surprised.

"Way to go, Red," laughed Charlie. "I thought you've been a little giddy around here lately."

Everyone laughed and Gladys blushed. After several long seconds, she spoke. "What'll you all have? The food's on me. This is a celebration."

They ordered lots of greasy food and carried on for hours, delighted in their friend's good fortune.

"Oh, I almost forgot," said Jules. "Jodeane sent me some money to help me get back to Texas. But I need help getting it cashed. I was hoping my good friends would have some suggestions."

"No problem," said Sadie. "Can you meet me at the branch where I used to work in the morning a little before eight? I have an appointment with Tom Duncan before the bank opens, and I'd be glad to ask him to cash it for you."

"You going back in the banking business?" asked Charlie.

"I'm going to see what I can find out about the new owners of the bank. Thought I might see if they had any openings."

"Oh, returning to the scene of the crime, are we?" Charlie cleared his throat. "Maybe we can make it a party. I'm meeting Lilly there to sign over the accounts to her."

Sadie turned to Charlie. "I don't know if I'd call that a party or not."

Jules held his coffee cup in the air. "Yes, let's call it a party," he laughed.

Chapter 24

Tom Duncan opened the door for Sadie when he saw her and Jules approaching the branch. "I can't believe you would darken this door—especially today," he said.

"What do you mean?"

"Today is the first day of April," he said. "Don't tell me you've forgotten the most traumatic April Fools' Day of your life."

No, Sadie had not forgotten. In fact, she had been anticipating this day for weeks, promising herself it would not affect her. It's just a day, she had told herself, a day like every other. But she had no idea how sick she would feel at the sight of her old workplace.

The office had barely opened and no other customers had arrived yet, which gave the place a sense of eeriness. As she stood in Tom's office Sadie's mind began to play tricks on her, and for a flash she thought she saw a masked man. Could it be another robber or someone who had come to play an April Fools' Day prank on her? She looked again and he was gone. Her imagination had gone wild.

" . . . management has a different philosophy and . . ." Sadie could hear Tom talking but she couldn't quite hang on to his words. She saw Charlie's truck pull into the west parking lot and park next to a new, dark green Ford Explorer. A thin, blond woman dressed in a pink business suit slid out of the Explorer as if she had been waiting for him. The sight of Charlie gave Sadie a sense of relief. As far as Sadie was concerned, the big man radiated safety and authority everywhere he went whether he was in uniform or not. Today, he looked handsome in jeans, cowboy shirt, and denim jacket. Sadie smiled. She had never seen him in a cowboy shirt.

Tom continued to talk. "I'm surprised they haven't already called you, Sadie. With Stan gone, they are . . ." Tom's voice once more slipped out of hearing range as she watched Charlie shake hands with Jules before he and the pink-suit lady walked over to a young girl sitting behind a desk in the far corner. Jules sat back down in one of the overstuffed chairs in the middle of the lobby and waited while Sadie visited with her old colleague. Sadie's thoughts drifted and she could see her fallen comrade at Jules's feet, still lying there with her sweater draped over his head.

"Sadie?" asked Tom. "Did you hear me?"

Sadie blinked and the blue berber carpet swallowed the image of Gordy's body. "I'm sorry, Tom. I guess this place is getting to me a little more than I thought it would." She sat in one of the chairs by Tom's desk.

"I was just saying they think Stan intentionally falsified the amount of loss to the insurance company after the robbery. They seem to be out of balance by several thousand dollars. Wouldn't that be something, Sadie. Of course, proving . . ." Tom continued speaking and once more her mind shifted. From the hallway leading to the back door, a man slipped into the lobby. Sadie watched him move in slow motion. His black jogging suit, the sunglasses positioned under the eye holes of his mask—all exactly as he had appeared that horrible morning one year ago. Except his gloves were missing. She could see his hands as they gripped two guns—one black, one nickel. Her heart jumped in her chest. Why wasn't someone doing something? She wanted to scream, to leap out of her chair and shout a warning to everyone. Where was Charlie? And then she saw the dark spot on the robber's hand.

"Oh, God. No!" The words flew from her mouth but she couldn't hear them. Her body propelled through space as if she were in a dream.

The masked man, sensing her movement, raised his guns and pointed them at her. Then, for a split second, he hesitated. The sound of gunfire echoed in her head as a bullet ripped through the air. His head jerked and his arms snapped toward the ceiling as he fell backward, still clutching his weapons. Visually, Sadie searched for the identifying marks on the fallen man's hand—the unmistakable results of a snakebite.

"It's Jaycee," she whispered before her world slipped into darkness.

When Charlie saw the masked man round the corner from the hallway, his hand instinctively moved to the high-rise holster on his right

hip where his service revolver rode under the cover of his denim
jacket. Without thought, he unsnapped the thumb break that held his
Smith and Wesson 357 in place and slid the weapon out in a fast,
effortless movement. In a fraction of a second, Charlie zeroed in on
the robber's head and mentally noted that he had a clear and unobstructed shot.

In his peripheral vision, Charlie saw movement in the manager's
office. As the robber leveled his guns at Sadie, Charlie squeezed the
trigger and the robber fell. Bone fragments, blood, and brains splattered on the nearby brick wall.

Charlie ran to the robber and kicked both guns away from the
body. He had seen this combination of weapons before and struggled
for a moment to remember. "I'll be damned," said Charlie aloud. "I
watched this asshole target-shoot." Then he turned his attention to
Tom Duncan, who held a wireless phone to his ear while Jules
crouched on the floor over Sadie. "Is she okay?" asked Charlie.

"I don't know," answered Jules in a shaken voice.

Sadie woke up to a noxious odor as the doctor moved the small vial
under her nose again. Sadie pushed his hand away and almost knocked
the smelling salts from his fingers.

"I think she's back," remarked the young intern.

Sadie's eyes began to focus and the doctor turned away. She could
see Charlie standing not far from the doctor and then she noticed
Lance Smith leaning against the wall near the door. She thought for a
moment and remembered seeing Jaycee. She tried to sit up.

"Whoa," said Charlie. "Let's not be jumping up just yet."

"What happened?" she asked. After a few seconds she added,
"Was it a dream?"

"More like a nightmare," the intern remarked as he left the room.

"Don't worry about it right now," said Charlie.

Sadie could see Charlie had clipped his badge to the front of his
belt. "Was it really him? Where did he go?"

"He's gone, Sadie. Just rest."

"Did he shoot me?" Sadie held her hands in the air for inspection
and then started searching her body for bandages.

"No bullet holes or blood," Charlie comforted her. "But you did
create quite a bump on your head when you fell."

Sadie turned her head away. "Is he dead?"

"I'm sorry, Sadie." Charlie waited for a moment and then asked, "Is there someone you want us to call for you?"

Sadie found it hard to think clearly. "Does anyone know I'm here?"

"I doubt it. But I'm sure the robbery attempt will hit the news soon. You know how they love a sensational story."

Lance spoke for the first time. "You want me to go out and see Eli and Mary? Let them know you're okay. Want me to bring them here?"

"No, no," said Sadie. "Don't bring them here. Tell them I'm okay and will be home in a little while. I'll meet them there. Tell Aunt Mary to make me some potato soup. That way she'll know I'm okay." Potato soup was her aunt's comfort food for everything. "I don't want them to get upset."

Without a word, Lance slipped through the doorway and was gone.

Returning her attention to Charlie, she asked, "Did you have to kill him?"

"It was you or him. Do you think I'd let him shoot you?"

Sadie closed her eyes and rolled onto her side, bringing her knees into a semi-fetal position as uncontrollable tears streamed down her face. She tried to reconcile in her mind what had happened. How could she have loved and hated the same man? How could he be the cold-blooded killer who murdered Gordy and set her on a life-altering path? It was madness. Nothing made sense.

A nurse appeared from nowhere and placed her hand on Sadie's shoulder, gave her a comforting pat, and moved on to another patient.

When Sadie woke up again, the room was dim and quiet. She rolled over, then sat up on her elbow when she heard movement.

"How are you feeling?" asked Charlie.

"I want to go home," she said.

Charlie took a slow drive to Sadie's house while he filled her in on all the information Lance had dug up on Jaycee. "His legal name was Johnny Cantor."

"Cantor?"

"Yeah, remember? Henry said that was the name on the car reg-istration of the car that woman crashed at your house."

"Cantor?"

"He had used the initials J. C. all his life, and I guess he worked it until it finally evolved into 'Jaycee.'"

"Where did 'Jones' come from, then?"

"Jones was his mother's maiden name."

"So?"

"He had started the wheels in motion to legally change his name to Jones in an effort to distance himself from his daddy, who is sit-ting on death row for murdering two women in Texas. Time's run-ning out and he's scheduled to be executed early next year."

"You're kidding."

"And besides that, two names probably came in pretty handy for someone who liked to string along more than one woman at a time."

Sadie felt disgusted, realizing she was one of those women. "How could he be the same person, Charlie?" she asked. "How could he have fooled me like that?"

"I think I told you one time, Sadie. He was a con. I could tell he was a player the day I met him at the hospital. How do you think his daddy ended up on death row? Maybe it runs in the family," Charlie laughed.

Sadie didn't appreciate Charlie's humor. "But, his voice. The robber had such a cold, distinctive voice. Jaycee had such a kind voice . . . so gentle. It just can't be."

"Evidently, he was pretty good at the game. He'd never been caught. His fingerprints are not in any of the state or federal data systems. But—I guess you should know—Jules identified him as the man he saw throwing the bag in the trash bin containing the sweatsuit and dye pack from your robbery. I wouldn't be surprised if he wasn't responsible for several unsolved robbery cases where the robber had the same M.O. Whether we'll ever be able to tie him to any of them may be another matter. It wouldn't surprise me if he was the one who killed your ex-husband."

Sadie shook her head. "Why would he do that?"

"Maybe they were in cahoots."

"Jaycee and Michael?" Sadie thought for a moment. "He was in town that evening. But that doesn't make any sense. Why would he kill Michael?" she asked again.

"Hard to say. Maybe he didn't like the competition."

"Maybe he thought he was protecting me."

"Where did you say you met Jones?"

In a quiet voice, Sadie answered, "At Gordy's funeral. Can you believe that? He was at Gordy's funeral."

The two rode in silence for a while and then Charlie continued to talk. "The strange part is, Lance said he found out the guy was a pretty good investor. On the surface it looks like he had more than enough legitimate money. Which leaves me to believe . . . he was in it for the thrill. Either that or he was extremely obsessed with money."

"Probably both." Sadie leaned her head against the car window. "Nothing is ever what it seems."

Chapter 25

Donnie Tenkiller pushed the accounting-room door open and pointed with his head at a stranger standing near the front of the store sipping on a bottle of water. "There's a white guy out here asking for Miss Waylay," he said, imitating the mispronunciation of her name.

Sadie raised an eyebrow and peered around Donnie's shoulder. A young man in a three-piece suit appeared to be completely out of place in the surroundings of the Eucha General Store.

"Who is he?" she asked.

"White guy."

"What does he want?"

"You."

"Thanks a lot, Donnie." Sadie flipped her hair behind her shoulder and walked around the counter to the cash register. "May I help you?" she asked.

"Miss Wa—?"

"I'm Sadie Walela."

"Hello, I'm Gary Peterson." He handed her a business card that identified him as an attorney with the Crown and Bailey law firm in Plano, Texas. "Is there somewhere we can talk in private?"

Sadie thought for a moment while she sized up the young man. His brassy flattop, freckled face, and gold wire-rimmed glasses made him look like he couldn't be far past puberty. His suit and briefcase reminded her of a struggling salesman.

"Am I supposed to know you?"

"No, ma'am. But I have some information you're going to want to hear."

Her curiosity overrode her caution. "Are you selling something?"

"Oh, no, ma'am. Nothing like that." He looked even younger when he smiled.

"I guess we could go next door to the drugstore. They have some booths we can sit in there." She turned her attention to Donnie. "I'll be next door if you need me."

Donnie, who had been eavesdropping on their conversation, nodded an understanding of her unspoken words. She knew he would check on her in a few minutes.

As the young man opened the door for Sadie, he pulled a handkerchief from his pocket and wiped his brow. Sadie wondered if the sheen of perspiration on the young man's forehead resulted from the combination of mid-July heat and humidity in northeastern Oklahoma or something else.

The drugstore, fairly empty of customers, offered a welcome blast of cool air. They slid into the booth nearest the back wall and ordered soft drinks from the young Indian girl working behind the soda fountain.

Wasting no time, the young man balanced his briefcase on the corner of the table and brought out a manila folder. When Sadie saw the name "Jones" written in large black letters across the front of the folder, her adrenaline surged and she became defensive. "What is this about?" she asked. She didn't want to have anything to do with the name of Jones.

Sensing her discomfort, Gary Peterson placed the briefcase on the floor and laid the folder on the seat next to him. "My firm has been handling the estate of Mr. John Cantor of Plano, Texas," he explained. "I understand he also used the name Jaycee Jones, which I believe is how you are familiar with him."

Sadie sat silently for a few seconds before answering. "You mean the man who tried to kill me?"

The young man's eyes widened ever so slightly. "No, ma'am, I'm not aware of anything like that. I do know the auditors spent a considerable amount of time on this account before the estate could be settled."

"Account?"

"Yes, ma'am. There was quite a controversy over whether the manner in which Mr. Cantor died would in any way void this policy. But I can assure you everything is in order. It has been examined with a fine-tooth comb. It is all legitimate."

"I'm sorry, Mr. Peterson," said Sadie. "Do you want to back up

Deception on All Accounts

and start from the beginning? Because I don't have the slightest idea what on earth you are talking about."

"Yes, ma'am, I'd be glad to. And you can call me Gary if you'd like."

"Okay, Gary. Let's hear it." Sadie sat back and began to sip on her soda.

"Let's see," he said. "We'll start with the investment account. Are you familiar with the investment account?"

Sadie shook her head. "Nope."

"Mr. Cantor, or Mr. Jones . . . . If you don't mind, I'll refer to him as Jones since that is the name he had been using for quite some time."

"Fine. Mr. Jones it is." Sadie chewed on the end of the straw from her drink.

"Mr. Jones opened a joint investment account in his and your name. He opened it with funds from the sale of a stock certificate from a bank—Mercury Bank, I believe."

"He did what?"

"We looked up the certificate. It showed your notarized signature."

"I know about that stock, Mr. Peterson. I told him to give it away. I didn't want it."

"It looks like he gave it to you and him."

"That was nice of him."

"Mr. Jones appears to have been a master at manipulating stocks. That small investment turned into a very hefty account in a relatively short time. It grew from less than a thousand dollars to over fifty thousand in less than a year."

Sadie lowered her chin and looked at him through wide eyes. "I beg your pardon?"

"I know it is hard to believe. Like I said, the auditors checked every entry on this account. It's as if he had a crystal ball linked directly into Wall Street."

"He probably did," murmured Sadie to herself.

"Anyway, once he reached the necessary amount, he bought two paid-up life insurance policies—one on you and one on himself, with each of you as beneficiary for the other."

"What?"

"Yes, ma'am. And now that he is dead the benefit is payable to you."

Sadie sat up straight and looked directly at the young attorney. "Now, let me get this straight. You want to give me some kind of blood money from this bank-robbing hoodlum who killed people for fun . . . and traumatized me for life and then tried to kill me?"

"Oh, no, ma'am. I can tell you quite assuredly, there is no bank-robbery money involved in this transaction. The FBI traced every penny this man had, including this account. No, ma'am. This is the result of the sale of a stock certificate in your name only."

"And he bought a life insurance policy with it?"

"Simplified, yes. Actually, he bought two. You can do what you want with the one he bought on you that named him as beneficiary."

"How could he buy an insurance policy on me without my signature?"

"Oh, he couldn't. But we have your signature, ma'am. Right here. Is this not your signature?"

Sadie took the document and stared at her name. No mistake. She recognized her own signature and remembered the day he had her sign documents for the sale of the stock. He had tricked her into signing something to purchase a life insurance policy on herself. Suddenly, it dawned on her that if Jaycee had killed her in the robbery and gotten away with it, he would have been able to cash in on her dead body.

"That son of a bitch."

"Excuse me?"

"Nothing." Sadie squinted and looked past the young man into empty air. "I'll think about it. I'm not sure I want anything, including money from a killer."

"I can understand that, but you might change your mind when you see the amount of the policy." He balanced an envelope in his right hand above the table.

Sadie thought for a moment and then snatched the envelope from his sweaty hand. She ran her thumb under the flap, tearing loose the seal. She pulled out the policy and thumbed to the last page. "This can't be right. How much is this for?" she asked. "One, two, three . . . there are six zeros after this 'one.'"

"Yes, ma'am."

"This policy is worth a million dollars?"

"Yes, ma'am."

"You're kidding."

"No, ma'am. All you have to do is fill out these forms with wiring instructions and mail them back to us in this special envelope."

"And he would have gotten a million dollars if something had happened to me?"

"Yes, ma'am."

"Geez, quit calling me 'ma'am.'"

"Yes, ma'am."

Donnie Tenkiller stuck his head in the front door of the drugstore. "Sadie, there's a call for you from a Mrs. Andover. Do you want me to take a message?"

Sadie looked at the policy in her hand, then at Gary Peterson, then at Donnie. "No, no. I'll be right there."

An array of eclectic headstones sat in seven rows, theater-style seating on a soft, sloping hillside overlooking the valley below. Near the top of the imaginary theater, Sadie sat at the base of an old, stately oak tree holding an envelope in her hand and staring at the new grave. The fresh flowers left by friends the day before had already begun to wilt, dying from the hot summer sun. The small, temporary marker staked at the top of the grave read "Agatha Gertrude Andover, Age 7." A ribbon on a nearby wreath elaborated: *We love you, Soda Pop.*

In the distance, Sadie could see Charlie's truck as he parked next to her Chevy near the entrance to the cemetery. He shaded his eyes with the palm of his hand, easily found what he was looking for, and walked up the makeshift road used only by hearses on funeral days. When he reached the oak tree, he sat on the ground beside Sadie without saying a word. They sat in silence.

Finally, Sadie spoke. "The new owners at the bank offered me a job."

"Really? You going to take it?"

"I don't think so," she said. "However, Stan's gone . . . he and Adam both. Got caught with their hands in the till when the new guys took over. Charged with embezzlement. They inflated the amount of the robberies to the insurance company. By quite a bit, I guess." Sadie turned to Charlie and asked, "Do you think they were in cahoots with Jaycee? He and Adam were pretty tight."

"I guess anything is possible. When the feds searched Jaycee's place, they found a master key to Mercury's branches."

"No." Sadie stared at Charlie.

"There's a lot of speculation about where the key came from," he said, "but no proof. The bank's records show it had never been issued to anyone."

"So that's how Melvin Crump got killed," said Sadie. "The answer to the mysteriously unlocked door that I never could figure out. I still don't know how he got the vault open." Sadie chewed on her lower lip for a moment. "Adam told me he misplaced a set of keys one time," she said. "But he never said anything about losing a master key. If he had, Stan would have fired him. Then, on the other hand, it's pretty much a moot point, because Adam's secretary was in charge of issuing keys. It would have been no problem for Adam to get another key without anyone finding out."

They sat in silence until Sadie spoke again. "You know, I always wanted to be a successful banker, but I'm not so sure anymore. I thought it was such a noble, upstanding career—not to mention the illusion that bankers make good money. Nothing ever ends up being what you think it is, does it?" A hummingbird hovered nearby, its wings fluttering invisibly. Sadie smiled and continued. "My grandmother used to tell me the important things in life were the simple things—like helping other people. The more you give, she'd say, the more you get in return. I think I know what she meant by that now. Life is so fragile, so short." Sadie stopped, looked toward the small grave, and shook her head. "She was just a kid."

"Yeah, I know."

"And now I have the means to help her." Sadie turned and looked at Charlie. "But it's too late."

"Maybe you can help someone else," he offered.

A car door slammed and they looked down the hill toward the small parking area at the gate of the cemetery. Lance Smith got out of his car and smiled and waved at the duo. He leaned against Charlie's truck as if content to wait for the two to return to their vehicles.

Charlie held his hand in the air for a moment, acknowledging his co-worker's arrival.

"You know, Charlie, I didn't want that money," continued Sadie. "But I've changed my mind."

"Really?" asked Charlie. "You know what they say, don't you?"

"No, tell me."

"Beware of the green frog."

"Oh, yeah?" Sadie's eyes sparkled. It had been a long time since she had heard money referred to as a green frog.

"An old Indian told me once," he said, "it's a white man's sickness—chasing money. You can never catch it. It's always jumping away, just out of reach. Chasing it only brings chaos into your life." Charlie looked off into the distance, grinned, and then added, "And since I'm a white man, I thought I'd pass on that bit of Indian philosophy to you."

"Yeah, I know, *yonega*," Sadie chuckled and then added, "but this Indian isn't chasing the green frog anymore, Charlie. This time it landed in my lap. And I think I can use it to help people like Soda Pop." Silence filled the air for a moment before she continued. "You know, so little kids can have wigs to wear when the chemicals that are supposed to make them better only rob them of their hair. So they can ride a horse if that's what they want to do. And their parents won't have to go to bankers, get down on their knees, and cry and plead for money to pay for medical treatment. So they'll have a chance to be more than just a kid before their life is ripped away." A tear spilled off her cheek.

"So, you've already decided to take the money?"

Sadie slapped the envelope against her knee. "Yep, I'm going to take the money. I want something good to come from all the misery I've gone through for the last year and a half, for all the suffering this little girl went through her whole life. I'm going to open a foundation and call it the Soda Pop Foundation so the spirit of that little girl can live on forever."

Charlie stood and offered Sadie his hand. She grabbed it and let him pull her into a standing position. He held on to her hand, and when she looked at him, he kissed her fingers. "You are one of a kind, Sadie. Extraordinary. And by the way," he pointed toward Lance, "there's the Indian who imparted that bit of wisdom to me."

She grinned, squeezed his hand, and said, "Let's go mail this envelope." Then she walked toward Lance, waiting below.

About the Author

Sara Sue Hoklotubbe (Cherokee) was born and raised in northeastern Oklahoma near the banks of Lake Eucha in Rattlesnake Hollow. After graduating from the University of Oklahoma, she spent over two decades in the financial institution business. During that time, she served in various management positions and taught banking classes at the local community college.

In 1996, Sara retired to a life of full-time writing. After living in other parts of Oklahoma, Hawaii, and Alaska, she recently returned to the heart of the Cherokee Nation. There, she lives with her Choctaw husband, reconnecting with the peaceful surroundings of her youth while she continues to write.

CPSIA information can be obtained
at www.ICGtesting.com
Printed in the USA
LVOW03s0023040418
572237LV00001B/45/P

9 780816 523115